One Little Prayer by Kimberley Comeaux
Louanne Wise, a precocious nine-year-old girl, yearns for someone to call "Dad" since her own died in the War between the States, and when she finds a man wounded in her woods, she feels her dreams could come true. But her mother may not be as easy to convince.

The Tie That Binds by Susan K. Downs
A band of fifteen orphans has arrived on a train from New York City, including Anna and Andrew Clymer who are determined to stay together. Luck has it that each child is adopted by a single parent, but it will take a miracle to get the two adults together and form a family.

The Provider by Cathy Marie Hake
Baby Talitha Halpern's mother died, and her father is locked in deep grief. Tiny and weak, she must be fed, but the only wet nurse to be found is a recently widowed immigrant whom Mr. Halpern finds unsuitable. Can a child's needs heal and bind two broken hearts?

Returning Amanda by Kathleen Paul
Prim and proper, four-year-old Amanda Greer steps off the train and is quickly separated from her older sister. She seeks out the town sheriff for help. What is a bachelor to do with a tiny child? He takes her to the church social hoping to unload her on some motherly female.

A Mother's Heart

FOUR HISTORICAL STORIES OF COUPLES BROUGHT TOGETHER
BY THE FAITH OF A CHILD

One Little Prayer © 2000 by Kimberley Comeaux.
The Tie That Binds © 2000 by Susan K. Downs.
The Provider © 2000 by Cathy Marie Hake.
Returning Amanda © 2000 by Kathleen Paul.

Cover Image © Corbis
Illustrations by Mari Goering

ISBN 1-59789-291-2

A Mother's Heart was previously published as *The Heart of a Child*.

All Scripture quotations are taken from the King James Version of the Bible.

Published by Barbour Publishing, Inc., P.O. Box 719, Uhrichsville, Ohio 44683, www.barbourbooks.com

Our mission is to publish and distribute inspirational products offering exceptional value and biblical encouragement to the masses.

 Member of the
Evangelical Christian
Publishers Association

Printed in the United States of America.
5 4 3 2 1

A Mother's Heart

FOUR HISTORICAL STORIES OF COUPLES BROUGHT TOGETHER
BY THE FAITH OF A CHILD

KIMBERLEY COMEAUX

SUSAN K. DOWNS

CATHY MARIE HAKE

KATHLEEN PAUL

BARBOUR
PUBLISHING

One Little Prayer

by Kimberley Comeaux

Chapter 1

One minute James Edward Larabee, a former captain of the Confederate Army, was riding on his horse through the woods, the next minute he was flat on his back. Stunned, he could do nothing but lie there for a moment, before his soldier instincts kicked in and he began taking quick inventory of himself and his surroundings.

The first thing he noticed was that his leg was covered in blood. Then, the most horrific pain he'd ever felt in his life exploded throughout his bloody limb, causing him to cry out. He'd been shot, he realized. But that couldn't be. The war was over; it had been over for nearly two and a half years. Why would someone shoot him?

The snap of a twig, then a movement out of the corner of his eye, caught his attention. He looked up and saw a hazy figure running away from him. He could barely make out the blue and black clothing, as the person darted through the trees.

"Hey! Come back! I need some help here!" he called several times, but the person just kept going.

It must have been the person who shot him. But why? It couldn't be an outraged Yankee who decided to use him for target practice. He no longer wore the gray pants trimmed in gold that were a sign of his involvement with the Confederate Army. If only he'd gotten a better look at the person who shot him. What kind of man would leave another to bleed to death? Or maybe it was a woman, he just couldn't tell.

Helplessness poured over him as he struggled to sit up. How was he supposed to get help? He had no idea where he was. And to top it all off, his horse had run off with all his belongings and money.

But he'd have to address that problem later. If he didn't get the wound bandaged, they would be finding a dead man instead of a wounded one.

Almost methodically, he took off his jacket, then pulled his shirt off, leaving only his long johns top, and began wrapping the shirt around his thigh, just as he'd done to wounded soldiers in the war. And as he pulled at the sleeves of the shirt, tying it tightly, he thought that it was ironic that he'd managed to escape the bullets during the war, only to be brought down on his way to start a new life. Had God forsaken him again?

The January wind cut through his clothes, and he stared at the sky peeking through the tree branches. He thought briefly of saying a prayer but decided that it wouldn't do any good. Had God listened when he'd prayed that his father and brother would return from the war? Had He listened when he prayed that their plantation would still be intact?

No. His father and brother died in the war and their

plantation in Dothan, Alabama, had been burned to the ground. His faith had died along with them.

The one saving grace had been the money that his father had buried in the family cemetery before they went off to fight. Daddy had put ten thousand dollars at the foot of Mama's grave. That cash was going to buy him a brand-new life out West. He'd made plans to purchase a saloon in San Francisco. All he had to do was show up, sign the papers, and hand over the money.

But now here he lay, probably bleeding to death, his horse missing. . .suddenly those plans seemed very far away. And though the pain in his leg seemed to lessen, the pain in his soul became worse. Bitterness ate at his gut as he silently laid one more accusation at God's door. What was next? Was he to die here? All he knew was that he was in the middle of a forest, somewhere in north Louisiana. There might not be anyone for miles.

But the sound of footsteps coming his direction quickly banished that notion. As it came closer, though, he realized it was a horse's gallop that he heard. He breathed a sigh of relief. His horse had obviously come back to him. If he could manage to get on the animal's back, perhaps he could find a doctor or at least someone who could remove the bullet.

He raised himself on his elbows and watched as the horse came into view. His eyebrows suddenly lowered and he frowned at what he saw next. Though it was his horse that was coming toward him, it was being ridden by. . . well, he couldn't really tell what was on Rebel's back.

When the horse was reined to a stop, the most strangely dressed little girl he'd ever laid eyes on looked down at him. For a moment, he could do nothing but gape at her attire. On her thin shoulders she had draped an old faded sheet tied at her neck. Her chest was decorated with pieces of tin sewn carefully to her thick brown blouse. But it was what she wore on her head that got his greatest attention. Sitting pertly on her golden curls was a uniquely carved-out. . .gourd!

After studying him for a moment through narrowed, suspicious eyes, she whipped out a wooden stick, holding it like a sword and pointing it at him. "What army are you with, sir?" she demanded in a high, extremely Southern-sounding voice.

He couldn't help but chuckle at her serious face. As if irritated, she jabbed him with the stick, hitting him in the chest. "Are you English or French?" she asked as she went to poke him again.

He quickly grabbed the stick before it reached him and yanked it out of her hand. "Listen, little girl, you've stolen my horse and poked me with sticks and I'm getting a little tired of—"

"How dare you address me as 'little girl'! I am Joan of Arc, and I've seized your horse! Now, give me back my sword so that I may slay you." She lifted her chin and held out her hand so regally that James couldn't help but admire her.

Suddenly the costume made sense—of course Joan of Arc would be dressed as a soldier. He quickly searched his mind, trying to remember whether Joan was French or English. "Uh. . .I'm French?" he tested carefully. He couldn't figure out if the little girl was playing a game or if she actually believed she was Joan of Arc.

She withdrew her hand and put it on her hip. "Well, in that case, I'll let you live."

He moved and then winced as his leg began to throb again. In her child's play he'd forgotten all about his wound. "Joan, I'm not going to live if you don't run and get me help. Someone shot me in the leg," he told her gruffly as he adjusted his makeshift bandage.

Suddenly Joan's eyes filled with horror as she noticed all the blood that she seemed to have missed before. "Goodness gracious, Mister! You're bleeding like a stuck pig!" she said, falling out of character.

She jumped down from the horse, her tin clanging as she ran to him and knelt down. He saw that she wore trousers under her skirt, and he put her age to be about nine or ten. Clearly old enough to understand how to get help.

"Yes, Joan, and that's why I need for you to—"

"That bullet's gonna have to come out!" Joan interrupted.

"I know that. I—"

"Someone must have thought that you were a deer! Don't you know not to go traipsing through the woods this time of year?"

James closed his eyes and took a deep breath, then opened them again. "Joan, could you just—"

"And here you are all dressed in brown just like a deer. Nope, that wasn't too smart!"

He narrowed his gaze at her. "If it's too dangerous to be in the woods, what are you doing here?"

She just smiled and pushed the gourd back off of her forehead. " 'Cause these are my woods! Ain't nobody gonna shoot me!" she exclaimed, looking at him as if he were the dense one. "And my name's not really Joan."

"Well, whatever it is, could you just—"

"My name's Louanne Wise. But you can call me Victoria."

He knew that he shouldn't ask but. . . "Why do you want me to call you Victoria, if your name is Louanne?"

"Because Louanne is so plain! Victoria is more. . . noble sounding, you know, like Queen Victoria! But it seems I am doomed to live out my existence with the name I was born with." She finished with a long-suffering sigh.

She then looked at him with renewed interest. "What is your name? You're not a robber or outlaw or anything like that, are you? Because if you are, I'm not supposed to be talking to you. Actually, I'm not supposed to be talking to anyone who doesn't live in Wiseville. I'm a Wise, you see, and practically everyone around here is kin to me one way or another; so it's all right if I talk to them. But I don't believe that I've ever seen you before!"

It was he that took the breath after that little speech. It made him tired just listening to her.

"My name is James Larabee of the Alabama Larabees, and I promise you that I'm not an outlaw. But I am going to pass out if I don't get this blood stopped," he grumbled, then added, "You know, Joan of Arc wouldn't allow a man to suffer out in the wild."

She thrust her chin up and adjusted the bed sheet around her shoulders. She was back in character. "Of course not. Joan of Arc can do anything!" Then she was quiet for a moment. "Except, of course, she didn't save herself from being burned at the stake. She should have come up with a better plan," she added with a frown.

"Louanne, honey, please. . . ," he groaned. "Get help."

"Okay." She jumped up and looked at his horse. "Can I take your horse?"

"If it'll help you get help faster, by all means take him."

With the skill of one who had been raised around horses, Louanne climbed on the back of the brown animal and took off.

ᄋᄋ♡ᄋ

As she galloped toward home, she thought about the man she'd left behind. He sure seemed like a nice person, even if he was just a little grumpy. She hoped that his leg would be all right. One of her uncles had come home from the war with one of his legs cut off at the knee. She didn't want that to happen to Mr. Larabee.

It seemed strange to find a man who wasn't kin in her woods. Strangers just didn't pass through Wiseville that often.

Then she got another idea. What if God had brought Mr. Larabee to her? She had been praying for God to send her a daddy, since He had her real daddy in heaven. Mama had told her to make a prayer list, and that was one of the first things she prayed for everyday, though Mama wasn't aware of it.

One of her many uncles was the preacher in town, and he always said that God worked in mysterious ways. Well, finding a shot-up stranger in her woods was the most mysterious thing that she'd ever come across! Surely, that must mean that he was the answer to her prayers! It made perfect sense!

As her house came into view, however, she wasn't sure that her mother would go running to help a man that she didn't know. Since Daddy's death, two years before, gentlemen had been flocking around her mama, asking for her hand in marriage. Mama never seemed very interested. She was always telling them that it just wasn't proper to come calling out at her house, since she and Louanne had no menfolk who lived with them to make it proper. She would allow only the cousins and uncles to visit. Louanne wished that her mother would marry someone. The man in the woods was as good as any of the men who'd come calling. If only Louanne could find some way to get her mother to meet him. Suddenly, an idea came to her. It was in the form of a lie. She got off the horse and ran to where her mother was coming out of the chicken coop.

"Mama! Come quick! I just found a man in the woods, and I think he's. . .dead!"

❧♡❧

James realized that he had dozed off, when a sound startled him and shook him out of his slumber. He saw that it was a small wagon being pulled by a horse, coming down the wooded trail.

The little soldier had done it! She'd gotten him help. He relaxed and closed his eyes again, waiting for them to reach him. He wondered if she had brought her parents with her. He hoped that she at least had gotten her pa. A woman would have a hard time lifting him into a wagon.

He heard the clatter of the wagon. He opened his eyes and saw a beautiful woman dressed in blue calico, getting down from the wagon. But other than the little girl and the woman, there was no one else. He shifted his weight to sit up but accidentally hit the wound against a rock on the ground. The pain was so intense he couldn't cry out; instead, he felt himself blacking out. He fought it, trying desperately to hold on to consciousness.

"You're right, Louanne. I think he's dead," the woman said.

Dead? He wasn't dead. . .was he?

"Why don't you listen to his heart, Mama?"

There was a pause, then the woman said, "Alright."

He heard a rustle of fabric, then the scent of honeysuckle flooded his senses and the touch of her soft hair brushed against his chin. He opened his eyes and saw her press her ear to his chest.

"My, you smell pretty," he said in his best Southern drawl, despite himself.

Her head reared and whipped around. Startled blue-green eyes flew to his face. "You're alive!" she charged and scrambled back. But in doing so, she lost her balance and tumbled to the ground.

He managed to lift himself to his elbows. "Of course, I'm alive. Didn't Louanne tell you that I needed help?"

The woman pushed herself upright and smoothed her skirts modestly over her ankles, while she sat a small distance from him.

"She said that you were dead!" she told him, sending Louanne a warning glare that future retribution was soon coming her way. Louanne began to play with the tin on her chest.

"Ma'am, please, I've been shot, and I need to get this

bullet out of my leg. . . ."

"Oh, my goodness! You're not an outlaw or something, are you?" Her hand was over her heart, a horrified expression on her pretty face.

Was everyone in this family suspicious of outlaws?

"Momma, someone shot him thinking he was a deer," Louanne chimed in helpfully.

An understanding look came over "Momma's" face. "Oh, dear. I'll bet that's what happened. You are bleeding pretty badly," she said carefully, as if trying to make up her mind about something.

Suddenly, she hopped up and clapped her hands together. "Well, I guess we need to get you aboard this wagon, don't we?" She looked at him as if measuring him up, then she glanced at the wagon. A worried expression overtook her face.

James grabbed a stick beside him. "Ma'am, if you can help me, I can lift myself up with this." He lifted one arm, while gripping the branch with the other. "My name is James Larabee, by the way."

The woman reached down to clutch his arm, and together they managed to bring him to his feet. He put his arm around her and leaned heavily on her shoulders. She, struggling to hold his weight, turned toward him. James found himself no more than a half an inch from her face.

As he stared into her eyes, his pain didn't seem nearly as bad. She seemed to feel it, too, because she stared back.

Before the war, James Larabee had courted some of the most beautiful young women around Dothan, but none of those compared to the petite angel who was looking into his eyes at that moment. None had the silky-smooth, soft peach skin nor the long brown eyelashes that framed her ocean-blue eyes. And, though most of her hair was wound loosely in a knot on top of her head, the rich chestnut color gleamed in the soft light of the woods.

"You never told me your name," he said to her, but he wished he hadn't spoken.

As if she'd suddenly become aware of their situation, she blushed hotly and looked away. "My name is Mrs. Tessa Wise," she told him, emphasizing the title.

James's heart sank, and he could feel the pain again in his leg as the euphoric feeling he felt at her nearness began to melt away. She was married. He was ashamed that he'd embarrassed them both.

But as she helped him slide into the back of the wagon, he reminded himself that it didn't matter—he wasn't in the market for a wife. Saloon owners didn't marry. That was no life for a family.

And besides, he had lost too many loved ones. He would not make himself vulnerable to those feelings ever again.

They set off in the wagon. The pain in his leg throbbed as he was jostled about, and he blamed his delirium for making him think of love. Tessa Wise was going to take out his bullet and perhaps let him bunk down a few days in her barn. Then he'd leave.

A whole new life was waiting for him, and he wasn't going to allow anything to stand in the way.

Yet, the whole time he repeated the words to himself, he couldn't get rid of the picture of those beautiful blue-green eyes.

Chapter 2

More than once on the journey back to her house Tessa Wise wondered what she had gotten herself into by offering to help James Larabee. She and her daughter were alone, and having a man at her house, injured or not, just wasn't seemly.

Of course, he'd just have to stay in the barn. But, then again, the barn was so drafty, and it was January, just a week after the New Year. Already this winter was proving to be a rough one and was predicted to be even worse later in the month.

She sighed and chewed on her bottom lip as she worried over her situation. Mr. Larabee was injured and he needed help. What would God think of her if she left an injured man to bleed to death? He was, after all, shot on her property!

That thought caused her to start chewing on her lip again. Who had shot him? Had they really mistaken him for a deer? And if so, why had they not come to him, seen their error, and helped him?

Tessa had the sinking feeling that it was one of her late husband's young cousins or maybe one of their friends. It would be just like them to shoot impulsively, get scared, and run away.

"Isn't he handsome, Mama?"

That little whisper from Louanne broke Tessa out of her fretting in a big hurry! "What did you say?" she demanded, also speaking in a whisper.

Louanne smiled and got closer to her mother's ear. "He is so handsome. Riding up and finding him just lying there in the forest was like something out of a fairy tale," she said dramatically while putting her hand over her heart.

"Oh, Louanne, I don't want to hear any of your nonsense! This man is not a prince, and if he was, he wouldn't be tromping through our woods in the dead of winter!"

Actually, her daughter did have a point. The man was quite nice-looking. He had dark, wavy brown hair that was slightly longish and curled at the collar. His nose was straight, but not too long, and his cheekbones were prominent, his jaw square and manly. But that doesn't matter, she told herself, shaking herself from the picture that she'd just conjured up. The sooner she got him patched up, the sooner he could be on his way!

"But he could be a prince exiled from his country and running from those who want to kill him!" Louanne insisted, getting herself all worked up, her voice growing louder with each word.

"I promise that I'm not a prince," their rider chimed in from the back of the wagon.

Mortified, Tessa sent her daughter a glare. "Please excuse my daughter, Mr. Larabee. She's got quite an imagination."

"Don't you worry, Mrs. Wise. I find your daughter charming," James Larabee told her, his lazy Southern drawl drawing out the sentence. Tessa thought his accent was quite nice. Different from the country accents of North Louisiana, there was something else in his voice. She couldn't quite pin it down.

When she glanced back, she noticed his eyes were squeezed shut in obvious pain and he clutched the make-shift bandage wrapped around his leg.

She quickly looked forward and snapped the reins. She was going to have to get that bullet out before infection set in.

ϑ♥ϐ

It took them more than a few minutes and a whole lot of effort, but they finally got Mr. Larabee into the house and situated in the spare bedroom. One of her brothers-in-law, J. T. Wise, was a doctor, and Tessa sent Louanne after him. Tessa, having served as a temporary nurse during the war, was well acquainted with digging bullets out of men, but she still hoped that J. T. could be found, just in case.

She mixed some laudanum in a glass of water and took it to him. "Here you go, Mr. Larabee. Just drink this, and it should help you to not hurt so bad."

As he took the glass from her, his fingers brushed against hers and their eyes met. Tessa quickly looked away and tried to hide the blush that she knew must be burning her cheeks. What was wrong with her? Why did this man affect her so strangely?

Tessa was carefully removing the shirt-bandage from around his leg when he spoke. "Uh, have you ever done this before?" There was more than a slight trace of worry in his voice.

Tessa lifted an eyebrow as she looked over at him. "Scared, Mr. Larabee?"

"Cautious, Mrs. Wise," he countered. Suddenly they both started to chuckle. It went a long way to ease some of the strain in the room.

She flashed him a smile and started cutting the fabric away from the wound. "As a matter of fact, I have done this before, so you don't have to worry. I patched up quite a few men in the war, both Confederate and Yankee. But if you're still uneasy, I sent for my brother-in-law, who is a doctor."

James shook his head. "I'm sure you'll do just fine."

Tessa gave him a smile that she hoped contained more assurance than she felt. As she examined the wound, she realized that the bullet was lodged pretty deep. She could see part of it, but she wasn't sure that she could get it out without causing him to start bleeding again.

She looked at her patient to ask him if he could feel the laudanum taking effect yet, but his eyes were closed. She gazed back at the wound, took a deep breath, then grabbed the large tweezers and went to work.

❧♡❧

James couldn't remember when he'd ever felt worse. Though his head was swimming with the medicine she'd given him, he could still feel the pain as the doctor dug out the bullet. He had to wonder: If it hurt this bad with the doctor doing the surgery, what would it have felt like with an amateur like Tessa Wise doing the job? He was just glad the good doctor had arrived in time!

But, it was all over with now. Doc had sewed him up and wrapped a bandage around his leg and told him that he wasn't to move for two weeks.

Two weeks! He didn't know who took the news worse, Tessa or himself. She had pulled the doctor out of the room in a big hurry, and he could still hear them whispering in the next room. Well, he wasn't happy about it either. Two weeks was going to put him off schedule, mess up his plans! He had a life to get on with, and this setback was fouling everything up.

Frustrated, he looked up to the ceiling and railed aloud, "Why me, God?"

"Why are you blaming God?" Louanne said from the doorway, surprising James. He hadn't even heard the door open.

"Why are you eavesdropping?" he countered with a smile.

Louanne, who was now dressed in a pretty green dress with a matching bow in her hair, skipped into the room and sat at the edge of his bed. "How else is a kid supposed to find out things?" she asked with a shrug. She then leaned over and put a hand to his head. "Are you feeling better?"

James squelched a laugh at her motherly action. *She must be imitating Tessa.* "Yes, ma'am," he drawled, playing along. "Doc Wise fixed me up."

"It was such a tragic thing that happened to you out there. I could just imagine that it was me who was injured on the cold, cold ground. . .waiting to die. . .all hope lost," she exclaimed dramatically, clasping her hands together at her chest. "Then, off in the distance a rider approaches upon a pure white steed and rescues me. He would be a prince and he would ask me to marry him!"

This time James did chuckle. "I've never heard anyone take an accident and turn it into a fairy tale. You're something else, Little Lulu!"

Louanne looked at him as though he had just offered her a giant piece of candy. "You called me Lulu! You know, my dad used to call me that," she said in an awed whisper. "It's a sign!"

James opened his mouth to comment then froze. "Used to?" he asked carefully.

"Yeah, my dad was killed in the war."

"I'm sorry," he told her, but his mind was whirling. Why had Tessa led him to believe her husband was still around? An elation he couldn't even begin to understand washed over him, but just as quickly, he squelched it.

Then he thought about what Louanne had said before that. "What did you mean when you said that it's a sign?"

"I can't tell you, right now, because it's a secret! But I can tell you that I was only kidding when I said that I thought you were a prince, earlier in the wagon. I know you're just a regular man." She got closer, as if she wanted to share a secret. "Princes have countries to run and damsels to rescue. They wouldn't be riding through our woods. Besides, I have another reason for knowing that you're not a prince, but I can't tell you that either. I can tell you it has something to do with God, though."

James sighed inwardly. God sure didn't make it easy for people to ignore Him. James wanted nothing more than to get on with his life and never think about God, and instead he was saddled for two weeks with what, apparently, was a deeply religious family.

"You sure do have a lot of secrets for such a little girl!" he commented absently, his attention shifting to his throbbing leg. The medication was wearing off and the pain was returning.

Louanne huffed and lifted her chin in the air. "I'm nine years old, Mr. Larabee. I'm hardly little." He grimaced, and she laid her hand on top of his. "You're looking ill again, Mr. Larabee. Is it hurting?"

He nodded, and she scooted off the bed. "I'll run in there and get Uncle J. T."

Louanne ran into the living room, but not two seconds later, she was back. She sighed a longsuffering breath and informed him, "Mama told me she'd talk to me later then sent me back in here."

She came around the bed and resumed her place beside him, taking his hand into her own. "I know what will help! I'll pray for you. Uncle Donald says that Jesus can heal the sick and afflicted, and since you were shot you're not really sick. I guess we can call you 'afflicted' so this should work," she told him matter-of-factly.

"Lulu, what does your Uncle Donald do?" he asked, though he was afraid that he already knew the answer.

"He's a preacher!"

With a resigned sigh, he nodded his head and let her pray for him.

No, God surely didn't make it easy.

❧♡❧

"J. T., just what were you thinking telling that. . .that. . . stranger that he should stay off his leg. . .at my house! I can't have a man stay here! What will people think?" Tessa charged at her brother-in-law. She was upset, not only at J. T. but at herself for the happiness that ran through her at the thought of getting to know James Larabee a little better. That didn't make any sense! She wasn't interested in any man, much less a stranger.

Dr. J. T. Wise just grinned at Tessa, a smile so reminiscent of her late husband that Tessa felt suddenly guilty. "Tess, everyone will think you're doing a poor unfortunate man a favor and doing your Christian duty by nursing him back to health. Besides, he really does need to be watched closely. Infection could easily set into that wound." He picked up his black bag and withdrew a couple of packets. "Give him this if he suffers any pain."

Tessa took the packets but still glared at J. T. "I don't like this, J. T."

"What do you want me to do, Tess? Take him home with me? I already have five kids that I don't hardly have room for! And with Carolyn heavy with the sixth, she wouldn't be too happy if I brought an injured patient for her to care for," he informed her with a pleading expression.

There were seven Wise brothers and every one of them could talk a flea into jumping off a dog. But she knew that he was right. Carolyn was in no condition to care for the stranger. Neither was the rest of the family. It looked like, whether she liked it or not, she was stuck with the man for two weeks.

And despite the butterflies in her stomach, she refused to be excited about it!

"Oh, alright! But it's up to you to explain this to

Donald. I don't want him upset at me for having a man in my house!"

J. T. grinned. "You know, Tess, I haven't seen a ring on the man's finger. . . ."

"Don't say it!" she screeched at him then, realizing her volume, lowered her voice. "Don't you dare try to play matchmaker, Jonathon Tyler Wise! We don't know this man from Adam!"

"That's no problem, Tess," he told her as he put on his hat. "You've got two weeks to get to know him better!"

With a growl, she grabbed his arm and marched him toward the door, grabbing his coat off the hook and stuffing it in his arms as she went. "Leave while you still can. Just don't forget to talk to Donald!"

He shrugged his coat on, and just before she shut the door, he added, "I'll tell him he needs to start polishing up on his wedding ser—"

The rest of his sentence was just a mere muffled sound behind Tessa's door. She chuckled and shook her head. That J. T. was something else! She didn't know how his wife put up with him.

Her smile faded as she focused on the door that led to the guest bedroom. She didn't understand why she found it so hard to speak with the man. He was injured and harmless, she reminded herself, but it didn't seem to help the butterflies that churned in her stomach. She knew that James Larabee was a gentleman—she could hear it in his voice and see it in his mannerisms. He was probably a very rich gentleman.

So what is he doing here?

With a determined tilt of her chin and a fortified

breath, she started toward the room.

She was about to find out.

Chapter 3

They were praying. Or, at least, Louanne was praying while James Larabee stared down at his covers. Tessa smiled as her daughter's earnest words went on and on. A talent she, no doubt, inherited from her uncle Donald, who was famous for his lengthy prayers.

Since she hadn't been noticed, Tessa took the opportunity to study James Larabee. Despite the pain etched across his features, he certainly was nice to look at. And those eyes of his. . .they were a mesmerizing moss-green color. Surely he'd had many a lady vying for his attentions back in Alabama. Had he ever married? Did he have children?

"And we ask all this in Your name, Amen!" Louanne finished off. James looked up about that time and caught Tessa staring at him with what she knew must be a dreamy expression on her face. Tessa quickly looked away.

It seemed she was destined to be embarrassed around this man every time they were together!

Pulling together her remaining shreds of composure, Tessa folded her arms and addressed her daughter.

"Louanne, why don't you finish gathering those eggs I'd started earlier. And don't forget to put on your coat!"

Louanne passed Mr. Larabee a look that said she was not happy with the request then stood up. "A daughter's work is never done!" she wailed as she left the room.

Tessa watched the door close then turned back to her guest. "Well," she said nervously, "how are you feeling?"

Mr. Larabee waved a hand at his leg. "It was hurting pretty bad, but it seems to have calmed down a bit." The last part of the sentence was spoken with a touch of bewilderment, Tessa thought.

She nodded and wiped her palms on her skirts. "Mr. Larabee, I. . .uh. . .I hope that you didn't take my getting upset earlier. . .personal, it's just that it took me by surprise and. . ."

"It's alright, Mrs. Wise. You and your daughter live here alone, with your husband dead and all, and I am a stranger. Worse than that, a male stranger. If you can just tell me where I can find a room to rent, I'll get out of here first thing."

She felt herself blush again. Louanne must have told him that her father was dead. Now, Tessa not only felt like a bad hostess, she was a liar, too. "No, I'm just trying to apologize, Mr. Larabee. Of course, you must stay here. We have plenty of room, and you're going to need someone to look after you."

She'd avoided making eye contact with him, until she spoke those last words. Then she looked up at him, and there it was again. That connection that said so much, yet made so little sense. She quickly glanced down.

He looked away, too. "Well, I surely do appreciate the

offer, Mrs. Wise." He paused then spoke again. "Why don't you pull up a chair and let me tell you about myself. It might make you feel more comfortable if you know who I am."

She looked back at him and smiled shyly. "I think that's a good idea. I have to admit that I've been curious about why you were riding through our woods," she replied as she walked over to the corner of the room and pulled the wooden straight-back chair to the side of his bed.

He grinned sheepishly as he watched her get comfortable. "Well, as far as traveling through your woods is concerned, a fellow in Mississippi told me about this trail. Told me it was the best way to get to Oklahoma where I'm supposed to meet up with a wagon train headed out to California."

Tessa shook her head in bemusement. "And now you're going to be late because someone shot you in my woods. You know I still don't know who would have shot you and run away."

James's face grew grim. "I don't know either, but I would like to report it to the sheriff. . .that is, if Wiseville has one."

"Yes, actually. . ."

James groaned and held out a hand. "Don't tell me it's another Wise brother!"

Tessa laughed, feeling more and more at ease with the gentleman. "I'm afraid so. And I'm sure he'll be over here along with the rest of the clan when they find out that you are staying here." None of them would be able to resist it. They'd been trying to fix Tessa up with every available man in the area and she'd had nothing to do with them. And now having a man living under her roof would definitely get their attention. Wanted or not!

The Wises were good people, but they just didn't understand why she wasn't interested in any of the men they'd introduced her to. It wasn't that she didn't want to marry again, because she did. In fact, she dreamed of having a husband again and being in the same kind of loving relationship she'd enjoyed with her late husband, Will. She wanted more children, too. But she had yet to meet a man she felt a connection to, someone she wanted to know better.

Until now. . .

"I hope that it won't cause you trouble, Mrs. Wise. I know how folks can gossip."

She waved off his concern. "You don't understand Wiseville, Mr. Larabee. They are like overprotective mama bears to those they consider kin. They will be concerned about my safety, not my reputation. They know that I'm a good Christian woman and would never put my relationship with God in jeopardy by doing anything. . .foolish," she told him, hoping that he understood her double meaning. She didn't want him getting any ideas, either!

"But you were going to tell me about yourself," she prompted, changing the subject.

"I am the eldest son of Andrew and Virginia Larabee of Dothan, Alabama. But I didn't know my mother very well, only from what my father told me about her. She died giving birth to my brother, Joseph. So it was just the three of us. We lived in a big plantation house." He smiled reminiscently. "Grew up living the pampered gentleman's life, I suppose, although Daddy kept his promise to Mama and made sure we were in church every Sunday. But that didn't keep us from being a little spoiled. The cotton was plentiful, and we had everything money could buy."

"And you feel guilty about that," she guessed, when he paused.

He stared at her for a moment as if trying to read her thoughts. "Yes, I guess I do," he relented. "That and the fact that we owned slaves. I grew up thinking that it was normal to own other people, but I now know that it's wrong. The system wouldn't have lasted, with or without the war."

He sighed and stared forward as if he were seeing something other than the wall. "When the war began, I immediately enlisted just like all the other men who lived around us. My brother followed. We were patriots, full of enthusiasm to do our part, but reality quickly invaded our zeal. We saw and did things that we never thought we'd have to do. It became a quest for survival and longing for the war to be over and done with.

"Then, I got news that my brother had been killed, and then my father. . .I hadn't even known that he'd en-listed! I just wanted to go home. It didn't matter that I'd been promoted to captain or that I'd managed to come through unscathed. The war had suddenly gotten too close, become too personal. It had taken away my family," he finished gruffly. He closed his eyes for a second then looked at her apologetically.

"Mrs. Wise, I'm sorry. I didn't mean to go on like this. I don't know. . ."

Tessa reached out and laid her hand on top of his. "It's alright, Mr. Larabee. I understand."

He shook his head and turned his hand palm up and grasped her fingers. "Of course you do. I'm not the only one who lost loved ones in that war. I didn't mean to drag up memories for you."

Tessa knew she should pull her hand away, but she found that she didn't want to. There was such comfort sitting there holding his hand and sharing his pain. A kindred bond pulled them together, one that she was unable to understand.

"Mr. Larabee, Will has been gone for three years, and I've made my peace with God about it." She noticed that he dropped his gaze when she mentioned God's name, just as she'd seen him do with Louanne, and she wondered about it. But she didn't pry. Perhaps she'd have the opportunity to bring up the subject later in the week.

The mood that had enveloped them earlier, however, had diminished, and she became self-conscious about holding his hand. Slowly she withdrew her hand and laid it on her lap.

"What happened to the plantation? Did you return to it?" she questioned.

His face grew grim. "It was burned to the ground, along with the cotton crops. My father had buried some money in the graveyard, just in case something like that happened. I decided to take it and start a new life."

Tessa studied his face as she felt the pain laced in his words. "By going to California?"

He nodded. "I'm going to buy a saloon out there."

"You're going to do what!" Tessa screeched as she

stood to her feet. "I'm housing a. . .a. . .bar owner?" She was so taken aback that she wasn't aware that she was screaming at him.

His eyes widened and he held out a hand toward her. "Now, Mrs. Wise, I don't own one, yet. I. . ."

"It's the same thing! You gave me the impression that you were raised in a Christian home! How can you even think about living such a lifestyle? Were you not raised to believe in God?"

Her question hung in the air as they stared at each other. "Yes," he answered, after a moment. "I was raised to believe in God. But I prayed every day for God to protect my little brother. That He'd return me safely to my father and our home. But it was all destroyed. It was as though God hadn't cared about me or heard a word that I'd prayed. Why should I keep believing in Him, then, Mrs. Wise?" he asked, his bitterness burning through his words.

Tessa slowly sat back down and stared at her hands. "I don't know why God chooses to answer some prayers the way He does or why He takes some folks and leaves others. I know that He has a plan that we can't even begin to understand and it's not for us to question. But we can also see the blessings that He does give us and be thankful for what we have."

James stared up at the ceiling. "And what do I have to be thankful for, Tessa Wise? You have family left. I don't."

Tessa stood up again, and this time she planted her hands on her hips and glared at him. "I could name a half dozen things right off the top of my head, James Larabee, but I'm not gonna! You are bound and determined to feel sorry for yourself and blame God. But when you are tired of doing that—tired of being bitter—then you need to look around and let yourself see what God has blessed you with and how He can bless you if you'd only let Him."

And before he could say anything to that, she scooted the chair out of her way and marched out of the room.

Well, I've certainly lost the art of knowing how to talk to a lady, James thought sarcastically to himself after the door closed behind Tessa with a snap.

Where did that suave, witty man go who used to know how to charm women of any age? Had his manners died along with his faith in God? Or was he intentionally driving her away because he felt she was getting too close?

Being here with Tessa Wise was just too comfortable, too easy. It was enough to make a man forget his plans, his goals. It could make a man start thinking of things he had no business thinking of, such as a family. A home.

No. He had to stay strong. He had to keep reminding himself of his original reasons for heading to California. He had to ignore the voice inside of his head that told him his mother and father would be disappointed in his saloon plans—that they'd want a better, moral life for him.

And he had to ignore the incredulous eyes of Tessa Wise.

ஐ♥ஐ

Outside, Louanne crouched down below the spare bedroom window, where she'd been eavesdropping on the grown-ups' conversation.

She propped her elbows on her knees and cupped her face in her hands. This was all so terrible! How were her mama and Mr. Larabee ever going to get married if they were already fussing?

She was going to have to do something about this! They weren't going to come together on their own, it seemed, so she was just going to have to help them.

But how? Suddenly she had an idea. In her fairy tales, everyone always lived happily ever after. Maybe she could get some ideas from her books!

Quickly she ran to the coop to gather the rest of the eggs so she could get back to her room. She had a lot of reading to do before sundown!

Chapter 4

About forty-five minutes after the doctor left, his brother Donald—the preacher—came over with his son, Earl. James held back a sigh as he shook the preacher's hand.

"It's nice to meet you, Mr. Larabee. We just wanted to come over and see how you were doing. J. T. told us about the accident," Donald told him.

James gave the man a shrewd look. "And to check me out," he guessed.

Donald grinned unrepentantly. "That, too. We all feel responsible to look after Tessa."

James nodded thoughtfully. "I don't blame you, Reverend. I hate putting her out, but it doesn't look like I have much choice," he said grimly, indicating his leg.

Donald frowned. "J. T. said somebody accidentally shot you."

"I wouldn't call it an accident, Reverend. For all I know the man had a clear view of me when he took me down. At best, I would call it carelessness and cowardliness. Whoever did this deserves to be punished. To leave a man to bleed to death is just as bad as deliberately shooting to kill. If Louanne hadn't found me, I could have died out there."

A quick intake of breath came from beside Donald. James turned his attention on Earl who was sweating profusely. "What's wrong, son?" Donald asked.

"I. . .uh. . .need to ask Aunt Tessa something," he muttered and quickly left the room.

Donald shook his head and looked back at James. "That boy's been acting so strange lately. Well, you remember how it is being seventeen. You don't know whether to act like a child or a man!"

James glanced at Donald then back to the door and smiled absently. "Yeah, I remember," he commented, but his mind was racing. Did Earl know something about who shot him? Acting strange was one thing. Nervous strange was quite another.

"Well, I'll let you rest, but before I leave, why don't I pray for you!"

James thought about declining, but Donald was already laying hands on him and bowing his head before James could get the words out.

James sighed and gave in to the inevitable. There was just no running from God.

Over the next four days, James got a visit from every one of Tessa's in-laws.

Sitting around visiting with the Wises' was about as comfortable as getting teeth pulled. James had the odd feeling that he had been put on trial and the verdict wasn't favorable.

The toughest came from the mother of all the Wise boys, Irene Wise. She sat in James's room and asked him about everything from his childhood to how many girls he'd courted. She specifically wanted to know why he was going to California. He hemmed and hawed and drummed up a passel of vague answers to satisfy her curiosity, but he doubted that she'd been fooled.

He'd gotten to know Tessa better, too. She'd overcome her shyness around him, and she seemed to want to talk to him as much as he wanted to talk to her. She was unlike any woman he'd ever met. It wasn't just that she was beautiful, there was something else about her, something fine—a real quality that made her special.

But now they were all gone—he hoped—and he could rest a little easier. Especially since J. T. had brought in a chair with wheels so that he could get out of that tiny little room.

It was late in the evening, and he watched from his chair as Tessa ran around the kitchen, getting supper ready. She laid out potatoes and peas to be shelled on the table then scurried around and started battering the chicken, preparing it to fry. She was doing everything so efficiently that he didn't want to break her rhythmic dance. But he was so tired of sitting and doing nothing that he spoke up.

"Can I help you do something?"

She looked up in surprise. "What do you mean?"

"I can peel potatoes. That used to be my brother's and my punishment when we were kids. We got to be pretty good at it," he said with a grin.

She looked at him with a raised eyebrow. "I don't doubt it!" she said teasingly. "Well, I never turn down help. I was just about to call Louanne in here to shell those peas. I'm sure she'll enjoy having her work cut in half."

She pulled out a chair from the table then helped him wheel his chair under where the potatoes were. As she let go of the chair he reached up and caught her hand.

"I'm sorry that you're having to cook extra and work harder just because I'm here. You need to know that I fully intend to reimburse you for everything, including room and board," James told her, enjoying the soft touch of her hand. He couldn't resist rubbing his thumb over the satiny skin. He was surprised when she didn't pull her hand away.

She did clear her throat in what James was sure was a nervous gesture. "Don't be silly, Mr. Larabee. It's no more work than usual, and I always make too much food anyway," she told him.

"Has it been hard, you know, being left to raise your daughter alone?" he asked, knowing it was none of his business but feeling a desire to know.

She looked at him, surprised that he'd asked such a question. Staring at him, she opened her mouth to say, "Don't be silly," then she stopped. She looked thoughtful then told him truthfully, "Yes, it has been hard. At times, I didn't think that I could make it. But the Wises have helped me along the way."

He stared at her probingly. "But they couldn't fill that void, could they?" he guessed.

She smiled sadly and gripped his hand harder. "No, they couldn't. But God did." She saw him turn his head and sigh, so she emphasized, "I know you don't like to hear that, but it's the truth. And He can do the same for you."

She let go of his hand and threw both of her arms in

the air. "That's all I'm going to say!"

He laughed, despite the fact that he was uncomfortable with the conversation. Even though she constantly nagged him about his relationship with God, it didn't lessen his fascination with the lovely woman. "Nothing you can say is going to offend me, Mrs. Wise. I don't want you to be afraid to say anything to me."

She gave him a bemused look. "Strangely enough, I'm not. I feel real comfortable talking with you, Mr. Larabee. You've been great company for Louanne and me."

He watched her talk, how her lips moved and smiled, how her eyes twinkled, how the curls fell about her face, having fallen from their topknot. He felt a quaking in his chest. It was the oddest feeling, and he wondered what was the matter with him. Was he getting sick? Or was he just becoming enamored with Tessa Wise?

It had been so long since he'd been attracted to a woman; he'd almost forgotten what it felt like. But had it ever felt like this before? He couldn't recall any relationship before that matched the intensity he felt for Tessa.

"I feel at ease with you, too. I can't tell you how much I appreciate your letting me stay here, Mrs. Wise. And it's not just because you're taking care of my wounds, but because you've made me feel a part of your family."

They stared at each other for a full thirty seconds before she cleared her throat again and backed up a step or two. "Well!" she said as she blinked a couple of times. "This family is never going to get to eat if we don't get busy!"

He smiled at her knowingly, pleased that she was so rattled. "Sounds good to me. Where do I start?"

She showed him what to do then called for Louanne, and soon they were all chatting while they worked.

James enjoyed watching Tessa talk to her daughter, the easy camaraderie that they shared. He really missed not growing up with a mother. His father had filled his head with stories of how beautiful and gracious his mother had been, but James now wondered if she'd have talked to him and played with him or if she would have been too busy being the grand lady of the plantation to do such things with him. He'd had a nanny, a large black woman who watched after him and kept him in line, but it wasn't the same.

Then his mind wandered to Tessa, the woman. What kind of wife had she been to Will? Had she enjoyed being married? Had she loved her husband too much to love someone else now that he was gone? It would be nice coming home to her, James decided. She absolutely fascinated him—she could tease and be quick-witted, then she could be gentle and nurturing. She wasn't the type to let people take advantage of her, but he had the impression that she would never hurt anyone's feelings, either.

Ah, but what did he know? He'd only known her four days! Maybe tomorrow she'd wake up and the sweetness and kindness would be gone. But he didn't think so.

What was it about her that captivated him so?

"Mr. Larabee, have you ever read *Cinderella*?" Louanne asked him as he picked up his third potato.

It took him a second to focus on what she was asking him. "*Cinderella*?" He thought a minute, then his brow cleared. "Oh, that silly little story about the prince and the shoe?"

Louanne looked at him with pursed lips. "I like that story."

"Uh. . ." He looked at Tessa for help, but she just smiled and shrugged her shoulders, putting the pressure all on him. "Well, what I meant was that I've always figured that story was more for. . .you know. . .girls."

Louanne sighed and rolled her eyes. "Okay, but let's think about what the prince did in the story. He runs after this pretty girl that he's never seen before, and all he finds is a shoe. Then he scours the whole countryside trying on the shoe to find the right owner, because he feels that this woman is his only true love. Don't you find that incredibly romantic?" she asked, wearing that dreamy look on her face that she wore every time she got dramatic.

He looked at Louanne then up at Tessa, who was eyeing him with interest waiting to hear his answer. She was enjoying this, the little minx! "Actually, I always thought that was a really dumb way of looking for her. Why couldn't he just look at their faces? If I'd found my only true love, I would think that I'd remember what she looks like."

Louanne narrowed her eyes at him, while tapping a pea pod on the table. "Let me put this another way. Let's say it's. . .oh. . .my mama!" she said as if she'd just thought of it. "And she was dressed up in a really fine dress of white silk and her hair was down and curly with roses pinned in it. She wouldn't look anything like she does now, so how would you know it was her?"

James looked at Tessa while Louanne talked and imagined her with that white dress on and flowers framing her lovely face. She would look just like a bride. Then again—no, he couldn't think about that.

Tessa looked up then and caught him staring, but she didn't look away. They stayed like that for mere seconds, but it seemed like an eternity.

"Louanne," he said, still looking at Tessa, "I can't imagine not recognizing your mama, even if she was wearing an old toe sack."

Louanne's laugh broke their connection, and James noticed that Tessa seemed flustered as she hurriedly turned back to her frying pan.

"That's not a very romantic thing to say, Mr. Larabee! You can't write a sonnet using the words 'toe sack!'" Louanne said.

James grinned. "Oh, I don't know about that. Let's see. . . Cardinals are red, but some birds are black, I think you're quite lovely in that old toe sack!"

Both Tessa and Louanne groaned in chorus at the terrible poem, and acting offended, James looked at them both. "If you don't like that one, I have lots more."

"No!" they quickly answered, then they all dissolved into giggles.

James savored the evening, watching Tessa and Louanne, enjoying the delicious meal. He knew with the life he'd chosen for himself it would probably not come again.

ᘒ♡ᘖ

Two days later, Louanne was still trying to come up with a way to get Mr. Larabee to ask her mama to marry him. They were talking, she'd give them that, but it was all too polite. Unless they got on the subject of California and Mr. Larabee's "plans," then they seemed to get all tense and they'd stop talking.

Louanne was baffled. What were his "plans"? Whatever they were, they must be something that her mama didn't approve of. And from the sound of the conversation going on around her at that very moment, she had a feeling it was about to get unpleasant once again.

"James," her mother began. Mr. Larabee had asked her to please call him that instead of being so formal. Likewise, her mama had asked him to call her Tessa. Louanne saw this as progress. "Do you still own the family land in Alabama?"

Louanne's eyes darted from Mama to Mr. Larabee, and from the look on his face, she had a feeling that he didn't like the question.

"Yes." That was all he said. Louanne looked at her mother—a storm was definitely about to brew.

"And. . . ?" Tessa prompted.

Mr. Larabee just shrugged his shoulders. "And what?"

"Do you plan to sell it?"

"No."

Mama's fingers were tapping on the table. Not a good sign. "What do you plan to do with it?"

"Nothing. Tessa, can we talk about something else?"

"I just don't understand why you didn't stay there and try to rebuild. That is your heritage, you know."

"Tessa, you cannot change my mind. I know you don't approve, but I have to do what is best for me, right now." Mr. Larabee's eyes were staring intently at Louanne's mama.

"I don't think it is best. I know God doesn't want that for you, James."

Mr. Larabee didn't say anything, and to Louanne's disappointment, the conversation came to a halt, just like it always did when they got on this subject or when Mama mentioned God. It seemed as if Mr. Larabee was mad at God about something, and her mama was trying to help him with it. Only Mr. Larabee didn't seem to want help.

Well, Louanne knew she had to do something or the rest of the meal was going to be miserable!

"Mr. Larabee, have you ever heard of the story of the Beauty and the Beast?"

Mr. Larabee looked at her with narrowed eyes. "We're going to discuss fairy tales again?" he asked warily.

"Louanne, this makes the fourth one that we've discussed. I think you need to start reading something else," her mother admonished.

"But don't you just love the part when Beauty rushes back to the castle and finds the beast dying. And just when she thinks she's lost him, she cries out in a pitiful voice that she loves him. Then, suddenly he starts changing into a handsome prince." Louanne looked at both adults. "I think we can learn something from this."

Mr. Larabee nodded in agreement. "Yes, we should keep our word. If Beauty had kept her word and come right back to his castle, he wouldn't have almost died in the first place!"

Louanne shook her head. "Okay, that is a good point. But I was talking about the main lesson about love."

"I'm not sure Beauty loved him as a man, you know. I think she just loved him like a friend or a. . .pet." Tessa chimed in.

"Oh, Mama! I was talking about the fact that love

changed everything!" Louanne stressed, growing agitated.

"Especially for the beast. All that hair had to be itchy!" Mr. Larabee had apparently already forgotten his tiff with Louanne's mother.

Louanne sighed and pushed a piece of potato around on her plate.

Tessa looked at Louanne with a mother's compassion and stroked a hand down her curly hair. "For you to see that in a fairy tale is very insightful of you. It shows that you are a very good reader!"

"It sure does," James piped in. "Not every child likes to read at your age. I can see that you are a very smart and clever girl."

She smiled at James. "Do you really think so?" Louanna asked, her face lit up with expectation.

"I sure do!" he answered with a wink.

The little girl was beaming with pride and happiness as she stared at James. "You know, I think I'll go and read right now! Uncle Donald bought me a new book just the other day!" She jumped up from the table and carried her plate to the sink.

"Good night!" she called as she ran to her room.

Tessa stared after her daughter for a moment then looked back at James. "You are quite good with children, James. I've not seen her that excited in weeks!"

He shrugged. "I like her. She's a sweet kid."

Tessa grinned at him. "And you're a good man, James Larabee."

His face reddened briefly, but he came back with, "You thought I was an outlaw when you first saw me!"

She giggled. "What else was I to think? I soon realized

that you weren't," she defended with teasing eyes. "But I am worried about this saloon business, and I'm not going to quit nagging you about it until you realize that you aren't cut out for that kind of life!"

James groaned as he leaned back in his chair, but Tessa ignored him. She told herself that it was for his own good! But deep inside, she knew it was also for her own.

Chapter 5

Tessa handed James the last dish and watched as he carefully dried it and laid it on the counter. It was night time and Louanne had already gone to bed. The two of them worked side by side as they had for the last four nights, since he'd gotten the wheelchair.

"You don't have to help me with these every night, you know. You are supposed to be resting," Tessa told him as she folded the dishtowel and laid it on the edge of the sink.

"It's just not in me to sit around and be useless. Besides, I've had more rest than any man could possibly need." He wheeled himself around the table and toward the door. "I think I'm going to get some fresh air. Want to join me?"

Tessa hesitated at the thought of just the two of them sitting in the moonlight. It was too intimate—something that a couple would do if they were courting. She should just say no and go on to bed!

"Okay. Let me just pour us some coffee and I'll bring it on out," she answered despite herself.

He smiled at her as he reached up to grab his coat

from the hook beside the door. "Sounds good."

Berating herself for being so weak where James Larabee was concerned, she reached under the cupboard and grabbed a couple of cups. She slipped on her own coat and went out onto the front porch while holding the cups of hot coffee carefully in her hands. She handed him one then took a seat in the rocking chair beside his.

"It's getting colder," she commented. "If I didn't know better, I'd say it felt like snow weather."

He nodded and took a sip of his coffee. "Tessa, I . . . ," he began then paused and tried again. "Tonight at supper, I didn't mean to be rude. I know you're just trying to help, but I—"

"Don't need my help," she finished for him. She cradled the warm cup between her palms as she stared down at it. "James, can you just tell me what made you decide to move to California? And why a saloon?"

He glanced over at her, then turned to look out at the moonlit trees before him. Crickets were singing and he could hear a couple of owls that seemed as though they were competing for who could hoot the loudest. And as he sat there on the small front porch, enjoying the crisp wind as it brushed his hair and chilled his face, a feeling of peace invaded his heart—a peace that he hadn't felt since before the war. Before he knew it, he was telling Tessa Wise things that he hadn't even admitted to himself.

"I don't want to have to think about home," he said quietly. "I don't want to look at things that remind me of my father or see people who knew my brother. I don't even want to do things that they would have done, so I don't have to think about them."

"Is it working?" she asked, compassion laced in her soft voice.

James thought about that as he gripped his cup. "No," he answered finally, truthfully.

"I thought about moving, too. When my husband's body was brought home, I couldn't even sleep in our room. Everything I touched had been made by him—the house, the furniture, Louanne's toys. . ." She drifted off and looked at him. "But I didn't have a buried treasure like you did, James. My parents have been dead since I was fifteen and my aunt whom I'd lived with had died that winter. I couldn't pack up and move off to a new place because I didn't have the money. And I'm glad I didn't."

She reached out and covered his hand. "I would have been running away from my pain instead of dealing with it. I wouldn't have known the strength and comfort that God has given me that has made me a stronger and better person. He can do it for you, James. Just ask Him!"

James held onto her hand and looked steadily at her. Part of him wanted to believe what she was saying. Wanted to obtain what she had been given, but he just couldn't seem to take that step. There was too much bitterness, too much pain. Would he ever be a whole person again? he wondered. It seemed too easy to simply ask for God's help and believe it would all be better, when he still blamed God for it happening in the first place.

"I can't. Not yet. Maybe someday."

"Then, I'll just keep praying that someday comes sooner than later."

He grinned at her, admiring her spirit. "You don't give up, do you!"

She smiled back at him. "Never!" she declared, letting his hand go and taking another sip of coffee.

He sipped while studying her over the rim of his cup. "What about you, Tessa? You ever going to marry again? It's been three years, hasn't it?"

Tessa threw him a dry look. "Now you're beginning to sound like J. T.! And the answer is yes. I do want to marry again, but as bad as I want more children, I'm not going to be in a hurry. God gave me a good man the first time, and I feel lucky that I was able to spend eight years with him. I know that He'll bless me a second time."

"Louanne says that you've had four offers of marriage in the last year," he couldn't help but mention.

He watched as she put a hand to her cheeks as if they were burning, and James had a feeling that they were. "She shouldn't have told you that!"

"You mean it's not true?"

"Well. . .yes. But she still shouldn't have told you!"

James began to chuckle. "Tessa Wise, the only thing that surprises me is that you haven't had more than four ask for your hand."

"Oh, for goodness' sakes!" she exclaimed and took another drink of coffee as if to hide her face.

"I know that if I were living here in Wiseville, I'd be asking for your hand myself!"

Suddenly, the teasing laughter left his voice and face. A stillness descended over them, and James found he could hardly breathe.

"You shouldn't tell me that," she said in a breathless,

panic-filled tone. She was staring down, not looking at him.

He mentally kicked himself, wishing he could take his words back, while knowing that they were true. "I know. I'm sorry. It's just that. . ." He stopped and ran an agitated hand through his hair. "I didn't mean to embarrass you, Tessa. Just pretend I didn't say anything, okay?"

She didn't say anything for a moment. Then, when she did, he had to bend near her to hear, for she spoke so softly. "If you lived here in Wiseville and had asked for my hand, James Larabee, I just might have said yes."

James sat there, so stunned at her admission that he couldn't even answer her when she suddenly brushed past him and said good night.

As he listened to the screen door slam behind her, he wondered if going to California was so important after all.

ಲ♡ಲ

The next morning Tessa watched from the corner of her eye as James wheeled himself into the kitchen. She noticed that he'd made good use of the tub of hot water she'd set in his room for him. She couldn't help but notice that his hair was curlier when it was wet, although it looked as if he'd tried to comb it down.

Goodness, she was nervous this morning. Especially after her little "confession" the night before. What had possessed her to say something like that? It must have been the moonlight and the romantic atmosphere. She was normally a prudent, levelheaded person. She never said things without thinking, never blurted things out that might embarrass her or anyone else.

Where was that levelheaded person last night? Certainly not sitting in the moonlight with James Larabee!

"Good morning, Tessa," he greeted, his voice low and husky.

She took a deep breath. *Just act normal!* she willed herself before turning from the sink with a fixed smile on her face. "Good morning! Did you sleep well?"

He looked straight at her with a frank expression. "To tell you the truth, no. I didn't sleep well—I tossed and turned all night thinking about what you said to me."

Okay. So much for acting as if nothing happened. She quickly turned back around, biting her lip and clenching her eyes tight. He wanted to talk about it? Couldn't he just leave well enough alone?

"Why don't you call Louanne to the table. Breakfast is almost ready," she said in a calm voice, deciding to ignore his comment.

"Come on, Tessa. Talk to me. What is going through your mind?" he pleaded, wheeling closer to her.

She fiddled with a stack of plates. "Why discuss it, James? What's it going to accomplish?"

He tugged at her skirt. "Tessa, I. . ."

She whirled around and confronted him. "You are going to California, and I'm staying here. You have plans that I cannot agree with or condone. I serve God and you don't. Are you saying that any of that is going to change?"

Minutes seemed to tick by as they stared at each other. Tessa's heart was beating so hard she wondered if James could hear it. A silly irrational hope sprang up in her heart, a hope that he would say yes. Yes, things were going to change. Yes, he would give up his plans. Yes, he would give God a chance.

But, of course he didn't say that, though he didn't exactly say no.

"I don't know what I'm saying, Tessa. All I know is that something happened between us last night. Something changed, and I don't want us to go back to the way we were before."

He reached up and took her hand. It felt so warm and safe enclosed in his rough palm. "Oh, James," she cried softly, "I just don't think—"

"Is breakfast ready yet?" Louanne asked as she skipped into the room. She skidded to a halt when she saw them quickly release their hands. Her eyes grew large as her gaze darted between them. "Y'all were holding hands!"

"Yes."

"No."

Louanne frowned. "Well, which is it? Yes or no?"

James intervened. "Lulu, why don't you set the table while I finish talking to your mama."

Louanne rolled her eyes and threw up her hands. "Nobody tells me anything!" she cried as she stomped to the china cabinet. "And my name is not Lulu today, it's Pocahontas!" This morning she had her curly hair in a pair of quirky-looking braids and was wearing a tan, fringed Indian dress over a pair of long johns.

James chuckled at the wild costume then looked back at Tessa. "We're not through discussing this."

She looked at him sternly. "Yes, James, we are."

He just smiled and winked at her as he wheeled himself toward the table.

Tessa's legs were shaking as she brought the dish of eggs and bacon to the table. What did this all mean? She just didn't understand the feelings that she had for James. They were too fast. Too strong. With her husband, Will, she'd fallen in love slowly. She'd known him all her life, yet she had to warm to him as more than just a friend when he began to court her.

But what she was feeling for James was instantaneous—something had happened the moment she'd laid eyes on him. It didn't make sense. He was a stranger. He would be leaving in just a week.

As she put the eggs on the table, she caught him staring at her and her legs became even shakier. What was she going to do once he left? Why did she feel as though she was going to lose something precious. . .something wonderful?

She shook off her thoughts, willing herself to quit fretting over something she had no control over.

She was taking the seat across from him when Louanne called out to her. "No, Mama. I've fixed this place for you." She motioned toward a seat next to James.

She narrowed her eyes at James, who shrugged his shoulders. "I didn't have anything to do with it!" he defended himself with an innocent look.

"Louanne, I always sit here," she explained, trying to figure out what her daughter was up to.

"Please, Mama!" she begged. "I went to all the trouble. . ." She let her voice drift off, sending her pleading look to her mother.

Tessa looked at James then back to her daughter. "Okay," she sighed and sat down in the chair Louanne indicated.

James nudged her with an elbow. "I think she's matchmaking," he whispered in her ear.

Tessa froze. Was that what her daughter was doing? Was that what all the silliness with the fairy tales had been about? She looked at Louanne and found her smiling at them, obviously reading something into their close position.

"It's a sign. . . ," Louanne said with an excitement in her voice, although it seemed as if she were saying it more to herself.

"You know, that's the second time I've heard you say that, Lulu. . .I mean Poca. What do you mean by it?" James asked curiously.

Louanne looked from James to Tessa, her expression hesitant. "I'm not sure I should say. . ."

Tessa had had enough. "Spit it out, Louanne. You've been acting strange. . .well, stranger than usual. . .and I want to know what's going on in that little brain of yours."

Louanne fiddled with her crooked braid. "Well, I guess I can tell this much," she said slowly. "I think that God meant for Mr. Larabee to stay in Wiseville. That's why he ended up in our woods."

Tessa stared at her daughter, worried. "Oh, Louanne," she said gently. "I know that you are enjoying Mr. Larabee's company, but that doesn't mean that God sent him to stay here."

"But there have been signs!" her daughter insisted. "I think that he was sent here for us, Mama! I mean Mr. Larabee's always looking at you, Mama, when he thinks you're not looking, and the same goes with you! I can tell you're in love with him!"

Now, Tessa was not only alarmed, she was embarrassed. She had been staring at James. Her face was burning so hot that Tessa doubted that it'd ever be normal again.

But then. . .James had been staring at her, too?

She wouldn't think about that now. She couldn't. Her hopes would run high, this attraction that she felt for James would grow deeper, and then she'd be left with a broken heart. Or had it already grown deeper? Had she already begun to fall in love with him?

And what about Louanne? She didn't want her daughter's heart to be broken when James left them. What was she to do?

"Louanne, honey. We need to talk about this!" she told her daughter. But Louanne shook her head.

"I know what you're going to say. You don't want me to get my hopes up, and I don't. I just have faith is all."

Tessa felt James take her chin into his hand and turn it toward him. She averted her eyes down, unable to face him.

"Is that true?" he asked softly. "Are you in love with me?"

"Uh. . .you know, I think I'll just take my breakfast in my room and let y'all talk about this," Louanne said with a smile on her face and excitement brimming in her eyes.

"No! Louanne. . . ," Tessa called out in a panic.

"Yes, thank you, Lulu. We'd appreciate that." He stared at Tessa as he spoke.

She was looking at him now, unable to look away.

"Are you going to answer my question?" he prompted.

"No."

"What if I told you that I'm falling in love with you, too?"

Tessa felt her heart skip a beat, and for a moment she couldn't seem to breathe. "It's too soon! We don't really know each other," she cried, trying to come up with excuses.

His hand left her chin and cupped her cheek, his thumb rubbing softly under her eye. "I don't understand it either, Tessa. And I don't want Louanne to get hurt. All I know is that I don't want to leave anymore." He paused a minute, thinking. "Why don't we do this: why don't we use this next week as a time to really get to know each other. It'll give us both time to make sure that what we're feeling is for real."

All the reasons why this suggestion was not a good idea drifted through Tessa's mind. But she knew that she would take his offer. Not only would she have time to get to know him better, she would have time to pray. That was the only way she would know for sure.

She smiled shyly at him. "Okay, I think that would be wonderful."

He grinned at her, his eyes shining with emotion. Then he leaned closer to her, and Tessa knew that she was about to be kissed. Part of her wanted to run, the other part of her wanted to lean closer.

The latter won. She met him halfway and touched her lips softly to his. He made a sound from his throat and pressed more firmly, moving his lips in a caressing motion over hers. It felt so wonderful. It had been so long since she'd been kissed.

As he gently broke away, he pressed a quick kiss on her cheek and looked at her. "You know you never answered my question, Tessa. Are you falling in love with me?"

She lovingly ran her gaze over his handsome features then smiled. "Yes, I think I am."

Chapter 6

Saturday evening, J. T. had brought by a couple of crutches and told James that he thought it'd be okay for him to get up and exercise a little. It felt so good to be able to move around, so James took the opportunity after the doctor had left to explore outside around the little white house.

The last four days since they had decided to examine their relationship had been truly life changing, James thought as he looked around the small clearing surrounded by tall pines. Tessa and he had made good use of their time together and had really gotten to know each other. He told her things that he'd never told anyone about himself. He hadn't meant to, of course, but Tessa just seemed to pull it out of him.

And he learned important things about her. He knew that she longed for a husband and more children. Since she'd been an only child, she had vowed that she would have a house full of children when she married. She had truly loved her first husband, but somehow, that didn't bother James. It just proved that she was the type of person who made good choices for herself.

He saw how she cared for Louanne, even teaching her at home, since they'd lost the town's schoolteacher in the last year. She was a caring and nurturing woman.

She was also a devout Christian, and she never stopped trying to get him to talk about his anger toward God. And it was working. There had to be something great about God for Tessa—who was such an intelligent, levelheaded person—to be so faithful to Him.

As he shuffled around trying to get used to the crutches, he took in his surroundings. The small barn was clean but badly in need of paint. The fences had been mended but were still sagging in places. He saw her garden, now dormant, and he wondered how hard she had to work to keep food on their table. He knew that the Wise brothers helped her, but they had families of their own. All that he saw around him had been tirelessly worked by Tessa.

He wanted to make life easier for her, somehow. She deserved better than this existence. *Are you planning on taking her away from all this, Larabee?* A voice in his head taunted him. *And what do you have to give her? A burnt-out piece of land that you are too cowardly to rebuild?* He didn't know what he could offer. He just knew that he wanted to be a part of her life, somehow, some way.

But was it possible?

"*Pssst!* Mr. Larabee!" A whispery voice called out to him from behind a tree. "Over here!"

James squinted in the darkness and made his way over to Louanne who was hidden in the shadows. "What are you doing out here? I thought you'd gone to bed!"

She stepped out into the moonlight where they could

see each other better. "When I heard you go out of the house, I knew I had to talk to you. It was a sign!"

James sighed. "I thought we were all through with this 'sign' business, Lulu."

Louanne rolled her eyes. "I know, but this was one I couldn't ignore." She then shook her head. "I've been reading *Romeo and Juliet*, you see, and when I saw that you were standing outside, I knew it would be perfect!"

"What would be perfect?" he asked guardedly.

"For you to present a soliloquy under Mama's window!"

"A soli. . . How do you know such a big word?"

"I read a lot," she told him with her usual panache. Then when he gave her a questioning look, she admitted, "Okay, so it was a vocabulary word from last month.

"But anyway, in *Romeo and Juliet*, Romeo goes beneath Juliet's window and. . .well, you remember, don't you? He tells her. . .well. . .I really didn't understand what he told her because it was something about the light breaking through the window over yonder and then something about being sick and green and eyes being in her head. . . But that doesn't matter! What matters is that Juliet really liked it when he did that! I think you need to do something like that under Mama's window!"

James bit his lip and tried not to give in to laughter. "You think she'd like that? Because you know that I love to make up poetry," he teased.

She looked appalled at that statement. "Oh no! You better not make up any of your silly poems. Why don't you just tell her how pretty she is and that you really like her!"

James pretended to think it over. "I don't know. What

if she doesn't come to the window? Then I'd look pretty dumb standing there talking to the side of the house!"

Louanne gave him a patient look. "She'll come, I promise." She pointed toward the house. "Look. There is her window over there. I'll go with you and sit underneath it where she can't see me. I'll tell you what to say, okay?"

"Well, alright. If you think that this will work!" he said as they made their way over to the window.

"Say, didn't Juliet have a balcony? I don't think it's going to have the same effect with her room being on the ground floor," he whispered.

"Shh!" she admonished. "It'll work. Now, just call out her name."

"Tessa," he whispered.

"You're going to have to say it louder than that!"

"Hey, Tessa!" he yelled, enjoying himself immensely.

"Oh, that was romantic!" she groaned, covering her head with her hands.

The window sash was suddenly thrown up and Tessa's tousled head poked out. "James, for goodness' sake! What are you doing out there in the cold?"

"I'm supposed to be reciting a soliloquy."

"A what?"

Louanne groaned aloud. "Tell her that she's beautiful!"

"Tessa, you look so beautiful, even though your hair is a mess!"

Another groan came from under the window, and Tessa stuck her head farther out. "Louanne? Are you out here, too?"

Louanne reluctantly got up. "I was trying to help Mr. Larabee court you, but it's proving to be just too difficult."

James laughed. "I tried, Lulu."

Tessa stared back and forth at the two of them as if they were crazy. "What does standing outside freezing to death have to do with courting?"

"She has a point, Lulu. I don't think it was near this cold when Romeo was yelling up at Juliet's window."

"I give up!" Louanne declared. "You two can just work this out on your own." With that she turned and made her way to the door.

James looked back at Tessa and her rumpled state. "You know, I wasn't kidding when I said you looked beautiful." He stepped closer and put a quick kiss on her lips. "Good night, Juliet!" he said with a wink, and before she could reply he was hobbling back inside the house.

❧♥❧

James knew that he'd changed. It was evident the next morning when he decided to attend the Sunday church service with Tessa and Louanne. She'd already missed one Sunday because of him. He didn't want her to have to miss another.

"Are you sure about this?" Tessa asked then bit her lip the way she always did when she was worried.

He stood up, balancing himself with the crutches. "I want to go with you. I just hope I'm not too casual in these duds. I had planned to buy nicer clothes when I reached San Francisco," he explained, looking down at his chambray shirt and dark blue pants.

"You look fine. This is Wiseville, not New Orleans!" She reached up and brushed a lock of hair back from his forehead. It was such a "wifely" thing to do that James couldn't help but wish he could be the recipient of her touches all the time. "Wife" was a word that was sounding mighty good to him.

"That's just what Sleeping Beauty would have done," Louanne said, "when the prince awakened her from her deep sleep. A lock of his hair would be hanging from his forehead, and as he drew back from his tender kiss, she would reach out and gently smooth it back. . . ." Louanne drifted off in a dramatic sigh, and she stood in the doorway of the living room, watching them.

"Oh no. Not the fairy tales again! I thought you'd given up on us!" Tessa groaned.

James grinned. "I need to buy you some good westerns to read."

Louanne looked appalled. "Those kind of books aren't romantic!"

"There's romance in them!" he defended with mock indignation.

" 'Hop on the back of my horse, Darlin', and help me round up the herd,' is real romantic! I read that once in one of J. T.'s western novels," Louanne told him dryly.

James just shrugged while throwing Tessa a conspiring wink. "He could have left her at home!"

Louanne groaned and headed toward the door. "I really am going to give up this time!"

"Promises, promises!" Tessa called after her.

Chuckling, James and Tessa looked at each other and then followed her out of the house.

❦

The church service was just as James expected it would be. They sang songs and listen to Reverend Donald Wise preach his lengthy but interesting sermon. He also knew that it would stab him with guilt about his anger toward God. He still couldn't yet make that step—that little, yet huge step that would bring him to a right relationship with the Almighty.

To her credit, Tessa never looked at him or asked him whether he was enjoying the service. She wasn't the kind to pressure. But he knew she was thinking about it.

James had the awful feeling that if he didn't make his peace with God—there would be no relationship between him and Tessa. But he couldn't do it for her, no matter how much he wanted to.

No. He had to do it for himself.

But he couldn't. Not yet.

When the service was over, the three of them made their way out of the sanctuary. James could feel his leg start to really ache, and he groaned.

"Are you okay?" she asked, obviously worried.

He gave her a brave smile. "Sure, it's just a little twinge."

"It's probably more than just a twinge!" J. T. said from behind them in a stern voice. "I said that you could get up every once in awhile. I didn't mean that you could gallivant all around town!"

"Aw, it's not bad," James said. "Besides, I didn't want Tessa to miss another Sunday."

Suddenly J. T. swung in front of them, stopping them from going out the door. He looked at both of them with shrewd eyes for a moment, then his mouth spread in a knowing smile. "Ahhh. . .I see."

Louanne glared at him. "Now, J. T. . . . ."

"Hey! What's going on with you two?" Donald chimed

in from the doorway where he'd stood to shake hands with his parishioners.

"They're courting!" Louanne blurted out.

James and Tessa looked at the little girl in surprise. "She's only teasing," Tessa told her in-laws quickly.

"Oh no, I'm not! James asked Mama if she was falling in love with him, and Mama said that she was!"

"Louanne!" Tessa scolded.

"Now, Louanne. Don't go upsetting your mother," James admonished.

J. T. raised an eyebrow. "Are you saying that it's not true, James?"

"Well, no. I'm not saying that."

"Oh, good gracious!" Tessa wailed, covering her red face with her hands.

Then Louanne told her uncles, "You see, God sent Mr. Larabee to be my daddy."

Chapter 7

J. T. and Donald Wise stared at the couple as if they'd just heard the best piece of news they'd heard in a long time. "Daddy, huh?" J. T. probed.

James tried to ignore them. And while he patted Tessa on the shoulders in a comforting gesture, he scolded Louanne. "Now, Lulu, I think you've said quite. . ."

"No, this is getting interesting," Donald interrupted.

"James, could we please go," Tessa pleaded.

"Uh, I think my leg is hurting, after all," James muttered, trying to get out of the sticky conversation. "Maybe we'd better head home."

He let Tessa go ahead of him, then he, too, brushed past the brothers, nodding at them politely.

"Yes, we want you to get well so you can walk without any pain," J. T. called out. "It's not very seemly when a groom limps out to meet his bride."

They ignored that particular comment! "Tessa, your face is red," James whispered in her ear as he hobbled down the steps of the church.

"I just never know what those brothers are going to come up with next!" she muttered, embarrassed. "I should be used to them by now. They are both such big teases."

"Tessa, we really haven't talked about what Louanne said, about me being an answer to her prayer. Now she's told her uncles the same thing. Does it upset you?" James ventured to ask.

Tessa bit her lip. "I was wondering if it bothered you."

James stopped and motioned Tessa off to the side away from the stream of churchgoers. "At first it scared me, but I don't think I'm scared about it anymore," he told her honestly.

"You don't?" she asked breathlessly.

James smiled a secret smile as he reached out to brush a dark lock of hair that had blown across her lip. Her skin was so soft to touch, and he ached to kiss her and hold her in his arms. He probably would have if they hadn't been standing in the churchyard in full view of the townsfolk of Wiseville.

"It's sounding better and better all the time," he told her as his hand trailed down her cheek.

"Is that faith I hear in your voice, Doubting Thomas?" she teased.

"Among other things, Miss Smarty! Don't get too smug, now!"

"I won't. I'm too happy to be anything but grateful."

"Yeah, me, too." They gazed at each other for a moment, not caring who was looking at them.

Could I really believe? James wondered. Could he let go of the past and all his bitterness and learn to trust in God again? Tessa made it all seem possible.

"Good afternoon, Tessa," a young woman said as she passed them on the sidewalk. She had a child on one arm and was running toward a fellow who was sitting in a wagon with another child a little older than the first.

"Hi, Mary!" she returned, and James saw her grin.

"Who's she?"

"That is Mary, and the man she's getting into the buggy with is her husband, Frank. She became a Baptist while he was at war, and since he's a staunch Methodist he was none too thrilled about it." She shook her head with amusement. "But they seem to have come to a happy compromise. He brings her to church every Sunday, then goes to his church down the street."

James laughed with her as he watched the young couple embrace and smile at each other. "It looks like it didn't cause too much trouble, though. They seem happy."

Tessa sighed a womanly sigh. "They are. He loves her very much."

"Do I look at you like that?"

She glanced at him with a saucy smile. "All the time."

He nodded. "I thought so," he said quietly.

She turned as if to steal a look at him, but he just kept on walking, smiling to himself and enjoying the feelings that were blossoming within him.

Then suddenly James came to a quick stop. Across the churchyard he saw a flash of blue and black. It triggered a memory. A memory of someone wearing that same jacket, running away from him.

His happiness evaporated into oblivion and old, comfortable feelings quickly replaced it. Feelings of anger and bitterness.

It was the man who shot him. It had to be!

Forgetting the pain in his leg, he started toward the

group of boys standing outside of the churchyard.

"James! Where are you going?" he heard Tessa calling out to him, but he ignored her. Anger was beginning to boil in him as he drew closer. Here he was, the man who left him to die.

"Hey, you!" he called out in a harsh yell. All seven of the young men looked up curiously at him, limping toward them. "You in the blue-and-black coat!" he said specifically.

The man, a boy really, answered, "What's the problem, Mr. Larabee?"

James came to a halt. It was Earl Wise, the Reverend Donald Wise's son. Rage spread through his whole body like a raging river. His limbs shook as he glared at the innocent-looking young man. This boy had been in the same room with him and had spoken to him when he'd first been shot. He had stood there as James had told Donald of what happened. And he'd never said a word.

"You are the one who shot me and left me for dead," he charged. "I saw this jacket when you ran away from me. What kind of man are you to let someone bleed to death?"

Earl stood there in shock, unable to speak at first. "M—Mr. Larabee, I. . .I didn't shoot you—"

"Don't lie to me!"

"James, what are you doing?" Tessa cried, running up beside him.

"It was Earl. He's the one who shot me."

Earl looked pleadingly at Tessa. "Aunt Tess, I promise I didn't—"

"James, you have to be mistaken. . . ," Tessa told him,

laying a hand on his arm.

He shook it off, feeling betrayed that she wouldn't believe him. "Where's the sheriff! I want this boy arrested!"

"I'm right here, Mr. Larabee," Daniel said in a calm voice as he walked up to the group. James barely noticed that the friends who were standing by Earl were all backing away from them.

"Sheriff, this is the man who shot me. I recognize the coat; it was what he was wearing when he ran away from me."

"Uncle Daniel, I promise that I didn't shoot him," Earl defended. He looked scared but was reluctant to speak, as if he were hiding something.

"Do you know who did?" Daniel asked shrewdly.

Earl looked down at the ground and kicked at a pebble with the point of his boot. "I lent someone my coat, Uncle Daniel. I had a feeling he had done something that he wasn't telling me, but I don't know for sure."

James let out a frustrated breath. "Quit lying! Why don't you just take responsibility for what you did!"

Tessa came around to stand in front of James. "James, please. Earl wouldn't lie. He's a good Christian boy who's been studying to be a minister like his daddy. He would have never left you there to die."

James looked at her, her eyes shining with tears and her cheeks flushed. He almost gave in. But old wounds had been opened and were urging him on. He couldn't think rationally. All he knew was that he'd been taken advantage of for the last time. This time someone was going to pay for his misfortune. And why wasn't Tessa standing by him? Why wasn't she demanding that something be done?

Didn't she love him? Where was her loyalty?

"Just because someone claims to want to be a clergyman doesn't make him a saint." He looked away from her, his face hard. "You know my feelings about God anyway. Stay out of this, Tessa!"

Tessa backed away from him. He could hear her sniffle and knew that she was crying, but he wouldn't look. "I thought you'd changed your mind. I thought you were a different man," she told him, then she ran to her wagon to where Louanne sat, trying to see what was going on. He heard the sound of the wagon's wheels as she pulled away, obviously too upset with him to even wait.

He hardened his heart against her words and looked back at the sheriff. "Are you going to arrest him? Or am I going to have to find someone other than 'family' to do it?" he growled.

Sheriff Daniel glanced at him with his knowing eyes, and James got the strange feeling that the man could see right through him. James looked away. Then the sheriff addressed Earl. "Who's the boy, Earl? The one you lent your coat to?"

Earl looked at his uncle then looked away, clearly torn. "I don't even know for sure, if it's him, Uncle. How can I rat on a friend?"

"Someone broke the law, son," his father, Donald, spoke up as he, too, joined the group. "Tell us who the friend is so Daniel can ask him some questions."

James's leg grew steadily weaker as he stood there watching them talk back and forth and getting nowhere with the boy. James shifted on his crutches, trying to relieve some of the pressure, but it did nothing to ease the pain.

He moved again but lost his balance, causing the crutches to slip out from under his arms.

The last thing he remembered was falling and hitting his head on something really hard.

෬♡෨

"I just thought I'd tell you that James is at J. T.'s office. He fell and knocked himself out cold," Daniel told Tessa, as he stood in her living room with his hat in hand.

Tessa's heart dropped, and she felt a panic rise up within her. "Is he alright?"

"Yeah, I reckon," Daniel said lazily. Tessa knew that he was playing this for all it was worth. She was going to have to drag the information out of him, it seemed.

"Come on, Daniel. Please tell me how he is," she pleaded.

He twirled his hat around a time or two. "Hmmm. You seem pretty upset about this. It appeared to me, out there by the church, that you'd washed your hands of that Alabama man. I wouldn't figure you'd care one way or another."

Tessa folded her arms around her waist and glared at her brother-in-law. "You are really starting to get on my nerves, Danny boy, so spit it out." He hated to be called that name, so his brothers and occasionally Tessa called him Danny boy just to rile him.

He sighed. "He'll live, if that's what you're worried about. But when he came to, he started going on and on about having Earl arrested. It took awhile for us to explain that the boy who'd borrowed Earl's coat confessed that he'd been the one to shoot him." Daniel shook his head. "It was Clevis Packard's son Ned. He's only thirteen, and he got scared when his gun went off and he hit James. He didn't know what to do, so in typical 'kid' fashion, he ran away and tried to pretend it didn't happen."

"Is James going to have him arrested?" Tessa asked.

"No. When he calmed down, he was able to talk to Clevis about the boy. Clevis agreed not to let Ned handle a gun until he's had proper lessons on how to handle one, and then only in the presence of an adult." Daniel looked down a moment then glanced back up at her. "But, you know, Larabee's still pretty mad at you, though."

Tessa eyes flew open in disbelief. "What are you saying? Why would he be mad at me? I should be mad at him for the way he spoke to me!"

Daniel shook his head sympathetically, as if he knew something that she didn't. "He's mad 'cause you didn't stand by him. I know that you were just defending Earl, but it came off to James like you were against him. When a man doesn't have any family to call his own anymore, and he thinks he's finally found someone to make a new family, he expects that person to be loyal just like family."

"Oh, for goodness' sakes, Daniel! I am loyal! But I couldn't let him accuse Earl when I knew that he was wrong!"

"You should have told him that when you didn't have a crowd to overhear you."

Tessa gazed at Daniel and then shook her head, looking away. "This is the craziest thing I've ever heard!"

Daniel just shrugged and flipped his hat back on his head. "Well, I'd best be on my way. I'm supposed to be setting up shooting lessons for Clevis's son so he won't be maiming anybody else in the future." He winked at her before walking out of the door. "You have a good day, now."

Tessa rolled her eyes and pushed him the rest of the way outside. "Good-bye, Daniel."

She then leaned on the door and looked up at the ceiling, lost in her thoughts. How could James be mad at her? It just didn't make any sense! She hadn't gone nuts in front of the whole church.

Chapter 8

As soon as Louanne heard her Uncle Daniel leave through the front door, she ran out the back. She'd eavesdropped on the whole conversation and now things were beginning to make sense.

James Larabee, her promised daddy, wasn't coming back. He wasn't going to be her daddy, and he wasn't going to stay in Wiseville. She had to do something and quick!

Like a rabbit, she darted through the woods as fast as she could, heading in the direction of Uncle J. T.'s house.

She would talk to James. Maybe she could make him not be mad at her mother.

After about ten minutes, she barged into her uncle's office on the front side of his house, slamming the door behind her.

"Whoa there, young'un!" J. T. scolded with eyebrows furrowed. "This may be a tiny little place, but it's still a doctor's office!"

Louanne, breathing hard from her run, brushed the stray hair from her face and looked determinedly at her uncle. "Uncle, I've got to see Mr. Larabee. It's a matter of life and death!"

J. T. just raised a lazy eyebrow. Apparently he didn't see

the urgency that his niece did. "Life and death?"

Louanne rolled her eyes and stomped her foot. "You know what I mean! If I don't get in there and talk to him, I ain't never going to get another daddy!"

"You're never going to have—" J. T. corrected.

"Isn't that what I just said?" she huffed then pleaded, "Please, Uncle J. T.!"

J. T. nodded toward the door that led to the small room adjoining his office. "Go on in."

Louanne let herself into the room, and she went to where James was sitting on the edge of the bed rubbing the back of his head.

"Mr. Larabee?" she called out softly.

James looked up and winced at the sudden movement. "Huh? Oh, hi, Lulu. What are you doing here?"

Louanne took a deep breath and sat in the chair in front of him. "I came to talk you into staying in Wiseville."

James looked at her with compassion. "Louanne, there is nothing for me here. I need to move on. . . ."

"But what about you and Mama! I know that you love her!"

James grew very still, then after a long pause he looked away. "That is really none of your business, Lulu."

Louanne let out an annoyed breath. "I've got two eyes to see with, Mr. Larabee! You going to deny it?"

James looked at her then and grinned. "No, I'm not. But it doesn't make any difference. Your mama and me just ain't suited. And besides, I've got plans in California."

Louanne nodded. "You're going to open up a house of ill repute."

James scowled. "That's not what I'm doing! I'm opening

a saloon! Not. . .not that!"

"Uncle Donald thinks it amounts to about the same thing," she told him with innocent eyes.

James picked at a string on his pants. "Well, it ain't."

They sat there silent for a moment, then Louanne reached out to grab James's hand. He looked at her with confusion.

"Well, since you're going to go away from us and leave us here all alone," she began with a dramatic tremor in her voice, "I'd better say a prayer for you, so that you'll be safe on your journey."

Prayers. James sighed and nodded, figuring, *What could it hurt?*

Louanne squeezed his hand gently as she closed her eyes tightly and began to pray. "Dear Lord, please be with my friend Mr. Larabee as he leaves on his journey. Keep him real safe and watch after him so that no Indians will scalp him along the way."

James bit his lip to keep from laughing at that comment, but her next words quickly squelched all humor.

"And, Lord, You know that Mr. Larabee is upset at You, and I pray that You will bless him so much that he'll not be mad at You anymore. He's such a good man, and I thought for sure that You had sent him to our woods because You wanted him to be my new daddy. But I guess it was just wishful thinking and not an answer to prayer like I'd thought."

She sighed as she said this, and James felt a lump the size of a boulder rising in his throat. She'd thought that James was an answer to her prayer. He didn't know what to do. How could a child have so much faith, when he as an adult had so little?

"I know that You love Mr. Larabee, Lord, just like Mama and me do. You see, I know this because I've been listening at the door," she added as if she felt the need to explain and confess.

"I'll close now, because I know that Uncle Donald already takes up a lot of Your time with his long prayers, but I thank You for letting me get to know Mr. Larabee, and I ask You again to please take care of him. In Jesus' name, amen."

James could do nothing but sit there and stare at the little girl for a few moments. Never in his life had he felt so loved, yet so despicable at the same time.

He'd spent so much time shaking his fist at God and blaming Him that he'd allowed bitterness to cloud his good thinking. And all that time, God had faithfully watched over him and brought him to a place that he could receive his heart's desire—a family.

Yet, he almost missed it.

But every man wised up sooner or later, and James was glad it was still sooner, at least he hoped it was where Tessa was concerned.

"Louanne," he said softly, raising her chin with his fingers. "Do you still want me for a daddy after all the ruckus I've caused with your cousin and all?"

Louanne nodded but then puckered her brow. "Yes, except I really didn't understand what all went on this afternoon," she explained.

James smiled. "That's alright. It's water under the bridge. Now, all that's left is to try to make things right with your mama."

"Well, now's your chance so you better make it good," a voice from the doorway said.

James looked up in surprise as Tessa stood there leaning on the doorframe with arms folded. "Tess!" He got up and limped over to her. "Will you please forgive me, Tessa? I didn't mean to cause all this trouble or to talk to you the way I did this afternoon."

Tessa reached out to take the hand that he held out to her. "If you can forgive me for not taking your side. I didn't mean to seem disloyal."

"It's a deal," he said, bringing her hand up to kiss it.

He then drew Tessa farther into the room and reached down to draw Louanne from her chair. "Now that the apologies are out of the way, I think we need to start talking about the future."

"Are you going to ask us to marry you?" Louanne asked with excitement, her smile beaming at them both.

James lifted an eyebrow. "Well, I don't know. Do you think that your mother will say yes?" he asked Louanne while looking into Tessa's shining eyes.

"Of course she will!" Louanne blurted out confidently then added as an afterthought, "Won't you, Mama?"

Tessa looked intently at James. "I can only marry a man who loves God as well as myself. Can you do that, James?"

"I realize that I've been blaming God wrongly, Tessa. Louanne was the one who opened my eyes to it. I've been complaining and railing at Him for years now, and all this time He's been leading me to a place of healing. He loved me despite my hatred. I can do no less than to love Him and put Him first in my life." James paused, then added, "And never ever doubt my love for you, Tessa. I loved you from the beginning."

Tessa smiled as her eyes shone bright with tears. "Then I can do no less than to answer your question. Yes, James. I love you and would be honored to become your wife!"

James leaned over and kissed her then. Brushing her soft lips with his own, he felt the love and passion for this beautiful woman rise up within him. Had he ever felt this way? Had he ever felt so much warmth and contentment? Everything he'd ever wanted or ever needed was surrounding him in this room.

❧♥☙

Tessa savored his kiss as she slid her arms around his neck and cuddled against him. Her heart thundered within her chest, and she could hardly breathe, but it didn't matter. She had been so worried just a moment ago, and now she was being given the wondrous gift of love for the second time in her life.

It was different this time around, greater somehow. Maybe it was because she was older and had been through tragedy and hardship. Whatever the reason, she knew that this man, this sweet, handsome man, was a gift from God, and she was going to spend the rest of her life thanking Him for it.

"I'm feeling a little left out here," Louanne said.

Their kiss ended abruptly as Louanne's words startled them both. They looked down at Louanne's knowing look and her tapping foot and started to laugh.

James put his arm around the pretty girl and tugged her into their family circle. "I don't want you to feel left out, Lulu. In fact, now that we're all here and talking about the future," he started to tell them as he threw a wink at

Tessa, whose cheeks were still red from their kiss, "I had an idea that just came to me, or maybe God gave it to me."

Tessa hugged them both. "What is it, James?"

He thought a moment, then told them, "It's about the money that I was going to take to California with me."

Tessa looked dismayed. "Please don't tell me you still want to go to California because, honestly, James, I really don't. . ."

"Shh. . . ," he hushed her, giving her a quick kiss on the lips. "I wasn't going to suggest that. But I wondered how you would feel about moving to Alabama," he mentioned hesitantly.

Tessa looked at him wide-eyed, then her face broke into a brilliant smile. "Oh, James! Are you thinking about going back to the plantation?"

He returned her smile. "I would like to, but only if you don't mind leaving Wiseville. I know that you have family here and—"

This time it was she who kissed him to make him quit talking. "I want to go. James, I think it would be the greatest thing in the world, to return to your heritage!"

He let out a breath. "But you know that there isn't a house left; just a few of the old slave cottages are standing. It'll be hard for a while."

"I don't care, James. As long as I have you and Louanne there, we can rebuild the Larabee Plantation together."

"Does this mean there's going to be a wedding?" another voice came from the door.

They turned around to see all the Wise brothers crowded into J. T.'s little office and all trying to see into the room. "Oh, for goodness' sake, J. T.! Don't you boys have anything else to do besides meddle in my love life?" Tessa asked, exasperated.

J. T. frowned and glanced at Daniel and Donald standing on either side of him. "No, actually we don't! James, there, is my only patient and he seems to be righter than rain!"

Tessa giggled. "Well, if it'll make you all go on and leave us alone, I'll tell you! Yes! We are getting married. Now, go away!"

"Ha! I knew it!" J. T. yelled. They all were talking at once, but at least they moved away from the doorway.

James gave Tessa another kiss and then looked down at his soon-to-be-daughter. "Is this like they do it in the fairy tales, Lulu?"

Louanne smiled with a dreamy look on her face that was familiar to them all. "Oh no! This was soooo much more romantic!"

James gave the girl a quick squeeze, then reached back for his crutch that was leaning on the bed. "Now, let's go catch up with Brother Donald so that he can marry us and we can be on our way!"

Suddenly horrified, Tessa looked at him as she followed him out the door. "Oh, James! You don't mean that we're going to get married now! Today!"

"The sooner the better!" he yelled over his shoulder as he made his way toward Donald.

Tessa threw her arms in the air. "But there is so much to do! I mean, I have to make a dress, get my house all packed . . ." Her voice faded as she ran to join her husband-to-be.

"This is the way *Romeo and Juliet* should have ended!" Louanne declared with much flamboyance and flair as she ran after them.

Kimberley Comeaux

Kim has been married twelve years to Brian, who is a music minister, a songwriter, and formally the lead singer for The Imperials. They have an eight-year-old son named Tyler. This family of Americans currently resides in Ontario, Canada. Kim turned her attention toward writing Christian fiction when she discovered songwriting wasn't for her, because she loves to read, especially romance. "I started out with an idea and before I knew it, I'd written a book-length story." Kim has two full novels published with **Heartsong Presents**.

The Tie That Binds

by Susan K. Downs

Preface

B etween 1854 and 1930 over 200,000 orphaned or abandoned children traveled via orphan trains from the east coast of the United States to points west in hopes of finding new homes. Through this industrious "placing-out" program, as it was referred to in those days, trains carried a company of children to rural communities where people would gather and choose a child. Typically, prior to the train's arrival, a local committee evaluated applicants to determine whether they could provide a good home for a child. However, few committees bothered asking whether those interested in adopting were married or single or why they wanted a child. Despite this loosely structured plan, many children found loving and caring families—thanks to the orphan trains.

Chapter 1

W ell, Miz Watson, I see you still haven't forgiven me for my proposal of marriage," Frank Nance rasped in a futile attempt at a whisper. Emma swept past Mr. Nance's imposing figure as he held the door open for her. Stepping out of the bright sunlight into the dimly lit interior of Shady Grove's Mercantile and Dry Goods Store, Emma found herself momentarily blinded. The stale, musty air tickled her nose, nearly making her sneeze.

The wind blowing off the prairie was unseasonably hot. But Emma couldn't blame the wind or the afternoon sun for the perspiration now prickling her forehead along her bonnet's brim. The presence of Frank Nance always caused her internal temperature to rise and her stomach to clench in irritation.

"Shush!" Emma responded curtly. "I've not told a soul about your proposal, and the last person I'd want to overhear is Katy Greene!" She scanned the store for a glimpse of the clerk who always made it her business to know everyone else's business. Emma's panic eased just a bit when she caught sight of the town's busybody assisting other customers at the far end of the store.

"Have it your way, ma'am. But the offer I made a year ago still stands. It's a cryin' shame for a pretty lady like yourself to be widowed—alone and childless—at the tender age of twenty-eight. Everyone in the county says we'd make a great lookin' couple. And you could close up that little seamstress shop of yours and be taken care of at home, where a woman belongs. Besides, I could sure use someone like you to help me out on the farm."

Emma gaped in disgust. "How dare you mention my age! Just how on earth did you know it anyway?" Without waiting for a response, Emma rushed, "You certainly have gall to even suggest that my seamstress shop is an inappropriate occupation for a lady!

"And, furthermore. . ." Widow Watson's corset under her starched white shirtwaist dug into her ribs, and she gasped sharply before continuing her tirade. The smirk of amusement on Frank Nance's face only added to her fury. "And furthermore, wheat farming must not be the easy job you boasted it would be when you gave up cattle-driving. Otherwise, you wouldn't be so determined to find a wife to take care of the homestead. And you think I should jump at your offer because I need someone to take care of me? Contrary to your obvious opinion, Mr. Nance, I am quite capable of taking care of myself. I do not need you—or any other man in my life, for that matter."

Emma punctuated her speech by turning abruptly and stepping to a glass display case, which held an assortment of scissors and knives. Surely, her curt rebuff would end this uncomfortable interchange. But even as she feigned an interest in the nickel-plated pinking shears, she could feel Frank's intense scrutiny. Did he suspect that her words had not been totally honest?

If the truth were known, she had often entertained the idea of remarrying. She didn't look forward to an entire lifetime of widowed loneliness. In fact, since Frank Nance broached the subject a year ago, she found herself imagining what life might be like married to this rugged outdoorsman. He obviously possessed the same adventuresome spirit she had loved in her departed husband, Stanley.

Stanley Watson had always been on the lookout for the next thrill. His death three years ago occurred when he tried to break the bronco dubbed "untamable" by every horse-tamer in the county. Stanley took their edict as a challenge to conquer the beast. But the bucking steed threw Stanley within seconds of his mount. Emma could never erase the image of her husband's lifeless body inside the corral fence. His neck snapped as he hit the ground, and her beloved, impulsive husband had died instantly. Still, it would have been the kind of death Stanley would have chosen had he been allowed such a choice.

Oh, but Stanley. Why did you have to go and die so young? Why did you have to leave me alone in this world? Emma struck up this one-sided conversation with her deceased husband as naturally as though he were standing next to her.

Why didn't the good Lord grant us children? I prayed for a child. Your child. If I had borne your child, my grief and incredible longing for you might be just a bit more bearable. How I wish I had more than just my memories of you. If we had been blessed with a child, I wouldn't even listen to the likes of Frank

Nance. But it's so lonely without you.

Her thoughts of Stanley caused her to shiver in revulsion at Frank's blatant offer for a loveless marriage. A marriage of convenience. She had known the man only briefly before he proposed. There hadn't been the slightest opportunity for love to grow between them.

Well, Stanley Watson and Frank Nance might have been kindred spirits, but Emma knew, without a doubt, that Stanley had been desperately in love with her—as she had been with him. Frank Nance, with all his good looks and lofty promises of comfort and security, couldn't give her the one thing she longed for most, someone to love, who loved her in return. Besides, unlike Stanley, Frank was a quiet, inexpressive man. Every time she pondered the possibilities of marrying Frank, she remembered the disastrous outcome of her own mother's second marriage to the stone-faced, stern Josiah Trumbull. What if Frank's silent disposition hid a personality as cruel as that hateful man's? Mr. Trumbull had ruined her mother's hopes for a happy life. He had driven Emma away from her mother and her home. Emma would remain single for eternity before she'd enter into the risky union Frank offered. His proposition was simply too full of unknowns.

Still, the persistent Mr. Nance wasn't quite ready to accept Emma's "no" as a final answer to his long-standing proposal. He sidled up to the counter, wedging his way between Emma and the scissors display. His voice slowly increased in volume as he continued in his attempts to weaken her fierce independence. "It isn't as though you have a passel of eligible men to pick from in these parts." Frank's nervous fidgeting with the suede fringe on his leather vest belied the cockiness of his banter. " 'Less'n you consider the undertaker McHenry. He's buried three wives already and has one foot in the grave himself—"

"Mr. Nance, please keep your voice down! And please pay me the courtesy of never addressing this matter again. A marriage for convenience's sake, whether it be your convenience or mine, doesn't interest me in the least. My answer of last year remains my answer today. *No!*"

Emma's final word echoed through the store and the attentions of Katy Greene and her customers immediately turned to the pair. The rotund store clerk's eyebrows rose in obvious question, but she swallowed her curiosity for the time being and simply said, "Mr. Nance, Miz Watson, I'll be with you directly."

"I imagine Katy Greene is havin' a field day with this orphan train business," Frank said, looking in the shopkeeper's direction. "It's created quite a buzz around town."

Despite her firm rejection of Frank's repeated proposal, Emma was slightly taken aback by his abrupt change in the course of their conversation. Was he, at last, abandoning his idea of marriage? Or did he have a new strategy in mind?

"Excuse me, but I'm afraid that I don't know what you're referring to," she snapped, wishing he would simply do his business and leave.

"No offense, ma'am, but a person would have to be as blind as a post hole not to notice that somethin's goin' on here in Shady Grove. Didn't you see the crowd in front of the *Gazette* office when you walked by?"

Emma glanced out the storefront window to see

a dozen or more of the town folk clustered around the newspaper office. Apparently, her inability to focus on more than one task at a time had left her, once again, oblivious to her surroundings. Emma's thoughts and energies for the past three days had been consumed with the completion of Lizzy Baxter's wedding gown. Sometimes, especially on days like today, she found it rather surprising that she could even walk and think at the same time.

Attempting to disguise her deficient observation skills, she turned to Frank and calmly replied, "The citizens of Shady Grove are in a constant state of ruckus. What has them stirred up now?"

Stepping up behind Emma, Katy Greene interrupted with her own answer. "Of course, it wouldn't concern you, Miz Watson—what with being a widow and all—but a rail car full of orphans is headed for our little village, straight from New York City. They're looking for folks who will adopt 'em and give 'em a good home. My husband Orville is on the screening committee. He says that several folks have already inquired about adopting these children and the *Gazette* only posted the notice in Monday's paper. He's hopeful that all fifteen of the orphans will wind up right here in Shady Grove. Why, we might even take one ourselves."

Frank, unobserved by the rambling Mrs. Greene, rolled his eyes at Emma in a look that could only be interpreted as an expressive. "Oh, brother!"

Despite his irritating ideas, he still possesses a certain boyish charm. The unwelcome thought caught Emma off guard. However, the feelings quickly passed as Frank, eyes twinkling, dashed aside any admiration Emma might have been developing for him.

"Perhaps I'll look into taking one of the boys, too. I've heard tell those orphans make good workers."

Even though his words seemed to be spoken in jest, Emma wondered if his teasing tone was a cover for his ultimate motive. Could this man truly be so cold-hearted as to adopt a child for the sake of gaining a helping hand? Emma's ears heated with anger at the very thought. It's bad enough that he would propose a marriage of convenience to a grown woman. . .but only an ogre would adopt an innocent child just for the work he could get out of him. Did Mr. Nance think that adoption was something akin to the purchase of a new pack mule?

She studied his classically handsome features, searching for some answers to her question, but she received none. His mahogany eyes simply reflected his own speculations and appraisals back at her. Under ordinary circumstances, Emma might very well find herself agreeably inclined to Mr. Nance's overtures. Fleetingly, she wondered if she might react differently were the man to at least show some sign of affection for her, some predisposition of falling in love. The thought left her stomach in a disgusting flutter.

An overwhelming urge to run back to the cocoon of her seamstress shop flooded Emma. She didn't want to think about Frank Nance any more today. He flustered her beyond reason, and she refused to stay another moment in this infuriating man's presence.

Emma turned to the shopkeeper and announced, "Mrs. Greene, I really must return to my shop. If you would do me the favor of gathering together the muslin I ordered, along with two dozen shirt buttons and thirty cents worth of seed pearls, I'll be back at four-thirty to pick them up." Then she whirled on her heels and clamored out the door, murmuring a perfunctory "good day, sir" as she passed Frank.

Politely picking her way through the townsfolk still clustered in front of the *Gazette* office, Emma managed to position herself in front of the posted news board. The bold WANTED headline seemed more appropriate for a bank robber than adoptive families, but the article that followed tugged at Emma's heartstrings:

WANTED!
Homes for 15 orphan children

A company of orphan children under the auspices of the Children's Aid Society of New York will arrive in Shady Grove Thursday afternoon, June 24.

These children are bright, intelligent, and well disciplined, both boys and girls of various ages. A local committee of five prominent Shady Grove citizens has been selected to assist the agents in placing the children. Applications must be made to and endorsed by the local committee, which will convene at the town hall on Thursday, June 24 beginning at 9 A.M. Distribution of the children will take place at the opera house on Friday, June 25, at 10 A.M.

Come and see the children and hear the address of the child-placing agent.

The engine of Emma's one-track mind began building up steam. As she turned from the signboard and made her way down the street toward her shop and home, her thoughts quickly traveled into uncharted territory.

Why not a widow like me? Emma mentally shot back a response to Katy Greene's earlier statement. Then, as naturally as she drew breath, Emma's thoughts turned into a silent prayer. *Lord, why not a widow like me? One parent would certainly be better than no parent whatsoever. And I would make a great mother! I have a lot of love to give. I could definitely provide a more suitable home for a child than the stonehearted Mr. Nance.* A spark of self-righteous indignation burst into flame, sending Emma's unspoken prayer to the far recesses of her mind.

The very idea that Frank Nance might even tease about adopting a boy as an extra farm hand. . . Emma's temples began to pound in anger as her thoughts turned, once again, to the infuriating farmer. *Why, if this committee might approve the likes of Frank Nance to adopt a child, surely I can convince them to recommend me!*

Chapter 2

Emma stepped from her spacious porch and across the threshold of her white frame home. Swiftly she rushed through the tastefully decorated parlor and into her workroom, where a worn rolltop desk held her Bible. Emma picked up the Bible and settled into the straight-backed chair that complemented the desk. The room was filled with the necessities of the trade: stacks of fabric in rainbow hues, dressmaker frames, two full-length mirrors, a privacy screen for the customer's convenience, and a treadle sewing machine—Stanley's wedding gift.

With the smells of new fabric surrounding her, she mentally pushed aside thoughts of work and fervently asked God for wisdom. In her typical daily routine of prayer and meditation, she studied her Bible in a systematic fashion. But today, with her thoughts flitting in all different directions like the evening fireflies, she found it impossible to concentrate on one particular Scripture passage. Instead, she thumbed through the yellowed pages of her father's aging Bible, asking God to give her some sort of promise or sign. Did this newborn idea of adoption stem from selfish motivation? Was she simply acting on a desire to prove something to Frank Nance? Or could taking an orphaned child as her own be a part of God's perfect plan?

Instinctively, Emma turned to Psalms—the book of the Bible where she had most often sought and found comfort following Stanley's death. As she skimmed the well-worn pages, her attention rested on a verse just above her right hand. Her index finger pointed to the Sixty-eighth Psalm and she started reading verses 5 and 6. She must have read this very chapter, these same verses, numerous times: "A father of the fatherless, and a judge of the widows, is God in his holy habitation." Yes. She distinctly remembered pondering the fact that God proved Himself a merciful and loving judge to widows such as herself. But never had the words of Psalm 68:6 leapt out at her like they did now. "God setteth the solitary in families."

Was the Lord showing her a sign? Could it be that a solitary little girl now rode on a train bound for Shady Grove, hoping and praying for someone to love and care for her? Emma knew full well the meaning of the word "solitary." These past three years since Stanley's death she had wallowed in loneliness and solitude. Now, her heart ached to think of a mere child facing life without the comfort and security of a home or family.

God setteth the solitary in families. Throughout the remainder of the afternoon the words rang repeatedly through her thoughts until they became a chant. Over the course of the evening, the melodious words turned into song as Emma bathed, washed her hair, and prepared for the next day. *God setteth the solitary in families. God setteth the solitary in families.* Like a soothing lullaby, the psalm soothed Emma to sleep.

ஐ♡ℬ

When the summer sun's first rays at last broke over the horizon, Emma threw back her bedcovers and sat on the side of her bed. As she glanced across her small, tidy quarters, the psalm still rang through her head. *God setteth the solitary in families.* Once the idea of adopting a little girl had taken root in Emma's mind, her thoughts refused to dwell on anything else. Miss Baxter's wedding dress remained unhemmed. She had even forgotten to return to the mercantile yesterday afternoon to retrieve her order from Katy Greene.

The early morning minutes moved slower than February molasses as Emma waited for the appointed hour that the committee would consider adoption applications. With each loud tick of the mantle clock, her conviction and determination grew. Adopting a child was the right thing to do. Emma pulled up her wavy chestnut hair. Then she stood in her undergarments before the open doors of her wardrobe and riffled through an assortment of dresses. As a seamstress, she didn't lack for clothes. But what would be considered appropriate attire for a widow hoping to adopt a child?

Finally, Emma settled on a dark green taffeta with a white lace collar and black velvet trim. If she were to err, Emma preferred to err on the side of overdressing. Besides, the green cloth brought out the emerald flecks of her otherwise gray eyes. She smiled with smug satisfaction at her mirrored reflection as she buttoned up the bodice to her dress. *They won't turn me down for lack of good looks.* The thought only briefly skittered through her mind, but it was swiftly followed by a rebuff for such self-admiration, lest it border on conceit.

Emma felt like a hostage to time, just waiting for the mantle clock to chime nine o'clock. By the time the clock rang once, announcing 8:15, she was already fumbling with her front door key as she prepared to leave. She couldn't wait one minute more. She really wanted to be among the first in line. Thoughts of tiny arms around her neck, night-night kisses, and playing peekaboo swirled through her mind as her black leather high-top boots clipped a staccato beat on the boardwalk. With certain determination, Emma headed down Main Street toward the town hall.

The swinging doors leading into the meeting room announced her arrival in grating squeaks as she stepped over the threshold. As she had hoped, Emma was apparently the first applicant to arrive. Seated in an intimidating row behind a long table were the two women and three men who composed the recommendation committee. In unison, this team of prominent Shady Grove citizens stopped their busy pursuit of shuffling papers and consulting one another to turn and stare at Emma. The sun's bright rays, spilling in from the high windows, seemed to create a dream-like chasm between Emma and the prospect of adopting a child. Her heart pounding with anticipation, she plunged into the sphere of light as if she were embracing the prospect of adoption all over again. With each of the twenty steps it took her to cross the room, the floorboards creaked in protest, but the noise sounded like nothing less than a sweet melody to Emma. Nothing. . .nothing could dampen her joyful anticipation. . .nothing. . .not even when she suspected the committee's silently scolding, *You're a widow. You're wasting our time.*

Twisting her handkerchief between perspiring palms, Emma cleared her throat and began, "I—I want to adopt a child. A ch—child from the orphan train."

෨♡ඏ

The silver conchos that decorated the outer legs of his tanned leather chaps clinked softly together as Frank Nance hung the protective britches on a peg just inside the kitchen door. Typically, he reserved his chaps for rides out on the range, but today he had worn them as an apron, of sorts, to protect his best wool trousers from getting soiled during his early morning chores. He had no Sunday-go-to-meetin' clothes, so his newest britches would have to suffice. The washtub, which he had pulled into the middle of the kitchen floor last evening, still held the soapy remains of his bath, the clouded water long turned cold.

Crossing from the kitchen to the parlor, Frank stood in front of the room's single adornment, a garishly gilded mirror that hung on the south wall. Only traces of the reflective mercury remained behind the glass, and Frank had to tip his head at just the right angle to catch a glimpse of his reflection. Frank licked his fingers and twirled the ends of his freshly trimmed moustache. Then, he ran his hand down his clean-shaven chin and gave his parted and bear-greased hair a final smoothing pat.

"There you are—all citified and sissified," Frank said to his reflection. "But if gettin' gussied-up helps me adopt a boy, then gussied-up I'll get." However, he hoped and prayed he didn't run into Emma Watson today, looking like he did. She'd for sure think he had gone soft. Or would she? Frank never knew just how that woman would respond. Where the doe-eyed Widow Watson was concerned, or any ladies for that matter, Frank didn't have a notion what to do.

When he had made a proposal of marriage to the young widow, he thought sure she would find his offer hard to resist. He'd been told on more than one occasion that he was a handsome man. He was strong and young and could provide security and stability to a wife.

Frank had never been one to drink or carouse, thanks to his saintly mother, who had raised him to practice good Christian morals and ethics. She had seen to it that he learned right from wrong. Surely those traits held the marks of a good husband. Even though he had not been a particularly religious man of late, he still tried his best to avoid any big sins.

His bachelorhood didn't stem from any odd deficiency or personality quirk. Only his previous profession as a drover along the Chisholm Trail had kept him single and unattached. He knew from watching the married cowhands that life as a cowboy and the duties of a husband don't mix.

After the death of his mother, which left him orphaned at age fourteen, Frank had ridden the range, driving cattle along the Chisholm Trail from Texas through Indian Territory and on into the Kansas plains. Frank learned quickly what it took to survive in the Wild West. Alongside his gun and a good horse, a cowboy needed a gruff exterior and a callused heart. Frank was an expert at keeping his emotions and opinions to himself.

But the need for cowboys to push longhorns along the trail had grown mighty slim, thanks to the ever-expanding railroad and the fencing in of the plains. Frank had traded his adventurous life as a cowboy for the comparatively mundane existence of a Kansas wheat farmer. Since this drastic change, he found the old familiar loneliness much more difficult to bear. But he found admitting his need for companionship a difficult prospect—even with Widow Watson.

He had hoped beyond hope that Emma would have at least given his marriage proposal last year a glimmer of consideration. The two of them would be a good match. But the Widow Watson made it perfectly clear that she was not interested in even entertaining the idea. Maybe he should have courted her awhile before stating his intentions. He hadn't known her all that well when he first proposed, but Frank was a man who made up his mind quickly, and he didn't see any sense in wasting time. Unfortunately, Emma seemed to think he was much too practical with his straightforward approach.

Despite what the prim and proper widow thought, no other woman interested him. Frank was not just seeking a marriage of convenience. In truth, most of the "conveniences" of his life were cared for by Pedro and Maria Ramirez, the husband and wife team whom Frank had hired to assist him on the farm. He wanted a life partner. He wanted Emma for his wife. Frank dreaded the thought of facing any more years alone.

When Emma snubbed him again yesterday, Frank determined then and there that he wouldn't wait forever for Emma to change her mind. Ideas of proposing to another woman certainly crossed his mind. Frank had been exposed to more than one coy smile from the collection of young maidens in Shady Grove. However, he had soon dashed aside any notion of marrying another. Thoughts of marrying someone besides Emma Watson simply held no fascination for him—not that he was by any means in love with her. She simply held the maturity and grace that appealed to Frank. Yes, that was it—maturity and grace, nothing more.

So, if he couldn't have the companionship of Widow Watson, he would turn his attentions to other things. The idea of adopting a boy rather appealed to him. While a boy could in no way meet his longing to have Emma for his wife, Frank's desire to be a father would be fulfilled in an adopted son. He and such a boy would be good friends. Best friends.

When Frank had told Emma he might take a boy from the orphan train, he had spoken the words in jest. But the longer he entertained the whim, the more he liked it. After all, he had been orphaned as a child himself. Certainly, he could relate to a boy who felt all alone in the world. As a father, Frank would have a lot to offer a son.

Slamming the back door behind him, Frank tromped across the well-worn path that led from the kitchen to the barn. The strong, earthy smell of hay mixed with manure assailed Frank's nostrils as he slid open the barn door. Shadow, the mustang that Frank had lassoed and tamed as a colt, nuzzled up to his arm as he slid the bridle into place. Within seconds after lifting his saddle from the top rail of the horse's stall, Frank had cinched the straps securely and mounted the steed for the short trip to town.

♥

Emma's impassioned appeal ultimately convinced the panel members to grant her the coveted and necessary commendation to adopt. The two women on the panel had actually been brought to tears as Emma expressed her deep loneliness since the death of her husband and her desire to relieve the desolation of an orphaned child. The Reverend Barnhart agreed that Emma was faithful in church attendance and would provide well for the spiritual nurture of a young soul. Even the committee's businessmen, mercantile owner Orville Greene and *Gazette* publisher Ben McGowan, nodded their heads in approval when Emma addressed the fact that she could teach her child the art and trade of dressmaking and thus assist the girl in becoming a useful and productive citizen of society. But their approval came with a condition: Emma would be allowed to choose a daughter only if no married couples stepped forward first to claim the child. Clutching the recommendation letter securely in her gloved hand, Emma backed out of the room, nodding her head in appreciation to the committee all the way to the door.

God setteth the solitary in families, her heart sang with joy as Emma stepped from the meeting chambers into the hallway that extended the length of the town hall. She found the passageway clogged with several applicants nervously queued in pairs. The first couple in line pushed their way past her through the open door, and Emma received little more than a curious glance or two as she zig-zagged her way through the small group and into the dust-filled street.

A cacophony of horses, wagons, carriages, and pedestrians met Emma as she closed the door.

"Are my eyes deceivin' me, or did I just catch you coming out of the town hall?" a familiar voice softly spoke in her ear.

Jumping, she turned to stare straight into the right shoulder of the towering man. Lifting her gaze to meet his, her breath caught at the sight of Frank's freshly scrubbed and strikingly handsome face so close to hers. The aroma of strong lye soap still clung to his whiskerless chin. The crow's feet that framed his dark mahogany eyes crinkled as he responded with a grin to her startled response.

"W—why, y—yes. I–I–I. . ." Mad at herself for stammering, Emma's shoulders tensed and her toes curled inside her boots. Why on earth was she reacting to this man like a schoolgirl in the throes of her first crush? Surely the noise and excitement of the morning were wearing on her, for she had never been so challenged in maintaining her composure with Frank. *Or perhaps you simply want to believe you have never been so affected by him,* a rebellious voice taunted. Emma clamped her teeth in aggravation. *Frank Nance holds no place—absolutely no place whatsoever—in my heart! Period! The very idea is nothing short of lunacy!*

"You didn't by any chance seek a recommendation from the orphan train committee, did you?" The mischief dancing in his dark eyes told Emma that he already knew her answer. But the sparkle quickly disappeared behind a veil of seriousness as he followed the unanswered question with another, more urgent inquiry. "Were your efforts met with success?"

Emma studied the face of this mystifying man. From her previous dealings with Mr. Nance, she had long ago concluded that, despite his dashing good looks, the man was incapable of feeling any deep emotion. Yet, as he stood before her now, his voice took on an almost pleading tone. Why were her adoption plans important to Frank?

Doggedly determined to regain her cool demeanor, Emma raised the coveted recommendation letter for him to see. "Fortunately for me, the committee didn't feel that a widow adopting a child was as absurd an idea as Katy Greene believed it to be. I shall be allowed the opportunity to adopt any young girl who is not claimed by a married couple first." Before Frank could examine the paper further, Emma slid it into her beaded caba.

"Now, Miz Watson, that's powerful good news," he enthusiastically replied, undaunted by her curt reaction. "After I left the mercantile yesterday, I felt sorry for funnin' around about this orphan train business. Truth be known, I gave the matter considerable ponderin' last night. I'm on my way to meet with the committee myself and see if I can't convince 'em to let me take a boy."

"No, Fran–er–Mr. Nance. You mustn't. . . You can't. . . Why, the very idea of you. . ." An all-too-familiar irritation surfaced as flashes of yesterday's conversation flitted through Emma's mind. Would Frank Nance really adopt a boy just for farm labor?

"And why not, Miz Watson? Why shouldn't I adopt a son? You've made it perfectly clear that you are unwilling to consider my proposal of marriage. Would you have me forever condemned to live a life of loneliness and solitude?"

His sincere words dashed aside all her previous negative thoughts. Never before had the man spoken so openly with Emma. His soul-revealing speech made her squirm uncomfortably against the snug taffeta gown. As she studied his features in hopes of confirming or denying his sincerity, the psalm that had replayed through her thoughts all morning now took on new meaning. *God setteth the solitary in families*. Could this scripture possibly contain a promise for someone like Frank Nance? The idea of his actually needing human companionship had seemed almost preposterous to Emma. Could she have somehow misunderstood this man? If so, was his proposal based on more than he had admitted? Her stomach produced a betraying flutter. *Stop it!* She wanted to scream.

"You're preachin' a double-standard, Miz Watson. One that's tipped in your favor, if you ask me." A note of irritation crept into Frank's voice as he continued, waving an arm in front of his face to shoo away a pesky horsefly. "Evidently, you believe adoption to be quite fine and dandy for a widow woman such as yourself but somethin' strange and suspicious for a bachelor like me.

"Don't get me wrong, here, Ma'am." Frank fixed his gaze on Emma's face, still whisking at the air to deflect the buzzing bug. "I admire your wantin' a child, and your gumption to see this business through. From what I can tell, you have the makin's of a wonderful mama. Just because you aren't inclined to marry again doesn't mean you shouldn't grab at the chance to raise a young'un, if such a chance comes along. But I reckon you shouldn't begrudge me the same opportunity."

With the force of a slammed door, a steely glaze hid the soft vulnerability that Emma had glimpsed, ever so briefly, in Frank's eyes. "I'd like to stay and visit with you all day," he said, glancing over his shoulder at the town hall, "but there's important business to tend to."

Tipping his broad-brimmed, gray felt hat, Frank excused himself with an exasperating smirk. "Oh and Miz Watson," he said, turning to face her once more, "may I say 'thanks' for plowin' the ground ahead of me and plantin' the idea that it's all right for an unmarried person to adopt. If all goes well with me and that committee, I'll see you at the opera house tomorrow."

Chapter 3

T he ever-present prairie wind blew down Main Street on Friday morning, swirling the dust into miniature cyclones and whipping at Emma's skirts. She instinctively held a rose-scented handkerchief over her nose to keep from choking on the dry air, heavy with the pungent smell of livestock and working men. She paused before crossing the road and surveyed the collection of people now congregating outside the opera house doors.

Katy Greene's squeaky voice carried above the crowd, prickling Emma's nerves like straight pins jabbing an un-thimbled thumb. "Well, Orville wants a boy. But I insist on a girl so I can dress her up like a little doll. There's just not much you can do to fix up a boy, don't you know. . ."

The mousy woman whom Katy Greene had cornered continued to bob her head in tacit agreement as the vociferous Mrs. Greene droned on. Ignoring the storekeeper's rambling babble, Emma anxiously fingered the blue satin ribbon on the gingham-wrapped parcel she cradled in her right arm. The package contained a china-faced doll with real hair the same chestnut color as her own. A gift for her daughter-to-be. Emma had spent several hours yesterday evening making the doll's frock out of this powder-blue gingham. On her sewing table back home lay another piece of the fabric. She planned to sew her new daughter a dress to match the one the doll now wore. But as she scanned the gathering assembly, doubts now punctured the confident assurance of impending motherhood she had felt just moments before. How many of these couples wanted girls? And exactly how many girls had the orphan train carried into town?

Emma forced these negative contemplations to the back of her mind and, once again, inspected the amassing band of townsfolk. Half a dozen farmers in bib overalls and their plump, plainly-dressed wives composed the majority of the prospective parents waiting to enter the opera house. Were they all hoping only to find a new farm hand from among the orphan train riders? Or did they truly want to provide a good home to a child?

Emma had witnessed the area farmers' gab sessions, which took place on the boardwalk in front of the Shady Grove feed store. She knew that a good many ill-conceived ideas came from these weekly meetings. If they discussed adopting for free labor, had Frank been among them?

Until her most recent encounter with him, she would have strongly suspected his being the mastermind behind any self-serving plot, despite the teasing tone he used when he mentioned adopting a boy to help out on the farm. Now she hesitated to charge Frank with certain villainy. For a few unguarded moments Frank Nance had revealed a different side, a vulnerable side, to Emma. Just those few seconds, when she saw softness and emotion in his eyes, caused her to question her previous conviction that he was totally callused and cold. Nonetheless, a few doubts still lingered.

But where was he? Just yesterday Frank seemed doggedly determined to follow through on his adoption plan. It was unlikely that he had changed his mind. Emma craned her neck to see if she could spot the one farmer she knew would stand head and shoulders above the rest. Still, he was nowhere to be found. Could it be that his request for a child had been denied?

A whistle sounded from the train station down the road, indicating that the appointed hour had come. Vaguely hoping to catch sight of Frank, Emma crossed the street and nudged her way to the opera house doors. No sooner had the whistle fallen silent than the garishly ornate double doors of the opera house swung open.

"On behalf of the Orphan Train Committee, I welcome you all," Reverend Barnhart exclaimed. "Please come in. Those of you who are here in hopes of being matched with a child, we ask that you find a seat among the first few rows of the auditorium. If you are here to simply observe the occasion, please take your seats toward the rear." The dignified and refined minister, bedecked in his black preaching suit, shook the hands of the men and nodded respectfully at the women as they filed past him, instilling an aura of solemnity among the people.

The freshly lit kerosene lanterns that lined the far aisles and front of the stage filled the air with a heavy, sooty smell. The lights' flickering shadows set a mysterious scene for this true-life drama, in which the audience would soon play the lead parts.

Emma discreetly found a seat in the third center row, next to the aisle. But once all the couples had taken their seats, an empty place remained beside Emma. Absently, she wondered if some of the couples assumed her spouse would soon arrive. The rest of the seats in the auditorium quickly filled with more than fifty onlookers from Shady Grove's curious citizenry. Seemingly, no one wanted to miss out on the biggest show to ever come to town.

Up on the stage, the rotund publisher of the *Gazette*, Ben McGowan, cleared his throat and shifted from one foot to another as he waited for everyone to find a seat. "Ladies and gentlemen," he began in his deepest bass voice. "We are gathered here today to witness a truly newsworthy and momentous event. For, within a matter of minutes, the young ones who arrived via the orphan train yesterday evening shall be escorted from the Imperial Hotel. Accompanying this band of orphans is the child-placing agent, Mr. E. E. Hill, who shall address this body before the matching of children to parents commences.

"But prior to turning our attentions to the business of the day, may I take just a moment to express my appreciation to the citizens of Shady Grove for the privilege and honor of serving on this select committee. . . ." The verbose newsman continued his pontification, blatantly stalling for time until a chorus of giggles and shushes filtered through the rear doors.

As one body, the crowd's attention turned away from the stage and toward the commotion. Emma shifted in her seat just in time to see none other than Frank Nance, grinning from ear-to-ear, jauntily striding down the aisle. On Frank's shoulders rode a toddler whose face was hidden under the brim of the ex-cowboy's weathered Stetson. Behind him children of various ages, shapes, sizes, and gender followed in a single line.

Just like the Pied Piper, Emma couldn't help but think, suddenly irritated by Frank's uncharacteristically childish antics. Did she owe her perturbed attitude to a twinge of jealousy? For not once—not even when he had proposed marriage—had Frank shown to her the kind of emotion he so freely displayed with the children. Then again, why should she care? The man meant nothing to her. *Nothing,* she insisted. Wasn't it she who had rejected him? Emma reminded herself that she was not the least bit interested in Frank Nance. However, her mind betrayed her as it insisted on meandering to another question. Was Frank capable of showing that kind of affection for a wife?

Immediately, she squelched any notions she might be developing for the man. *He is not a dedicated Christian,* she firmly told herself. *Even if he is handsome, even if he declares his undying love and devotion, he never darkens the church door!* Emma simply could not involve herself with a man who did not share her passion for the Lord.

When the "orphan parade" reached the stage steps, Frank lifted the tot from atop his shoulders and uncovered the cherub's face as he retrieved his hat. A gentle pat on the young boy's backside sent him scurrying onto the stage to find a seat. Relieved of his charge, Frank turned to search the audience until his gaze rested on Emma and the vacant seat to her left.

Scrunching down in her seat, Emma dug her fingernails

into the red velvet armrests, hoping and praying that Frank would find another place to sit. But a quick scan of the lantern-lit room told her there were no other seats as close to the front as the one next to her. Would she ever shake this man?

Bringing up the rear of the orphan processional, a gentleman with an infant in his arms walked to the center of the stage and said, "As he's taking his seat, I'd like to extend my sincere thanks to Mr. Frank Nance for coming to my aid today." Seemingly nonplused by the hubbub around him, the man intercepted the baby's reach for his glasses while introducing himself as E. E. Hill, the child-placing agent from New York City. While he spoke, he pushed his spectacles back up the bridge of his nose with one thumb before securely clutching the infant's curious fingers in his grasp. His crumpled suit looked as though he had slept in it for several nights.

"Unfortunately, one of the young orphans amongst our party fell ill," Mr. Hill continued. "And my assistant, Mrs. Ima Jean Findlay, found it necessary to remain behind at the Imperial to care for the ailing child. Mr. Nance happened to be eating breakfast at the hotel and observed my single-handed struggles with the children. He graciously volunteered to assist."

Frank, who had already left the stage and was heading for the empty seat next to Emma, paused to respond. Although he spoke softly, the acoustics of the room caused his voice to reverberate throughout the audience. "No need to say 'thanks,' Mr. Hill. I was happy to help out.

"But I don't mind tellin' you. . ." Frank pointed with

his hat in the direction of the squirming children. "Herdin' cows is a heap easier than corralin' them kids!" A ripple of lighthearted laughter filtered through the crowd as he came to a stop beside Emma.

"Is it all right with you if I sit there, ma'am?" Frank whispered as he nodded toward the empty seat. Emma sensed, without even lifting her gaze from the package on her lap, that every eye in the building was watching this exchange. Her face heated and the tops of her ears stung with embarrassment over the attention now focused toward her.

Unlike yesterday, when she wanted to wear her best to impress the committee, today Emma had purposefully tried to shrink into the shadows and remain inconspicuous. As the only widow woman seeking to adopt, she didn't want to endure a morning full of stares. She had even chosen a nondescript brown muslin dress, rather than one made of a finer material or brighter color, for the express purpose of blending in with the crowd. But the boisterous Mr. Nance seemed intent on including her in his spectacle.

What had gotten into him, anyway? Never before had Frank behaved in such a frivolous fashion. Without verbally responding to his request, Emma shifted her skirts to allow him to squeeze past her and occupy the vacant seat. Then, with a flick of her wrist, she opened her whalebone and lace fan and began waving it furiously in front of her face. Despite the early hour, the room already felt uncomfortably stuffy and warm. But then, Frank's presence seemed to always elicit a heated reaction in Emma. In the past she experienced the heat of irritation. But this morning something else was certainly mixed with the irritation, which exasperated her all the more.

"Good mornin', Miz Watson. I reckon you were wonderin' if I was gonna show. Well, here I be. And you'll be happy to know that the committee also approved the likes of me." He waved his approval letter tauntingly in front of her.

A flurry of smart retorts flew through Emma's thoughts. However, when she raised her head to respond, she was struck by the gleam of excitement in Frank's eyes and she held her tongue. The vexation that typically accompanied her every encounter with this man now softened. She didn't want a sour mood to spoil this special day for either of them.

Emma, blinking rapidly, tried to hide the smile of anticipation that bubbled up from within. Frank wasn't the only one excited. The ambiance of the day so swept over Emma that she found herself actually complimenting Mr. Nance.

"You seem to have a real gift for dealing with children. I must confess, I am impressed." The words startled Emma, but not half as much as the spark of admiration that sprang into Frank's eyes. Flustered, she fanned herself all the more fiercely and nodded toward the stage. "We'd best turn our attentions to the platform, or we may miss something."

Forcing herself to stare forward, Emma wondered whatever possessed her to offer such a coquettish response. Now, she was nothing short of awkward and uncertain of her every move.

Up on the stage, Mr. Hill handed the baby boy he had been jostling to one of the four older orphan girls seated behind him. He smoothed his coat lapels and cleared his throat before turning to address the crowd. "I realize that many of you are anxiously waiting to be matched with a child, but first we must outline the procedures we will follow and establish a few ground rules. . . ."

Mr. Hill continued with his remarks, but Emma's attentions were compellingly drawn to the children seated behind him. As she focused on the children, Frank's imposing presence seemed to blur. Each of the boys wore new knickers, suit coats, starched white shirts, and neckties. The four girls were outfitted in identical navy blue cotton dresses and stiff white pinafores.

Only four girls, Emma noted with a twinge of disappointment. *O Lord, is one of them to be mine?* She eagerly studied each of their faces as she prayed. They were all a bit older than she had expected them to be—at least nine or ten years old. None shared any obvious physical characteristics with Emma. None reminded Emma of her deceased husband, Stanley. Yet, as they doted and fawned quietly over the baby boy placed temporarily in their care, Emma was favorably impressed with their tenderness and affection toward the child. They appeared polite and well behaved. Certainly Emma could welcome any one of these four girls into her home.

Out of the corner of her eye, Emma caught a glimpse of Frank discreetly waving at the toddler boy whom he had carried "horsy-back" style into the opera house. The youngster scrunched his shoulders and returned Frank's greeting by waving with both hands. Emma simply shook her head in bewilderment at this mystifying man. What had happened to the always logical, practical, emotionless Mr. Nance? If the truth were told, Emma liked the new Frank much better than the old. Still, only time would tell whether the changes were lasting and sincere or just another self-serving scheme.

"In conclusion. . ." Mr. Hill's closing remarks jarred Emma from her daydreams, and she forced herself to focus on his words. "Before we call the first couple to come and select their child, let me emphasize two key points. These boys and girls understand that they are here in hopes of finding a new home. Unfortunately for several of them, their search for a family will not end here—for we have fifteen children among our group, including the one that is ill, and only a dozen homes which have met the standards for committee approval. Despite the unfavorable odds, we will not force any child over age eight to go with a family. The ultimate decision rests with the orphan. If they do not feel comfortable with any of the couples here today, they will board the train with us and travel on to the next town. Our journey west will continue until all of the children have been placed in suitable homes."

Without turning his back on the crowd, the speaker took three steps back and stood between two young boys who were poking at each other. Mr. Hill's close proximity to the youngsters immediately caused them to cease their banter and sit up straight in their chairs.

"Secondly," Mr. Hill continued, "there is a one-year waiting period between child-placement and legal adoption. If, during that period, a family is grievously dissatisfied with the child placed in their care, as has happened on a very rare occasion with our placements, the family should contact us immediately and the child will be removed from the home."

Mr. Hill paused just long enough to pull a large white handkerchief from his back pocket and wipe the perspiration from his brow. "I believe that concludes my remarks. Approved couples will be called in random order as their names are drawn from this hat." He held a black top hat high into the air. "As I call your name, bring your letter of recommendation and join me on the stage. We will meet with our two single candidates for child placement following the matching of all married couples with a child. All right, shall we begin?"

Emma nervously licked her lips and scrutinized the four girls. Would one of them remain for her? She relived that seemingly supernatural assurance which had swept over her when she was approved to adopt. As she looked at the limited number of girls, new doubts assailed her.

The children were instructed to stand and line up across the front of the platform. As soon as the girls stood, they huddled around the oldest one, who held the baby in her arms. The younger boys eagerly jumped from their seats, each trying to shove his way to the front of the line. The older ones took a military stance, their faces solemn and stony. But Emma couldn't help but notice one boy, about ten, who lagged behind, his chin drooping to his chest. His frail body and pale complexion added to the aura of gloom on his face, and he stood a full step behind the others. *Why, what a sad little boy,* Emma fleetingly thought. However, her concentration quickly shifted to

Katy and Orville Greene, whose names Mr. Hill had just called.

Without a moment's deliberation, Katy walked straight toward the four girls. Emma nervously chewed on her fingernails as she tried to guess which girl the annoying Mrs. Greene would chose. To her amazement, Katy reached out and took the dozing baby boy from the arms of his young caregiver. "Oh, Mr. Hill, Orville and I have always wanted a baby boy," Katy gushed. "This is simply a dream come true."

Emma's jaw dropped in amazement. Turning to Frank, she nearly choked on her surprised exclamation. "Why, I distinctly heard Katy say that she had to have a girl!"

Frank rolled his eyes. "That woman's more perplexin' than a two-headed cow!"

Shaking her head, Emma chuckled as Katy carried her new son down the aisle and out the back door while Orville stayed to complete the necessary paperwork.

The next couple called to the platform were strangers to Emma. They appeared shy and withdrawn, obviously the type of folks that preferred to keep to themselves. Straightaway, they walked toward the wan and fragile boy who trailed behind the others. The husband and wife bent to talk with the child, their words inaudible to everyone but him.

"No!" the boy protested, his determined voice ringing out in sharp contrast to his meek demeanor. "I won't go with you. I don't want no new family." Emma leaned forward in her seat, straining to catch the snatches of the ensuing discussion between the boy and Mr. Hill. But she started when Frank nudged her forearm.

"You watch, that boy's gonna be mine," he whispered, beaming like a man who had seen his destiny.

Chapter 4

What on earth are you talking about?" Emma sputtered. "That boy obviously has more problems than two parents could hope to handle, let alone one. Besides, I thought you wanted an able-bodied worker to help out on the farm." As the sharp words left her mouth, Emma wondered if she should have voiced them. "I mean, he certainly looks too feeble and peaked to assist anyone in that regard. Why would you want to take on such a child? Really, you are full of more surprises than Katy Greene!"

"I know this sounds strange, comin' from the likes of me," he said with a tinge of mockery lacing his words. "But there is no logic or reason behind my hunches. There's just a certain feelin' deep down inside of me. I believe I could really help that boy. And as for being full of surprises, well, I suppose that's true. There's plenty about me you don't know." Frank tugged at the end of his moustache as he continued. "I am not the heartless monster you insist on making me out to be. This isn't the time or the place to discuss the matter, but I believe that a little hard work ain't goin' to hurt a boy. Fact is, a hard work ethic might be one of the most valuable things a father could pass on to a son."

Her thoughts a mass of confusion, Emma looked at Frank and then back up to the pasty-faced boy. Although Frank's words were spoken almost tenderly, they echoed the stern sentiment she, as a young girl, had heard her harsh and despised stepfather express many times before.

Emma's own father died in battle during the Civil War, and her mother, left nearly destitute, had remarried Josiah Trumbull when Emma was eight years old. From that infamous day until the cold March morning when she finally screwed up the courage to run away, Emma had been forced to work like a slave girl in her own home. Although sympathetic, her fearful mother could only cower in submission and resignation to this tyrannical man. Mr. Trumbull's unwieldy insistence that a child be taught the value of a hard day's work robbed Emma of childhood's simple pleasures, and she grew old long before her time.

Would Frank treat this young boy with the same oppression that she had suffered under Mr. Trumbull's authority? Or was he speaking the truth when he pronounced that he was not the heartless monster that she had surmised him to be? Could Frank show true affection for a child? Emma longed to believe that the latter would be true. The poor boy cowering on the stage didn't appear able to withstand much more trauma in his young life. If any child needed a loving, stable home, it was this pathetic specimen of a child.

Emma found herself hoping that Mr. Hill could convince the boy to go with the reserved couple now looking to take him home. Then Frank would be forced to turn his attentions to one of the other orphan boys. But the melo-drama now unfolding on the opera house stage continued as Mr. Hill turned his back on the pathetic waif and addressed the mild-mannered pair loud enough for the first few rows of the audience to hear. "If you don't mind my interference, I believe I know the ideal child for you. First, however, I need to ask. Would you consider a girl, or did you have your hearts set on a boy?"

The wife, twisting a handkerchief nervously, looked up to her husband and shrugged her shoulders in submissive deference to his wishes. "We're open to either, Mr. Hill," the balding man replied, running a hand over his smooth head. "Which child did you have in mind?" At this, Mr. Hill led the couple toward the cluster of twittering girls.

"She seems to be the perfect match for them," Frank whispered when the oldest of the orphan girls meekly nodded her assent to Mr. Hill. She stepped between her new parents and waved a timid good-bye to her friends as they walked off the platform.

That leaves only three girls, Emma figured fretfully. *O Lord. Is one of them going to be mine?* Her crumbling assurance that she was going to become a mother on this day dwindled as Mr. Hill proceeded through the list of married couples, for soon there were two girls remaining on stage. Then only one.

Despite her vested interest, Emma couldn't hold back her tears of joy at the sight of Ty and Rebecca Brownstone walking up to the platform and warmly embracing the last orphan girl. The Brownstones' only daughter, Sarah, had drowned two winters ago, after skating onto thin ice. Ty and Rebecca's acceptance of this orphan girl, who strikingly resembled their Sarah, signified their readiness to recover from their grief and lovingly parent once more.

However, hot tears of disappointment supplanted Emma's tears of joy when the Brownstones escorted their new daughter down the aisle. Emma's final hope for a child exited along with the departure of this last orphan girl. She could not begrudge the Brownstones a fresh start. Nor did she resent any of the other couples who had chosen the other three girls. But how could she have so totally misread the will of God? Emma had felt such a peace in her decision to adopt. Hadn't God given her Psalm 68:6 as her own special promise or sign? Had her secret wishes and desires superseded God's plan for her life? Hadn't her motives been pure?

As her mind filled with more unanswered questions and doubts, Emma whisked away any evidence of tears with the back of her gloved hand. Why would God deny her a child? Why? Hadn't she faithfully served Him and sought His will? Emma ground her teeth and forcefully swallowed the knots of anger nearly choking her. Anger toward God for rejecting her request to be a mother. And, however illogical, anger toward Frank Nance, for his earlier premonition about his child appeared likely to come true.

The auditorium began to quickly empty as the final adoptive couple approached the stage. Standing next to Mr. Hill, the pair faced the five remaining orphan boys. After several long moments of contemplation, they moved closer to the anemic, sour-faced boy who had so vehemently refused to go with the first couple. Perhaps the child's clear need for love and attention was tugging at many hearts. With his arms folded across his chest, the pathetic little urchin once again shook his head back and forth in refusal when Mr. Hill asked him if he wanted to go with the nice gentleman and lady to their home.

"Mr. and Mrs. Fletcher," Mr. Hill's voice echoed through the emptying auditorium, "I sincerely regret the obstinate nature of this boy. Rest assured, I shall have a stern word with him about his behavior today. However, you would surely be happier with one of these other fine and well-mannered young men." The placing agent cast a quick scowl in the direction of the offending youngster as he steered the Fletchers toward another boy.

Seemingly content with their newly matched son, this final couple made their way off the stage. As they left the hall, Mr. Hill stood at the edge of the platform and watched them depart. "Andrew Clymer, I'd like to speak with you over here," he said, motioning with his index finger for the skinny, sad-faced boy to join him. The youth stepped away from the other three boys, who seemed resigned that they had not been chosen this round.

As if he were ensnared in the plot of a classic play, Frank leaned forward, his every attention on the child he had declared would be his.

"Andrew, I don't mind telling you—you try my patience!" His stern but gentle voice floated from the stage, despite his attempts to speak confidentially. Placing his arm around the orphan's shoulder, Mr. Hill tenderly chided the child. "Don't you know, you are only hurting yourself and postponing the inevitable? You should have jumped at the chance to have a new family like the Fletchers. Nice folks like them don't come around at every train stop."

The chastised boy clutched the rim of his new hat as he calculated his response. "I ain't goin' nowhere without my sister, Mr. Hill. Not as long as I have any say."

"Er—um." Clearing his throat, Frank gently touched the top of Emma's hand. The brief pressure of his fingers against hers sent an unexpected tremor of tingles racing up her arm. Since Stanley's death, occasions for even the most casual of physical contact with a man were few and far between. But had she reacted so because a man touched her or because Frank touched her? Blinking in confusion, Emma tried to concentrate on his words.

"Excuse me, ma'am, but could you let me by?" Obviously, Frank had no inkling of Emma's response to his touch, for he focused solely on the boy. "I'd like a chance to speak to that boy and Mr. Hill."

"Certainly." Emma's knees began to tremble uncontrollably and fresh tears welled in her eyes as she shifted in her seat, allowing the preoccupied Frank to pass. "I suppose I should be going now, anyway," she muttered, a wave of loneliness washing over her. Not since the months immediately preceding Stanley's death had Emma felt so bereft. And her growing reaction to Frank Nance only heightened her despair and frustration.

She looked around the large hall to see that only a handful of spectators remained. Emma pulled her caba and the package containing the doll close to her chest in preparation to leave, but the peaks and valleys of emotion she had traversed over the past few days now sapped her strength. Suddenly, she didn't trust her trembling limbs enough to stand. She closed her eyes and drew a deep breath as she waited for her strength to return.

In this reflective moment, Emma's mind replayed a sentence just spoken by the boy being chastised on the stage. *I ain't goin' nowhere without my sister. . .not as long as I have any say.* At once, a strong dose of curiosity dashed aside thoughts of leaving. Her eyes popped open in time to watch Frank approach Andrew and Mr. Hill. What did the boy mean when he said he'd go nowhere without his sister? There were no girls left on the stage. Immediately, Emma recalled something she had dismissed earlier. Mr. Hill said an orphan was sick at the hotel. Was the sick child this boy's sister—a girl? A spark of hope ignited in her soul.

Frank knelt on one knee in front of the child. "Listen, I really think you need to come home with me," he said in the usual straightforward manner, which left Emma wincing in memory of his proposal to her.

"Yes, why don't you try and talk some sense into him," Mr. Hill interjected. "I've talked to him 'til I'm blue in the face, but my words seem to fall on deaf ears."

Rising to his full height, Frank towered over Mr. Hill. The child-placing agent took Frank by the arm and ushered him aside.

Emma leaned forward, straining to hear Mr. Hill's words as a new flood of possibilities caused her palms to moisten with anticipation. Once again, the psalm of promise began a slow etching on her mind. *He setteth the solitary in families.*

"The situation is this," Mr. Hill said, his whisper once again audible from Emma's close vantage point. "Andrew's four-year-old sister, Anna, is the one I mentioned earlier as being so sick. She contracted a nasty case of whooping cough, and we couldn't possibly bring her out in public until her health improves."

The words seemed a command for Emma to rise. Still clutching the box containing the doll, she tiptoed toward the stage in hopes of catching his every word. Evidently there was another orphan. A girl. And her name was Anna. *He setteth the solitary in families.* Her heart pounded ferociously as fresh tears stung her eyes.

Anna. My grandmother's name. Emma mouthed the name again silently. *Anna. O Lord. Is this the girl meant for me?* The prayer wove in and out of Emma's soul as Mr. Hill continued.

"Fact of the matter is, we can't proceed with our journey until she gets better. She might not survive another day on the train. You see how thin young Andrew, here, is?" Emma's gaze followed Frank's and Mr. Hill's as they surveyed the boy. "Well, he's plump as a melon compared to little Anna."

Mr. Hill released Frank's arm and approached Andrew, laying a gentle hand on his shoulder again as he spoke. "We don't like to separate family members if we can help it, but so often we must. Certainly, splitting up siblings and placing them in good homes is preferable to the street urchin's life they would lead in New York City.

"I see no other way but to wait 'til Anna's better and then place her with a family farther on down the line." Mr. Hill slowly shook his head from side to side. "But Andrew's luck is going to run out soon. He's passed up several gracious offers from folks willing to give him a good home. There aren't many couples looking to take on a ten-year-old boy as puny as he is. It sure isn't likely that we can find a family to take both him and Anna into their home."

He setteth the solitary in families. He setteth the solitary in families.

"Might I have a word with you, Mr. Hill?" Emma called out, unable to remain silent a moment longer. What had begun as a prayer and a hunch now blossomed into certainty. Little Anna surely was the child God had meant for Emma all along. Her skirts swished beneath her as she scampered up the stairs onto the stage. "I believe I can recommend a reasonable plan."

Emma's boots tapped loudly against the wooden platform as she hurried forward. Due to the quick traverse onto the stage and her nervousness over this hastily conceived plan, she was short of breath. She put her hand to her heart and gasped as she addressed Mr. Hill. "Why not. . . let—let me. . .take Andrew's sister?" She was finally able to fill her lungs sufficiently to finish the sentence without halting. "And place Andrew with Mr. Nance?"

Emma cast a sideways glance at Frank. From his puzzled look, her atypical behavior had left him mystified for a second time within a morning's span. His bewilderment was understandable. Rarely did she act so impulsively.

In all honesty, she should have discussed the matter with Frank first. For, if they each took a sibling, they would surely be forced to face one another with frequency. In light of their current situation, such regular encounters might prove uncomfortable at best. The varying questions flitting across Frank's face reflected Emma's own thoughts.

Have I given this matter sufficient thought? She had been so confident that this was God's plan that she hadn't even paused long enough to breathe a prayer. Well, she couldn't stop now. Emma would smooth things over with Frank later, if need be.

Nervously grinding her boots into the grit on the stage floor, Emma continued pleading her case with Mr. Hill, not daring to look at Frank. "You see, sir, the two of us are acquaintances, and I'm sure we could come up with a suitable visitation arrangement for the children. We've each been approved to take one child."

Emma rummaged through her purse and pulled out her prized paper, hoping that her sweaty palms didn't cause the ink to run. "See, here's my letter from the committee."

"I think you've come up with a satisfactory plan," Mr. Hill said, giving the proffered document a perfunctory skimming. "No doubt Anna's recovery would be hastened under a mother's care. And if you could manage to take her home today, the rest of us could catch tomorrow morning's train for Dodge City. Still, I'm not the one who needs convincing." He tucked his thumbs under his suspender straps as he turned to face Andrew. "What do you think of this nice lady's idea?"

Before Andrew could object, Frank crouched down and looked the young fellow square in the eyes. "The plan seems perfectly logical to me. Don't you agree? It wouldn't bother you none just havin' me as your paw—and no maw, now would it?"

Andrew shook his head slowly from side to side. "No, sir. I wouldn't mind. I'm used to not havin' no womenfolk around, less'n you count Anna." He threw a sheepish glance in Emma's direction as he explained. "You see, my mama died when little Anna was borned. Then, two years ago, our granny that watched after us joined Mama in heaven, too. That left our papa to take care of us kids the best he could.

"Not havin' a mama don't bother me one bit. Truth is, I kinda take to the idea." Emma caught Andrew warily looking at her once again. "B–b–but. . ." The boy hesitated before speaking his mind. "But, my papa always tol' me that if anything ever happen' to him, I was to watch after my little sister and take good care of her. I always promised him I would. Last March, our papa died whilst savin' me and Anna when our apartment buildin' burnt. So, as long as I'm still breathin', the promise I made my papa is a promise I aim to keep.

"Please don't take no offense," Andrew said, bowing his head submissively before the trio of adults. "I'm not meanin' any disrespect. But I don't see how I can watch after li'l Anna if you split us up."

"Take your time and think things through, young man." Emma sandwiched his right hand between her gloved palms. "You and your sister would live close to one another. Mr. Nance's farm, where you would live, is on the outskirts of town. I live right here in Shady Grove—just a block or so down the street.

"I promise you, little Anna would have a loving home and she'd be a real comfort and companion to me. You see, my husband died a few years back and I've been awfully lonely ever since.

"If you go to live with Mr. Nance on his farm, as he's asking you to do, I'm sure he'd allow you to visit Anna frequently. Now, wouldn't you, Frank?"

At the casual use of his given name, Emma shot a glance at Frank to see if he'd noticed her slip. His dancing gaze met hers, obviously enjoying this first crossing of verbal propriety. He briskly nodded as a smile tugged at the corner of his lips. "Certainly, Emma," he replied, seeming to take great pleasure in emphasizing her given name. "You know I'd do anything I could to help the boy keep a solemn vow."

Emma turned her attention quickly back to Andrew before Frank could see the color rising in her warming cheeks. If only the man were more. . .were more affection- ate and. . .and dedicated to the Lord. . . .

"I'd love your sister, Andrew, and I'd take good care of her," Emma rushed, intent on sweeping those disturbing thoughts about Frank from her mind. "What do you say? Can we at least give it a try?"

Chapter 5

F rank rose from his kneeling position to tower over the boy. He jumped brusquely back into the conversation before Andrew could respond.

"The idea makes good sense to me. Remember, your sister's sick. You don't want her to have to get back on that train again if you can help it, now, do you? And you've no guarantees that a better situation will come along. Might pay you to be reasonable about this. What do you say?"

Frank looked down at his pant legs and began slapping at the dust his knees had gathered while kneeling on the well-traversed stage. "I could sure use a young man such as yourself to help me out on my farm."

Oh, Frank. Hush, will you? Emma wanted to scold him aloud. *Let the boy think things through for himself. Don't you realize that you always push too hard?*

Fresh fears gripped Emma as she watched him talking to the boy. Before her eyes, Frank was rapidly returning to his forever logical and emotionless ways. Perhaps she had acted too hastily in proposing this placing-out plan. For despite the fact that she was gaining a daughter, it also meant that this poor little boy would be going to live with Frank.

In her eagerness to parent his sister, had she sentenced Andrew to a fate worse than orphanage life—a future with a duplicate of her stepfather, Mr. Trumbull? Whatever it took, Emma would not allow such a tragedy to occur. Andrew Clymer didn't know it yet, but if the need arose, he had a formidable ally in her. Then she remembered Frank with that toddler. Sighing in resignation, Emma hoped Mr. Nance would disprove her concerns.

The boy's ashen face appeared paler still as he bit his lower lip and contemplated the situation. He stared at the floor for several long moments while the adults waited for his reply. With the toe of a new black leather shoe, he kicked at a loose slat in the wood floor and haltingly began. "W–w–well. . .I suppose we might give it a try. Mrs. Watson seems like a nice lady, and bein' as how she's a widow and lonely and all, I know Anna would keep her in good company." Andrew tossed Emma a weak smile before throwing his head back to look up at Frank.

"Mr. Nance, sounds like you could use a hand on your farm. But you'll have to teach me, sir. I ain't had no experience working in the out-a-doors."

"Now, Andrew," Mr. Hill said, "I believe you have made a wise and mature choice. I'm confident you will be very happy with Mr. Nance. But let me remind you, this agreement works two ways. Mr. Nance may decide to return you to our care if you do not behave yourself in a manner befitting a proper young man. Is that understood? You are not to cause this kind man any trouble. Rather, you are to be a help to him."

Mr. Hill turned to Frank and Emma. "An agent from the state will come by Shady Grove to check on all our orphans in a few weeks. After that, we expect to receive a report concerning the children at least twice a year. If there are problems, you may certainly contact us at any time."

"So, the matter's settled then," Frank stated, reaching for the agent's hand and enthusiastically pumping it up and down. "Where's that contract I'm supposed to sign?"

Mr. Hill turned to retrieve the necessary paperwork from a table set up just off the stage, but Andrew called after him, a fresh note of panic in his voice. "Wait. I can't go with Mr. Nance yet. I've got to tell Anna good-bye."

Instinctively, Emma reached out to offer motherly comfort and assurance to the boy, but she stopped and hastily pulled her arm back to her side. The three remaining boys slumped in wooden folding chairs, awaiting instruction from Mr. Hill. Emma understood the nature of young boys well enough. If she were to hug Andrew in front of his friends, the act would thoroughly embarrass him. Instead, she affirmed him with an assuring wink and turned to Frank.

"Mr. Nance, I know you're itching to get back to your farm. Undoubtedly you've got work to do and I hate to impose. . . ." Her voice trailing, she worried that Frank would think she was overstepping her boundaries by meddling once again. But his nod gave her the courage to go on.

"You'd be doing me a real kindness if you'd allow Andrew to be the one to tell Anna of their separate placements before you leave town. Such news would be better coming from him than from a stranger like me—and he'd have a chance to say his proper farewells."

Andrew nodded his appreciation to Emma for interceding on his behalf. And when both Frank and Mr. Hill agreed to her request, she watched the boy's fretful countenance relax.

As soon as all of Frank's and Emma's child-placement legalities had been tended to, Mr. Hill shoved the official documents into an already bulging leather case and prepared to go. Then the rag-tag parade of orphans and adults marched, by twos and threes, down the stage stairs and out the opera house door.

After breathing the fumes of burning kerosene all morning, Emma eagerly filled her lungs with the dry June air as she led the processional toward the Imperial Hotel. Mr. Hill fell into step beside her, followed by Frank and Andrew. The three older orphan boys brought up the rear.

Emma attempted to appear attentive when Mr. Hill launched into a verbose anecdote about a recent adventure on the orphan train. But in actuality, she was straining to catch the conversation between Frank and Andrew as they walked behind her.

Above the squeaks and clatter of passing buggies, Emma could hear Frank answering his new son's rapid volley of questions about life on the farm. By the sound of the boy's interested voice, a transformation was beginning in the sullen child. A smile played at the corners of Emma's lips while she eavesdropped on their amiable conversation. She prayed that all her worries about Frank's coldheartedness were invalid.

This unmarried farmer might very well be the perfect father for the boy after all. Andrew needed someone like Frank—someone to devote undivided attention to him. Emma's smile of pleasure became an inner chuckle as she thought that, perhaps, Andrew might soften Frank's rough edges a bit as well. Surely a ten-year-old could chisel into that granite heart. Teach him how to love. Get him ready for a wife. . . Frank had a long way to go before Emma would reconsider his proposal of marriage, but she'd seen a glimmer of hope in his reaction to Andrew today.

The swinging signboard of the Imperial Hotel came into view, and Emma's pulse pounded in her temples. A marriage of a different sort replaced all thoughts of Frank. For today she and Anna would enter into the union of mother and child. Refusing to succumb to cold feet, Emma had already committed "to have and to hold" Anna as her daughter from this day forward. She had accepted and assumed responsibility for the child—sight unseen.

The anticipated moment of first meeting drew nearer with each clipped step she took down the boardwalk. Soon Emma's dream of a daughter would take on flesh and bone. The group followed Mr. Hill through the Imperial's frosted glass doors, across the lobby, and into the hotel's ornate sitting room. The lavish furnishings and gilded fixtures created an air of opulence that seemed out of place in the prairie town of Shady Grove.

"Miz Watson. . ." Mr. Hill removed his top hat and picked at invisible lint on its brim. "I'd appreciate it if you'd just have a seat for a few minutes and allow me to situate these boys in their rooms. Then, I'll accompany Andrew to his sister's bedside as he shares the news of their placement with her. Someone will come to fetch you soon, ma'am, so you can meet little Anna."

Pushing his bent, wire-rimmed spectacles up his nose, the agent's sagging shoulders testified to his fatigue as he turned to address Frank. "I appreciate your patience, sir. I know you're anxious to get your boy home. I don't expect this to take long. Please excuse us." Mr. Hill offered a courteous bow to Emma, then led Andrew and the other boy out of the room.

From across the lobby, Andrew glanced over his shoulder and waved at Frank. The beaming new father returned the gesture as the boy disappeared up the stairs. "Well," Frank said, turning to face Emma, "there's no use in standin' if we can sit. After you." He motioned to two empty chairs beside the grand piano.

Emma perched on the edge of the overstuffed chair and settled her package and purse on the lamp stand as Frank plopped into the seat next to hers. "I'm glad to see that you aren't upset with me for suggesting that I take Andrew's sister. I wasn't sure just how you would respond."

"I thought your idea was a grand one. Why would I have been upset? Fact is, I'm still hopin' you'll reconsider my proposal of marriage. The way I figure, this new connection we share with Andrew and Anna will increase my chances at changin' your mind." He produced an audacious wink that left Emma with no choice but to reach for her lace and whale bone fan and wave it furiously in front of her face.

"Mr. Nance," she said firmly, "there is no reason for you to continue—"

"No reason, Emma?" he teased.

"Really! Would you please—"

"The facts are, ma'am, either you're warmin' up to me or my name's not Frank Nance."

"My feelings for you in no way—"

"So! You do have feelin's for me?"

"I never said that," she insisted, glancing across the lobby at the distracted hotel clerk.

"Well, regardless of what you care to 'fess up to, my offer does still stand."

"So does my rejection! You need to know, Mr. Nance, I am a woman of deep faith. I could never—absolutely never—marry a man who—"

"Hey! I've got faith!"

"But you never darken a church door!"

"I'll go to church if that'll make you happy." He smiled hopefully.

"I'm terribly sorry, but we seem to be miscommunicating in the most severe manner. I'm talking about—about—what I'm tryin to say is—is. . ." She snapped the fan closed.

"Well, go on."

"I would never marry a man who isn't dedicated to the Lord—with his whole heart. I'm talkin' about more than just a shallow acknowledgment that there is a God."

"I'm not a heathen, by no means, Emma," he drawled. "I've been a Christian since my maw led me to the Lord when I was about Andrew's age."

"But is Christ Lord of your life. . .or are you?" The question settled between them, creating a chasm that she knew would never be removed unless Frank could answer in the affirmative.

With the question left unanswered, Emma walked toward the white marble fireplace. Before turning her back to Frank, she caught him watching her with an esteem she had not previously seen on his countenance. Strangely, she sensed that, for the first time, she had somehow gained Mr. Nance's complete respect. How odd that the very issue that separated them would also deepen his regard. Firmly pivoting away from him, she awaited until Mr. Hill returned.

Regard? Did Frank Nance perhaps care for Emma more than he had admitted?

"Are you ready?" A renewed burst of energy seemed to enthuse the agent as he appeared in the arched doorway. "If so, come on with me. Andrew did a fine job of preparing Anna to go with you. She seems excited about meeting her new mother."

Emma skittered lightly across the lush oriental area rug to grab her beaded handbag and the gingham-wrapped baby doll. Frank rose from his chair while she gathered her things. His dark eyes reflected the sincerity of his apology as he spoke. "I'm sorry about forever bringin' up my proposal. There wasn't any call for my bein' so selfish while you were waitin' to meet your little girl. I hope all goes well for you upstairs. That's the gospel truth."

"Thanks." She glanced up to see those dark eyes spilling forth with words unspoken. And for the first time, Emma admitted to herself what she had desperately wanted to deny. Despite her attempts to voice her dislike of him, Frank Nance had stirred her pulse for many months.

Nervously excusing herself, she joined Mr. Hill in the hotel lobby and forced all thoughts of Frank's proposal from her mind. A lightning bolt of anticipation seemed to shoot through her, and she shivered with giddy energy. She would have taken the stairs two at a time had no one else been watching.

Mr. Hill led the way down the carpeted hall to the door marked 2-D. Without bothering to knock, he turned the brass doorknob and swung the door open wide, then waited for Emma to enter ahead of him. She stepped past him into the austere room to see a thin woman, dressed in black, sitting in a straight-backed chair next to the room's lone window. The weary woman gave Emma a cursory nod in greeting, making no effort to stand.

At the head of the brass bed, holding onto a post, Andrew stood as though guarding royalty. But the sad-faced child Emma had observed at the opera house was gone, replaced by a grinning ten-year-old. "Here she is, Anna," Andrew bent over the bed and exclaimed. "Your new mama. See, I told you she was pretty."

Nothing could have prepared Emma for the breath-catching moment that followed. A knot of emotion clogged her throat. Goose flesh erupted down her arms. Tears blurred her eyes and spilled onto her cheeks. For eyes the color of roasted chestnuts, big and round as coat buttons, now peeked timidly over the top of crisp white sheets. The flush of fever painted rouge-red circles of color on the child's cheeks. A mass of flaxen ringlets framed her china-doll face.

She's the most beautiful little girl I've ever seen, Emma thought as she approached the bed. *And she's my daughter. My child.* Anna reached out to Emma with twig-thin arms and, in that simple act, erased any of the new mother's misgivings about adoption. Emma rooted her maternal bonds the instant she scooped the child into her arms and held her close. As she buried her hands in Anna's curls, she knew she held the miraculous fulfillment of God's promise. The Lord had answered her prayers.

God setteth the solitary in families. The psalm that had become Emma's constant prayer was now her song of celebration. But another scripture verse joined her chorus of praise. Echoing Hannah of Old Testament days, Emma's heart sang, "For this child I prayed; and the LORD hath given me my petition which I asked of him."

Yes, the Lord had surely heard and answered Emma's prayers.

☙♡❧

Thirty minutes later, Emma stepped over the threshold of her daughter's bedroom with Frank and Andrew close behind. "This is your very own room, sweetheart," Emma announced to the flushed, fevered child Frank carried in his arms. "I fixed it up just for you."

Anna's dark eyes grew round with wonderment as she surveyed the room. White Irish lace curtains adorned the windows. A cushioned rocker stood in one corner, ready to soothe both mother and child. On the dressing table sat a lace-trimmed basket, brimming with hand-sewn hair ribbons of every hue. The pearl-handled mirror with matching brush and comb looked too pretty to use.

"I'll just pull back these blankets and we'll tuck you right in." Emma turned back the bedding and vigorously plumped a down-filled pillow before motioning to Frank to lay down the child. She wanted to open the bedroom window and circulate the stifling air, but she feared that a breeze, perhaps filled with dust from the road, would aggravate Anna's croup. As they had prepared to leave the hotel, Anna had suffered a severe coughing spell. Emma wanted to avoid a repeat of that painful episode, at all costs. The window remained shut.

Under the watchful eyes of Andrew, Frank gingerly settled the four-year-old between the starched white bed linens. From the end of the bed, Emma shook out a light-weight summer quilt and spread it on top of the sheets. Then, smoothing the covers as she worked her way around the side of the bed, Emma wrapped them snugly around the wisp of a girl so that only her little head poked out.

Beneath the layers of bedclothes, Anna cradled her new doll baby, refusing to relinquish her treasure even momentarily. Emma couldn't resist the urge to brush back the tangled mass of blond curls from Anna's forehead and deposit a feather-light kiss.

Straightening to ease the crick in her back, Emma noticed Andrew standing in the middle of the room, still holding the small parcel of Anna's things. She walked to the boy and extended her hands to accept the twine-tied package.

The curious boy, relieved of his burden, craned his neck to inspect every inch of Anna's new quarters. "She ain't never had no room of her own before," Andrew said as Emma shook out Anna's new dress and hung it in the cedar wardrobe. "Until we went to the orphanage, she always slept with me."

Emma detected a twinge of jealousy over his little sister's good fortune as Andrew posed a question to Frank. "Uh, Mr. Nance, do I get my own room at your place, too?"

In response, Frank reached over and ruffled Andrew's mousy brown hair. "You can take your pick from several rooms on the second floor of the farmhouse. The folks I bought the farm from had a passel of kids, so they built the place real big.

"But, boy, if you keep on referrin' to me as Mr. Nance, you'll be sleepin' in the barn. What don't you just call me 'Paw'?"

Andrew scratched his head and studied his new shoes. " 'Pahw,' huh?" he said, attempting to mimic Frank's southern twang. "If that's what you want, sir, I'll try."

"Well. . ." Frank hesitated. "You might have to ease into this 'Paw' business. I understand your feelin' awkward and all. Take your time. I won't push you none. And I was just funnin' with you about makin' you sleep in the barn." The laugh lines extending from Frank's eyes creased deeply as he smiled at Andrew.

Watching this bonding interaction between father and son, Emma felt a familiar fire rising in her cheeks and causing her palms to perspire. But the frustration and anger she had once felt in Frank's presence didn't cause this flood of warmth. This heat stemmed from her happy surprise in seeing again—as she had on several occasions throughout the day—a pleasantly different side of Frank. Emma longed for Frank to understand what she was trying to tell him in the hotel lobby.

"All this talk about home reminds me that there's plenty of work waiting for us at the farm," Frank stated, ushering Andrew toward the door. "The cows will be beggin' for milkin' soon. You'd best be tellin' your sister good-bye."

"Emma. . .er. . .Miz Watson. . ." He paused to expose her to humorous scrutiny.

Her cheeks warming, Emma needlessly fussed with Anna's covers.

"Unless there's somethin' else you're needin' from us, we'll see ourselves out."

She glanced up just in time to see Andrew instantly tense at the pronouncement of his imminent separation from Anna. "Wait!" Emma blurted, desperate to ease the boy's fears. "None of us have had a chance to eat lunch yet, and I left a pot of beef stew warming on the stove this morning. I can throw a meal together in a matter of minutes. It's the least I could do since you've been so kind to carry Anna home from the hotel and all."

Frank lifted his head and sniffed at the air. "I've been smellin' your cookin' since I walked in the door. I was hopin' you'd ask us to stay. Andrew, why don't you look after your sister for just a bit while I help Miz Watson set the table for dinner."

"I've got an even better idea," Emma interjected. "Let's prepare meal trays for us all. We can eat right here in Anna's room, so she won't need to be left alone."

"Lead the way, ma'am." Frank waved his arm in grandiose fashion, pointing to the open door. "Or would you rather I just follow my nose?"

Preceding Frank into the kitchen, Emma walked straight to the cupboard and began pulling soup bowls from the shelf. As she placed them on the counter next to the potbellied stove, Frank stepped beside her and lifted the lid from the iron soup kettle. A cloud of fragrant steam escaped into the air. Inhaling deeply, he leaned over to Emma and asked, "What can I do to help?"

When he spoke, her hands traitorously quivered as she spooned stew into the bowls. Emma had not been alone in a room with a man these past three years. She was far from prepared for the rush of growing excitement Frank's presence evoked. In the hotel lobby, he expressed his suspicion of her reaction to him, and just knowing that he suspected made her quiver all the more. Emma reminded herself that just two days ago she had stormed out of his presence, hoping never to see him again. But had she really desired to rid her life of Frank?

She handed him the soup ladle, resisting the urge to look into his eyes, lest her renewed resolve disintegrate. "You can take over this chore, if you don't mind. I need to slice up some bread."

In the moments that followed, Emma scurried about the kitchen collecting the makings of an impromptu feast. On one tray, she placed the soup bowls and a crockery pitcher of buttermilk. On another, she precariously piled plates of thick slices of cheese, sourdough bread spread with strawberry jam, and a molasses pie. While she worked, she chattered incessantly, reliving the day's Christmas-like excitement, leaving no opportunity for Frank to comment. At all costs, she couldn't allow him to suspect her vulnerability.

Within half an hour, Frank and Andrew sat on the homemade rag rug in the middle of Anna's room and crisscrossed their legs in preparation for their indoor picnic as Emma arranged the trays next to them. When she announced that she would offer grace, the ten-year-old sheepishly dropped the cheese he held halfway between the plate and his mouth. And although she had a lengthy list of blessings for which she wanted to give thanks to the Lord, she kept her prayer brief. She didn't want to torture the young boy.

Emma watched in amazement as the scrawny Andrew inhaled his meal. Judging by the way he attacked his food, he hadn't eaten his fill in quite a while. Frank protested when the boy grabbed the last piece of bread, but he consoled himself with a generous slice of pie.

"Save some appetite, son," Frank teased the boy. "I'm roastin' you an elephant for supper and I'll be expectin' you to eat it all." Andrew, whose face was buried behind his bread, stopped eating just long enough to confirm that Frank's words were spoken in jest.

"You keep eating like that and I'll stay busy making you bigger clothes." Emma chuckled.

"You're a good cook, ma'am." Andrew wiped the jam from his mouth with the sleeve of his shirt. "I ain't eaten this good since our granny died."

Unfortunately, Emma's efforts to feed Anna were not met with Andrew's same measure of success. The infirmed child allowed her new mother to spoon-feed her only three bites of stew before she pursed her lips together and refused to eat more.

When the meal had been consumed and Andrew had all but licked the plates dry, Frank stood to his feet. "Andrew and I will carry these trays back to the kitchen for you, then we'd better be gettin' home. The boy's right, though, Emma. You are a great cook."

Despite the pleasure his praise evoked, Emma refused to look directly at Frank, for fear of repeating her earlier heart-fluttering reaction. She rose from Anna's bedside and stacked the bowl of barely-touched stew on top of the other dirty dishes. "Perhaps you and Andrew could come for dinner after church a week from Sunday? Lord willing,

Anna should be better by then." *And I'll have my emotions back under control,* she added silently.

"Yeah, I be better then." Anna's hoarse whisper floated from the feather bed, soliciting smiles from all the others in the room. But even this brief attempt to contribute to the conversation brought on a fit of barking coughs. Emma hurried to her side and, scooping the child into her arms, began rocking Anna back and forth.

After several long seconds of violent crouping, Anna began gasping for air. Emma looked at Frank for assurance, but instead saw genuine concern in his face.

"I'd best be gettin' Doc Gilbert, don't you think?" The rhetorical question needed no answer, for he and Andrew were already headed for the door.

Chapter 6

Poor little thing is weaker than a kitten, Mrs. Watson. She's so worn out from coughin' that she fell fast asleep in the middle of my examination." Dr. Gilbert softly closed the door to Anna's bedroom and joined the anxious trio of Emma, Frank, and Andrew in the hallway.

"That croup of hers does sound mighty bad. I expect you're gonna fret over every coughin' spell, seein' as you're a new mama and all." Shady Grove's aged physician stroked his bushy gray beard as he spoke. "But listen to me and believe me when I say, I'm sure the child is goin' to pull through, what with your good nursin' and attention.

"There are several things you can do to help her." The doctor's soothing voice took on a serious tone as he rattled off his list of instructions. "First off, soon as I leave I want you to hang a wet sheet near her bed to put moisture into the room. That should help control her cough. And, don't let her lie flat. Keep her propped up so her airways are clear. One good way to do this is to hold her and rock her. You probably wouldn't mind that, now would you?"

The doctor set his black leather bag on the hall runner and stooped to fumble through its contents. "Now, she will likely fight you over it, but you must persist. I want you to give the young'un a teaspoon of this elixir every time she starts a coughin' spell." He pulled the cork stopper and passed the bottle under Emma's nose. "I want you to smell it 'fore I leave it with you, because most folks think it's ruined when they get their first whiff."

She jerked her head back instantly, her eyes watering at the pungent stench.

"Hey, let me smell," Andrew said, boyish curiosity oozing from him. The doctor obliged his request and all the adults laughed aloud at his sour face. "Cowboy howdy!" he exclaimed. "I hope I don't never get sick."

The doctor resealed the dark glass container and handed it to Emma. "I know it smells powerful bad. Made it myself from onions, garlic, paregoric, and spirits of camphor mixed in with honey, and I know the potion works. Other than this, the only other medicine I can recommend is time. The cough should run its course in a few days."

Emma stuffed the amber bottle of cough syrup into her apron pocket as the physician picked up his bag and prepared to leave.

"We'll follow you out, Doc," Frank said. "I need to get the boy settled and tend to my chores.

Pinching the crown of his felt hat between his finger and thumb, he politely tipped the headpiece toward Emma before donning it. "Andrew and I will see you a week from Sunday for lunch, if your offer still stands."

"Certainly," she replied. "I'll save you two a place on our pew at church as well. Service begins at ten-thirty."

"Well. . ." His lips formed into a stubborn line. "I'll make certain the boy is there."

So that's it. That's your answer, Emma thought, while gritting her teeth. He had not fully answered her questions about his relationship with the Lord in the Imperial Hotel's lobby. Until now. And the obstinate tilt of his square chin suggested that Frank Nance wouldn't bow at an altar in prayer for any woman.

That's all fine by me, Emma thought as Frank and his son stepped onto her massive porch. *If and when you do decide to give your all to the good Lord, it needs to be something for yourself, not for me.* Nonetheless, the dull ache in Emma's spirit attested to her keen disappointment.

But no sooner had she shut the door on her three visitors than a sole, painful cough rang through the house, dispelling all thoughts of Frank's infuriating ways. She paused briefly, her back against the door, and took a deep cleansing breath. Emma's prayers had been answered. She was a mother now. But did she have the skills necessary to nurse such a sickly, frail child? Pinpricks of fear stabbed ever so lightly at Emma's euphoria.

Holding her breath against the hope that there would be no new coughs, she peeked around the door into Anna's bedroom. The wisp of a child had awakened and was sitting up in her bed, stroking her doll's hair. Her daughter. This precious little girl with big brown eyes—her daughter. Anna's soft voice would soon call her "Mama." The two of them would share the same family name.

Had only a few hours lapsed since Emma first laid eyes on her? The thought seemed odd as she surveyed this heartwarming scene. Anyone would think, to look at Anna now, that the little princess had always ruled from this quilted throne.

One week later, Frank leaned against the front porch railing and finished his morning cup of coffee as Andrew crossed the barnyard to begin his morning chores. In just a week's time, he had seen tremendous changes in the boy. Thanks to Maria's starchy Mexican dinners and the hours they'd spent together outdoors doing chores, Andrew no longer looked sickly pale and starvation thin. Emma was sure to be surprised when they showed up for lunch the day after tomorrow. The imagined scene left Frank smiling in amusement. He derived certain pleasure at the prospect of proving to Emma that a few days' work did any boy a good service.

Frank looked forward to Sunday afternoon for other reasons as well. He wanted Andrew to see for himself that Anna was all right. Despite the growing camaraderie he and Andrew shared, Frank knew the boy worried about his sister constantly. Several times throughout the course of a day, Andrew would turn to him and ask how he thought Anna was getting along. Seldom had he witnessed such fierce loyalty in grown men, much less a child. His devotion to his sister constituted more than a deathbed promise made to his father that he was honor-bound to fulfill. Andrew obviously cared deeply for Anna. Yes, for the boy's sake, he was anxious for Sunday to come around.

But Frank wouldn't be honest if he didn't admit that he was anxious for Sunday to arrive for his own sake as well. Over the past week, when he'd lain down to sleep, a pleasant memory replayed over and over in his mind. Miz Emma Watson had been nothing short of flustered in his presence since that meeting in the general store.

And Frank was beginning to look back on their yearlong acquaintance and suspect that she might have been trying to hide her true feelings for quite some time.

However, a new problem now surfaced with the fair lady. She said she wanted a man who was more committed to the Lord. At first, her comments had amused him. Then, they had angered him. How dare she be his spiritual judge? But now, her words had grown into a recurring mantra in his mind and left him less than comfortable. The truth of the matter was, he knew he could do better by the Lord. Much better. And now that Andrew had come along, the boy deserved the same kind of religious upbringing Frank had been given. But he just wasn't certain he was ready to turn the whole thing over to the Lord. He was nice and comfortable keeping the Lord at arm's length.

Tossing the cold dregs of his coffee into the cracked dry ground next to the porch, he stood and dismissed the disturbing thoughts. *We could sure use some rain,* Frank said to himself as he studied the morning sky. The wispy, streaked clouds didn't hold much promise of breaking this insufferable hot and dry spell. Scanning the horizon, Frank was seized by a strong sense of foreboding for a peculiar gray haze enveloped the western wheat fields. At once, Frank noticed the faint, unpleasant acrid smell that always accompanied a distant fire. His gut twisted in dread. He had heard that a plague of grasshoppers had turned the skies black over Colorado, leaving devastated crops in their wake. But grasshoppers did not produce such a smell. Frank decided to investigate.

Just then, Andrew emerged from the chicken coop and began scattering feed. Frank paused a few moments more to watch his son. The boy's shoes quickly disappeared beneath the brood of bantam chickens as the birds pecked frantically at the seed, their red combs bobbing feverishly. "You've been cornered by chickens, son." Frank laughed with a father's pleasure, and Andrew waved happily to his pa.

Feeding the chickens had become one of Andrew's favorite chores, for when he was done he could hold the cheeping chicks that filled a warming tray just inside the hen house door. Frank had long ago forgotten how much fun such simple pleasures could bring a boy. He had caught himself laughing and smiling more in the past few days than he had in many years. A boy was good for a man's soul.

Suddenly, the gravelly bark of a coonhound in the barnyard shattered the early morning quiet to announce the arrival of a visitor. Frank stepped off the front porch and waved in greeting to a worried-looking man mounted on a sweating, stamping horse. After a brief exchange of words that confirmed Frank's former suspicions, the rider turned his horse, spurring the animal into a full gallop as he rode toward the rising sun.

"Andrew, come here, boy. I need to talk with you." Frank, his stomach clutching ever tighter, didn't wait for the puzzled child to catch up with him. Instead, he hurried into the barn and set about the task of saddling Shadow. Andrew was panting by the time he reached the busy stall.

"Listen, there's a grass fire threatenin' to destroy the Taylor farm, and they're roundin' up as many neighbors as they can to help fight the blaze. I've got to go and see what I can do to help. What with this confounded drought and all, if the Good Lord doesn't help us, them hungry flames will soon spread onto our own land.

"Oh, and Andrew, I realize you don't speak Spanish, and Señor and Señorita Ramirez's English ain't too good. But when they get here, do your best to explain things to them. Draw pictures if you have to, but the smoke should speak for itself. I expect Pedro will come and help us as soon as he gets the word. I don't have time to gab about it. I'll be home just as soon as I can. Maria will watch after you when she arrives. Until then, you are to stay here and tend to your chores, do you hear? I don't need to be worryin' about you on top of everything else."

"Yes, sir. I understand. Don't you fret about me. I'll be just fine."

♔♡♕

Andrew watched until Frank rode Shadow over the horizon, then he turned and walked slowly back toward the chicken coop to complete the first of his unfinished chores. The warm prairie wind blew the smell of smoke into the barnyard. A rush of painful memories seized him as, in his mind's eye, he saw his father rushing back into the burning apartment to rescue Anna. Was he to lose another father to the flames? Did some kind of curse follow him?

And what of the fire? Would it spread into town and perhaps burn the Widow Watson's seamstress shop? His father's dying words now haunted him: *Watch after your little sister. Take good care of her.* Yet his new pa's words seemed a direct contradiction to his duty: *You are to stay here and tend to your chores, do you hear? I don't need to be worryin' about you on top of everything else.*

But if he stayed at the farm, Anna might die in the fire.

What had he done, allowing a stranger lady to take on his responsibility while he'd headed off to play on the farm? He must check on Anna. Now. When last he'd seen her, Anna had been frightfully sick.

Chapter 7

T he fidgeting Anna danced in front of the full-length mirror as Emma attempted to pin a straight hem into her swaying full skirt. "Honey child, please!" she begged, licking a bead of blood from her pin-pricked finger. "Hold still for just a minute more."

"But, Mama, I'm pretendin' to be a princess. I can't wait for Andrew to see my new dress." When Emma sat back on the floor, the pinning job sufficiently complete, Anna began twirling around the seamstress shop until the stiff taffeta floated on air.

Anna had surprised them all with her strong will to recover from whooping cough. Each day, she spent more and more time out of bed, and the doctor was calling it nothing short of a miracle. Today, only an occasional cough remained. So for the past day, Emma and Anna had been excitedly making plans for Sunday and the child's first public appearance. Their initial item of business had been to make Anna new clothes for the occasion. A remnant piece from Emma's emerald green taffeta dress proved large enough to piece together a matching "coming out" frock for Anna's first time at church.

No doubt, Katy Greene would twitter that such an outfit for a child was frivolous. And, no doubt, Katy's words would be true. Still, there were times that called for more than a little frivolity.

"Hallo, Anna? You in there?" a voice warily called through the opened window.

Emma and Anna paused to exchange a nonplused stare. "Andrew, is that you?" Emma asked, hurrying toward the window.

"Yes'm," Andrew said, shuffling his feet. His dark eyes brimming with concern, he stuffed his hands into the pockets of his work britches. "I was worried 'bout Anna—"

"Andrew!" Anna squealed from behind.

"Come to the front door," Emma said.

As she opened the door and the boy hesitantly stepped into the parlor, Emma wondered where Frank might be. She scanned the street, bustling with the usual early morning activity, but saw no sign of the boy's father. At once, her heart twisted with a twinge of concern and perhaps a touch of regret at his absence.

Before Emma could interrogate Andrew, Anna ran from across the room and threw her arms around his neck. "Andrew, I'm all better now. And my mama made me a new dress." A slight cough followed her words, and Emma patted the child's back, hoping the excitement over seeing her brother wouldn't instigate a coughing spell.

"That's good news, young'un," Andrew said, tousling her hair. "I was worried about you. That's why I came around." He cast a shamefaced look toward Emma before bowing his head. "I hope you aren't too mad at me, ma'am.

I didn't mean to startle you none."

"Where's your pa?" Emma glanced out the door once more to verify Frank's absence as new thoughts whirled through her mind. Had the boy run away because Frank worked him too hard?

"He don't know I'm here. The neighbor's fields were afire and he took off on Shadow to offer his help. That smell of smoke made me want to see Anna somethin' fierce." He drew his sister close to his side. And, despite the boy's attempt at bravado, Emma noticed his bottom lip quivering while he spoke. "I snuck off 'fore Pedro and Maria arrived for work, and if I don't make it back home before Pa gets there, I reckon there'll be grief to pay."

"You're probably right about that, but I'm not about to let you out of my sight. You can't just go traipsing around the countryside—not without your pa knowing your whereabouts and especially if there's a fire. I don't care if you are all of ten years old." As she looked the boy up and down, she inwardly praised Frank for the healthy changes: the glow of his cheeks, the noticeable weight gain, and his fresh-scrubbed cleanliness. Perhaps Frank Nance was a better father than Emma ever imagined.

His year-old proposal became an undeniable possibility in Emma's spirit as she fussed over starting breakfast for Anna and Andrew. Certainly, if Frank were such a good father, he might easily be a good husband. Her heart palpitated at such a rate that Emma could barely stir the hotcake batter. Her previous concerns that Frank might be like her stepfather began to melt like wax before the fires of respect. Andrew showed no signs of being overworked and under-loved—something Emma had readily sensed in a child on more than one occasion. On the contrary, Andrew seemed to be blossoming under the care of his new father.

With all the discretion she could muster, Emma tried to pry more information from the boy as she worked at the stove. She desperately wanted to verify her assumptions as fact. She asked about their daily routine and the chores that he'd been assigned, looking for the slightest hint of Josiah Trumbull tyranny. But young Andrew was full of nothing but praise for his new father. He held Frank Nance in highest esteem. And Emma was certainly beginning to think Frank deserved his son's admiration. Wistfully, she envisioned the four of them as a family.

O Lord, she prayed. *Is there anything I might say to make Frank realize his need of a deeper walk with You?*

All morning, Emma prayed that prayer. And by the noon hour, she had certainly begun to pray for other concerns as well. Frank still had not come after Andrew. While she understood that Frank didn't actually know Andrew's location, Emma also figured he would start looking for the boy at her house. Even though the task of fighting a fire was certainly time-consuming, she was beginning to worry about Frank. Andrew had lost one father in a blazing inferno; surely God wouldn't allow him to lose another. Her soul trembled in dread as she tried to stay yet another of Andrew's questions about his father's absence. Instead, she directed the children back to the spacious kitchen to sit at the sturdy oak dining table.

She had no sooner set the plates of beans and cornbread in front of the children than pounding resounded from the front door. She caught her breath, wondering if

Frank were the visitor.

"That's probably Pa," Andrew said, his eyes bright with expectation.

"Probably," she said, her heart singing with hope. After removing her apron, she tucked stray strands of hair back into her chignon. The more she encountered Frank, the more Emma fretted with her appearance. Just before opening the door, she pressed her lips together, hoping she wasn't unusually pale after her long days and nights of nursing Anna while trying to keep abreast of her sewing schedule.

But when she opened the door, all concern for her appearance vanished. A gasp slipped from her lips at the sight of the soot-covered man who stood on her spacious porch. If Emma hadn't expected him, she would not have recognized Frank. All the hair had been singed from his face. The lack of eyebrows and lashes added to his wild-eyed look of terror. He held his hands cautiously in front of him, exposing several blistered burns.

"Andrew's missing," he blurted, forgoing salutations as he stepped inside. "He's nowhere to be found at the farm, and Pedro said he's not seen hide nor hair of him. Is he here by chance?" Frank craned his neck to look past Emma. He seemed oblivious to his serious injuries. His only concerns were for his son.

"Yes, he's here. And he's fine," she replied, touching his forearm in concern. "But you don't look as if you are. We must send for Doc Gilbert to care for your burns."

"I'll see the doctor in good time," he said, stepping past her. "I've got more important matters to tend to first. I'd like to take a gander at Andrew, just to set my mind at ease.

Then, if you don't mind, I need a private word with you."

Turning, he paused long enough to expose her to a pleading gaze. She caught her breath, wondering exactly what Frank had in mind. She had made her conditions clear in the parlor of the Imperial Hotel. Could it be that Frank had at last understood his need of a total surrender to the Lord? Emma had prayed for exactly that all morning!

Her mind whirling with the implications of the moment, Emma led the way back to the kitchen and watched as Frank crouched slowly and painfully on one knee next to Andrew's chair. For several long moments, he stared intently at the gaping boy. "You had me scared spitless!" Overcome with emotion, Frank closed his eyes tight.

Andrew's lips shook. "I'm sorry, Pa." He flung his arms around Frank's neck. "I know you tol' me not to go, but. . ."

Although Frank winced painfully, he did not discourage the boy's affection. Instead, he gingerly rested his burned hands against Andrew's back.

"The fire!" Andrew continued. "I was worried ta death it was gonna spread to town and kill Anna. And now you. . .you. . .you've been burned up, just like our papa!" Andrew choked on a sob. "Please don't die. . .don't die! I promise. . .I promise, I won't never run off again."

Emma pressed her fingers against her trembling lips and rushed toward Anna, now fretting because of her brother's outburst. She scooped Anna from one of the sturdy oak chairs and held her close. "Don't worry, little one," she crooned. "Everything is fine."

"Andrew's cryin'," she whined. "His pa is all burned up."

"Yes, but he's okay. Everything is fine."

The budding love expressed by father and son dashed aside any remaining doubts that Frank Nance was indeed a wonderful father. . .that he would indeed be an exceptional husband. The man had at last begun to allow Emma to see his true emotions. *O Lord, if only he would let down the barriers with You.* Certainly, Emma realized that these boundaries Frank had erected between himself and others were the very boundaries that were keeping him at a distance with God.

At last, Frank assured Andrew that all would be well and he was indeed fine. After a quarter hour of Frank's calm and assuring words, Andrew finally turned his attention back to the beans and cornbread. Frank grimaced as he rose to face Emma. "Do you think Andrew can look after Anna here in the kitchen for a short spell so you and I can visit in the parlor? There's somethin' I'm needin' to get off my chest."

"Don't you think we should at least put some salve on those burns first?" she asked, settling Anna in front of her noon meal. "I keep a jar right here next to my stove." Chattering nervously, she riffled through the cabinet next to the potbellied stove in search of the illusive ointment. "Seems like I'm constantly splattering grease on myself," she said, barely able to concentrate on the words tumbling from her lips. For all she could think of was Frank, standing so close to her. Despite herself, she began to wonder what it would feel like to have his arms around her. Was he about to restate his proposal? And if he did not profess a renewed love for the Lord, did she, have the spiritual strength to refuse him?

As Emma continued in search of the elusive salve, a

tense silence settled between them, and she began an internal, heavenward plea. *O Lord, give me the courage to stay with my decision, despite the fact that I. . .that I think I am fall—falling in love with him.*

"The salve can wait a few more minutes," Frank insisted from close behind.

Emma stilled. Her heart pounded. Her palms moistened.

"This is important, and I don't reckon it will take too long."

Swallowing, Emma silently turned from her task and moved toward the parlor, not daring to look into his eyes. A quick glance over her shoulder proved Anna and Andrew still sufficiently distracted by their meal. All the while she walked toward the parlor, Emma prayed for courage and strength and wisdom. She paused beside the French doors and watched as Frank walked toward the front window, complemented by lace curtains. A tense silence followed, and Emma knew that Frank Nance was deeply troubled.

"Old Man Taylor lost his life today," he said. "And I came close to losin' mine." Frank pivoted to face her. "We had formed a bucket brigade and were attempting to douse the flames of his burning barn when a support beam gave way, sending a portion of the barn roof down on top of us and buryin' Mr. Taylor in flame. I had the wind knocked out of me for a time. As quick as I could, I tried to rescue the old man, but to no avail."

Wearily, he rubbed at his blackened forehead with the back of his wrist. "During those moments everythin' you said to me at the Imperial Hotel started to make a heap of sense. All I could think was that I was really livin' my life for me and. . ." He paused to swallow. "And how far from the Lord I had strayed. . .and just how much I. . .I love you, Emma." His words came out on a broken whisper.

Her eyes filling with tears, Emma laid a trembling hand against her chest.

"And if you want the gospel truth, I think I've been in love with you for a good deal longer than I ever wanted myself to know it." He closed the distance between them and reached to touch her cheek, only to wince with renewed pain.

"We need the doctor—"

"No. Not until I've had my say. I prayed all the way from the farm for two things: that Andrew would be here and that you'd. . .you'd reconsider my proposal. This time, I can promise you, I don't have a single convenience in mind, Miz Watson." His pain-filled eyes produced a mischievous twinkle. "And I can also promise you that the Lord has grabbed my attention and I've done my business with Him." He paused to hold her gaze, his eyes revealing a sincere man. "This isn't any religion of convenience either. The Lord has taken hold of me like He never has before."

Tears trickling from the corners of her eyes, Emma nodded in understanding.

"If only you could find it in your heart to try to love me—"

"Oh, Frank. . ." Emma choked on a sob. "I think I've been on the verge of falling in love with you for months. And all morning I've prayed you'd say just what you've said. I—"

Emma's words were cut off by Frank's whoop of joy and his lips pressed firmly against hers. And in that moment Emma once again understood what it felt like to be madly in love with a man. . .and to have a man madly in love with her.

♋♡♌

In the hallway, Andrew, holding his sister's hand, peeked into the parlor to see his pa and Anna's ma kissing. "Yuck!" he whispered. Turning to Anna, he wrinkled his nose.

A soft giggle escaped Anna. "I like your pa."

Dashing aside his aversion to the grown-ups' kiss, Andrew picked up his sister and twirled her around. "Good! 'Cause it looks like he's gonna be your pa, too!"

Epilogue

Crisp autumn air swept off the Kansas prairie and down Church Street as Andrew and Anna clambered up the wooden steps leading into the white frame church. "Whoa. Wait up, you two," Frank called after them. "Give your ol' paw and mama a chance to catch up.

"Anna, did you say hello to the Reverend?" At her father's prompting, the just-turned-five-year-old curtsied politely to the pastor, then wiggled her first loose tooth for him to see. In the meantime, Andrew had already escaped inside.

"Mornin', Reverend Barnhart." Frank removed his hat and extended his right hand, still pink and scarred from the June fire. "We've got us a beautiful day to worship!"

"I do believe you'd say the same in the midst of a cyclone, Frank. I hope you never lose your enthusiasm for serving the Lord!"

"Seein' as how He's blessed me, I'd be a lowdown skunk if I didn't give Him praise." Before he could expound any further, Anna reappeared from a brief sojourn into the inner recesses of the sanctuary and grabbed both Frank and Emma by a sleeve.

"Come on, Mama, Pa. Church is gettin' ready to start and Andrew's savin' us a seat right down front." Frank's eyes crinkled in quiet laughter, and he exchanged a look of parental pride with Emma while Anna dragged them down the center aisle.

When the Nance family had situated themselves on the second pew, Emma gently nudged Frank and nodded for him to look at the children. He turned his head toward Andrew just in time to see the boy playfully stick his tongue out at his little sister. Before Frank could interfere with this sibling squabble, Emma leaned over and whispered into his ear. "Seeing him act like a kid does my heart good; how about you?"

Emma secretly intertwined her fingers in Frank's as he offered to share a hymnal during the opening song. Then, Andrew and Anna, Emma and Frank joined their voices in heavenly harmony while the congregation sang,

"Blest be the tie that binds
Our hearts in Christian love;
The fellowship of kindred minds
Is like to that above."

Amen.

Susan K. Downs

Adoption has played a big part in Susan's life. She and her minister-husband adopted three of their five children. While missionaries in Korea, the Downs family lovingly provided foster care for babies waiting to be adopted. Susan also performed many duties at the Korean agency that assisted their family with two of their three adoptions. She states her favorite assignments were those times when she was able to play "stork" for adoptive families. She escorted dozens of babies from Korea and delivered them into the arms of their expectant adopting parents.

Following the Downses mission service and their return to the States, Susan served for several years as the Russian adoption program coordinator for an adoption agency in Texas. This agency got its start in 1887 by placing children from the orphan trains.

Presently, Susan resides in Ohio and serves as a fiction editor for Barbour Publishing.

The Provider

by Cathy Marie Hake

Dedication:

This book is dedicated to my parents,
Roy and Elvera Smith.
Even when Daddy held no spiritual commitment,
Mom was a steadfast believer.
God used her faithfulness to woo Daddy
until he accepted Christ.
The Lord has blessed them and
used them in mighty ways.
For your example, your love, prayers,
and even for the discipline,
thanks, Mom and Dad.

Chapter 1

I'm sorry, Steven. I tried my best."

Steven Halpern stared at old Doc Willowby and shook his head in mute denial of the terrible truth.

"Jane was too weak. I did all I could, but it wasn't enough." Doc handed him a small bundle and murmured, "It's a girl. She looks to be healthy, but she's a tiny slip of a thing. They are when they come early like this. Keep her warm, and try to feed her watered-down cream with sugar added to it. Do you have any bottles?"

Steven looked blankly at his housekeeper. She nodded, but he didn't even feel a flicker of relief.

"She'll need to be fed every other hour. Give her an ounce each time for the first two days, then two or three ounces after that."

"I can't do this." Steven thrust the baby back, unable to even look at her.

"You have to. She may not make it, but you owe it to Jane to try." Doc gently slid the baby back into his arms. She'd begun to wail. "I'll let you comfort one another."

Doc left, and Steven walked over to the window. Rain pelted the pane. Every last angel in heaven had to be weeping to create such a storm. Stunned as he was, he couldn't even join in. He drew a shattered breath and looked down, ready to hate the child who had cost him his sweet Jane; but she was such a tiny mite, he couldn't dredge up such an ugly emotion. A fluff of dark down covered her head, and her lips puckered. He'd never seen anything as small as her hands. She accidentally found her fingers, sucked on them for an instant, then let out a small mewl of disappointment.

The next morning , the baby gummed the bottle nipple. Her cry was a tiny bleat of woe. Steven stared at her, then looked at Mrs. Axelrod. His housekeeper carefully turned the baby around, gently patted her back, and said, "Things are ready. Tom's gathering the hands."

Steven rose from the leather wingback chair and slowly crossed the floor. The planks rang with each step. He had to go out there and lay his wife to rest. Everyone waited while he built up the nerve. Jane had been a dainty woman, a lady of refined taste and delicate sensibilities. Out of respect, Steven scraped the mud off of his boots on the porch steps before heading toward the grave. By the time he reached it, his boots were caked again, but he was too numb to notice.

"Preacher Durley wasn't in town," Mark said, "so we'll all just recite a Psalm and Mrs. Axelrod can pray."

Steven kept his eyes trained on the plain pine box and nodded. Jane deserved something far nicer than that pitiful coffin. He'd failed her all around. She'd felt puny since the day she told him he was to become a father, so he hadn't detected any difference in her these last few days. Still, he should have sent for Doc Willowby sooner.

Maybe then he might have been able to save her once her laboring began.

"The Lord is my shepherd," the men about him began. He wanted to shout at them. Why did they talk about a shepherd when they were laying his wife to rest on a cattle ranch? "Yea, though I walk through the valley of the shadow of death. . ." No man walked there—he was dragged through, and the ground was covered by millions of jagged stones of memory that caused his soul to bleed.

Steven didn't hear the rest of the recitation, the hymn, or the prayer that followed. He stared at the gaping hole in the dirt and tried to convince himself this wasn't real. Mrs. Axelrod pulled him from his thoughts when she put the baby in his arms. "Go on back into the house," she ordered. "Mark will make sure things are finished up here."

He trudged over to the porch and had to muster courage before going inside. The fragrance of Jane's lavender perfume lingered in the parlor. It sharpened the edge of his grief. Mrs. Axelrod steered him to a chair and pressed another bottle into his hand. "Best try to feed her. She sounds hungry."

Twenty minutes later, Steven worried, "She's only swallowed once, and she choked on it."

"I'll make up another bottle and use black strap molasses instead of sugar. Maybe that'll work."

Throughout the day, they tried in vain to get the baby to eat. Her wails grew weaker. Steven raked his hand through his hair and stared out at the new grave. He could not bear to think Jane was there. Even worse, he couldn't imagine failing her by letting the child she'd died to birth falter and die, too. "We have to do something," he rasped.

ℭ♡ℬ

Lena Swenson let out a cry of outrage. She ran from the soddy with Lars' old rifle. Sorely tempted to aim true, she paused a second, then lifted the muzzle into the air and fired. The rifle recoiled and slammed into her shoulder. It hurt terribly, but not as bad as the sight of the cattle still standing in her cornfield, happily munching away.

She fired once more, then took off her apron and paced into the cornfield. Though she whirled the fabric in the air and slapped one of the huge black beasts, Lena reaped no reward for her effort. One cow turned, gave her a baleful glare, and continued to munch on the cornstalk.

Lena smacked the animal again and accomplished nothing more than making her hand sting. She had no choice: She hastily saddled up her old plow horse and rode in. She started herding the strays from her corn when two men rode up. "Your cows are eating my corn!"

"The fence was down," one drawled. He kneed his mount forward and forced another cow into motion.

Lena waved her hand at the trampled crop. "What about my corn?"

The second man knocked his hat backward on his head and swiped his sleeve across his damp forehead. "Hot as it's been, that stunted crop wasn't going to come to much."

"I still counted on it!"

He shrugged. "Your man can come reckon with the boss."

Lena reared back. Her horse danced to the side, and she struggled to handle her mount and emotions. "He is dead."

"No, ma'am. Mr. Halpern ain't dead. It was his wife."

Lena looked back up at them. Her voice shook as she clarified, "I didn't know of that passing. I was speaking of my own Lars."

The man's eyes narrowed. "You mean you're a widow woman? Out here all on your lonesome?"

She sat straighter in the saddle. "No, I am not alone. I have a son."

"We didn't get word of the death or the birth."

Lena looked back at the soddy. "Please get your cows out of here, or I'm not going to have any corn left at all."

"Yes'm."

She lightly tugged on the reins and rode her horse back to the barn. It took very little time to unsaddle him, then she went back to the soddy. Johnny was wailing, so she picked him up and jounced him on her shoulder.

Not having seen another soul in a long time, Lena desperately wanted to visit. She looked about and strained to think of what she could offer as refreshments to the men before they left. She had a few ounces of coffee beans left. Johnny sat on the table as she tossed the beans into the grinder and spun the handle.

"Ma'am?"

"Yes!" Lena scooped Johnny into her arms and stepped back into the bright sunlight. "I was going to make some coffee. You'd like to stay and have a cup, perhaps, *ja?*"

His leathered face creased into an apologetic smile. "Sorry, ma'am. What with us burying Mrs. Halpern this mornin', we don't dare lollygag. That's a mighty fine-lookin' son you've got. Big."

"Thank you." Lena's maternal smile froze as Johnny twisted in her arms and started to nuzzle a button on her bodice.

The cowboy cranked his head away and stared over at the corn. "I'll say something to the boss. Might be a few days before he decides what to do."

"I understand." Lena hastily hoisted her son up to her shoulder. "Thank you for coming to fetch the cows."

"We'll repair the fence."

"Please give Mr. Halpern my condolences."

He turned back, stared at her for a long count, then glanced around. Lena suddenly felt ashamed of her homestead. The crops were pitiful. With the wheat shriveling and corn heat-stunted, she'd be lucky to have enough food to get her through next winter. Last night's downpour, though welcome, wouldn't be enough to turn the tide. Her garden looked bedraggled. Had she even combed her hair today? She couldn't bear to see the pity on the stranger's face, so she dipped her head and busied herself with patting Johnny's back.

"Ma'am, you have my condolences, too."

His raspy tone nearly ripped away the thin veneer of self-control she'd developed over the solitary months. Tears welled up, but she blinked furiously to keep them at bay. Unable to speak for fear of dissolving into a fit of weeping, she bit her lip and nodded.

"I'd best be going."

After he left, she went inside and put away the coffee. There wouldn't be more until next year. No use wasting it on just herself when it was really too hot to enjoy a scalding cup.

Johnny nursed, then she settled him in the wicker basket and carried him out to a shady spot by the barn. "Boris, guard." Her hound lay down, and Lena picked up an ax.

She needed to chop firewood for cooking and heat for the approaching winter.

She'd already found a lightning-struck tree and hacked sections of it into manageable pieces so the horse could drag it back to the homestead. Since she wouldn't need to haul water today, this was an opportune time to take care of stocking the woodpile.

The ax was big for her hands, but she'd learned to use its weight to her advantage. Lars could have split the wood into pieces with a single blow, but it took her several. Each swing pulled at her shoulders, each blow jarred her; but she did what she needed to, and with each piece she stacked, she tried to think of another hour of winter warmth for Johnny.

Her thoughts turned toward Mr. Halpern. She knew nothing of him at all other than he was a rich rancher. It was a shame he'd lost his wife. Lena knew first-hand how losing a mate tore at the soul. She looked across the yard to the broken fence and prayed, "Dear Jesus, please comfort Mr. Halpern."

Her gaze fell back on her cornfield. Mr. Halpern's cows had virtually destroyed her crop. She hoped he was a fair man. Maybe he'd simply settle by sending over two barrels of cornmeal and some canning jars of corn.

"Jesus, You taught us to pray for our daily bread. I'm worrying about supplies for winter. I know I'm supposed to trust You to provide, but I'm so scared. The rain was good, and the wheat might still be a fair crop. After harvest, I'll have to leave the farm untended when I take it to the mill. Here I am again, fretting. I don't want to be greedy, Father, but please provide." She lifted the ax and swung yet again.

৵♡৲

Mark tapped on the kitchen door and stuck his head inside. "Mrs. Axelrod?"

"What is it now?" she sighed as she stood over the stove.

"Um, well," he shifted from one foot to the other and played with the brim of his hat. He held it in front of himself and seemed to find it inordinately interesting. "A small section of the east fence went down in the storm. Half dozen heifers got into the farmer's corn."

"Mr. Halpern can't be bothered with that tonight," she snapped. "It won't make much difference. He can make restitution in a few months when he's not so troubled."

"I would have thought so, too; but, well, this is different. It's a widow woman over there. Her man died."

"She wouldn't be a widow if her man hadn't died." Mrs. Axelrod wearily wiped her hands on the front of her apron. She used a thick cotton pad and lifted the heavy cast iron skillet. Very carefully, she poured tan-colored creamy liquid into a bottle and muttered worriedly, "Death stalks in threes—but I'm doing my best to be sure the third's not that little babe."

"I never put any store by that old adage."

Mrs. Axelrod sighed. "Tell the woman Mr. Halpern will pay up."

Mark nodded. "From the looks of it, she's gonna need it. She's poor as dirt, and she's got a son, too."

"We can't be bothered right now. In a month or two, when the crop would go to market, she and the boss can settle."

"It wouldn't go to market, ma'am. From the look of

things, it would go right to her table."

"Are you telling me she and her boy are going hungry?"

"Can't rightly swear to the fact that she is just now, but I'd reckon she's pert near close to it. She's slender as a willow. On the other hand, her babe is fat as a butchering hog." He watched as Mrs. Axelrod struggled to stretch the ugly black rubber nipple over the glass bottle. "One thing for sure—she may well be struggling at most everything else, but she don't have to mess with none of that kind of gear."

Mrs. Axelrod froze. She turned slowly and asked, "Are you telling me the babe's still a nursling?"

"I believe so." Mark grinned. "Poor woman turned three shades of red when he started rooting on her gown."

"Lord be praised! Go saddle up the boss's horse!"

Chapter 2

Steven heard the ring of the ax before he saw the neighbor woman. He shifted in the saddle and awkwardly clutched his daughter. For such a tiny, lightweight bundle, she was difficult to hold. She'd starve if he didn't get something into her soon. He wanted nothing more than to be left all alone, but the privacy of his grief fell second to providing for the child Jane had wanted so desperately.

As his horse walked past the crops, Steven judged them to be in grave trouble. She'd been on her own, so the widow hadn't plowed and planted much. He figured the corn plot to be only an acre, and the wheat wasn't quite twice as large. The soddy looked like a hovel for beasts instead of a habitation for humans. *How can anyone live like this?*

He spied the woman. He'd never met her—farmers were a blight on the land, and being neighborly with them went against his principles. She was tall and slender, but her shoulders were broad. He'd expected to see her in widow's weeds out of respect for her husband, but she wore faded blue calico. Sweat darkened the back of her bodice and made big rings beneath her arms. Mud caked the bottom ten inches of her gown. He'd never seen such a filthy woman. For an instant, he almost turned to go, but the babe in his arms whimpered and reminded him he couldn't afford to be picky.

The woman stood with her legs spread wide apart and twisted as her arms moved upward in a smooth arc. The ax in her hands almost robbed her of her balance, but she shifted her weight. The ax cut through the air, hit a section of wood, and split it. Both halves fell to the ground. She set down the ax, took up another piece of wood, and positioned it. As she reached for the ax again, a dog growled a warning and started to bark.

The widow woman wheeled around and clutched the ax before her. Her blue eyes were wide in a pale, dirt-streaked face. She stared at him as she sidestepped several yards toward a wicker basket. The dog stood guard over the basket and continued to growl.

"Hello. I am Lena Swenson."

Her voice sounded husky, as if she hadn't spoken in several days. Even with her singsongy Swedish accent, it shook a little, too. Steven stared at her and wondered what she thought she was doing, living alone like this. "I hear you're a widow now."

She recoiled from his blunt words, and Steven knew the sickening flavor of the grief his words caused. Her lips thinned and she said nothing, but she shifted the ax in front of herself. Her fingers clutched the handle so tightly, the knuckles went white.

Hackles raised, the dog stood beside her. Its growl took on a sinister pitch. "Call off the dog."

She shook her head.

He heard a whimpering sound. She cast a furtive glance at the basket. A wail quavered from it, and the color bled from her face. "I think you'd better leave, mister."

He wanted to. He wanted to ride off and never look back. The last thing he wanted was to place his clean little baby in the arms of this slovenly woman. Most of her silver-blond hair straggled out of an untidy knot on her crown. Jane would have swooned at the thought of such a person ever touching her beloved child. His daughter let out a soft bleat. He had no choice. Either he asked this woman to help, or he'd lose the baby, too.

Steven locked eyes with her, steeled himself with a deep breath, and said, "I heard you might have milk."

She blinked, then nodded. "My cow is fresh."

He let out a mirthless bark of a laugh. "Not your cow. You." She didn't react at all, so he flipped back the edge of the blanket. The baby made a pathetic squeak as sunlight hit her tiny face. "My girl is hungry."

Lena's mouth dropped open. She stared at him in shock.

"I heard you had a baby," Steven continued. "From the sounds of it, he's aiming to get some chow. Bluntly put, I want him to share with my daughter."

After a few seconds of silence, he swung down out of the saddle. The bundled baby occupied his left arm. He drew a pistol with his right hand. Lena gasped. "Lady, send that dog off, or I'm going to plug a bullet in him. I won't have him threaten my daughter."

"*Ruh,*" she ordered. "*Sitz.*" The dog sat and went silent. The woman studied Steven and said, "Boris will not harm you if you are friendly. Put away the gun."

"I'll holster the gun if you put down the ax."

"You must put the gun in the saddle holster and step away from your horse," she countered.

Steven grew impatient. "Listen, lady—my baby is starving, and you're acting like we're trying to swap horseflesh."

Lena sucked in a deep breath. "Is she sick?"

"No. Hungry."

"Put her in the cradle in the soddy, then step back out. I will go in and feed her."

He had no choice. The woman was dirty as a pig, but the baby needed something quick, or she'd dwindle. Her crying was pitifully thin, but constant. He'd give in for this one feeding, then find another way to take care of matters. Steven pivoted about, strode to the soddy, and went inside.

It was worse than he'd expected. Shafts of late afternoon sun angled through the doorway and illuminated walls made of huge slabs of grassy dirt. An iron bedstead took up a third of the space. Fresh splotches of mud dripped down from the ceiling and plopped onto the red and blue quilt. A rough table and two rickety chairs, a small three-drawer bureau, and a cradle comprised the remainder of the furniture. The tiniest potbellied stove he'd ever seen took up the far corner. Crates and shelves lined one wall. On them sat jars, crocks, sacks, a few bottles and barrels, and candles. Her poverty stunned him. Steven stood still for a moment, then did as she asked. He set his daughter into the cradle and paced back out.

She'd lifted her son with one arm. He was old enough

to lift his head and look around. His gown ruched up, displaying a pair of reassuringly chunky legs. Lena still awkwardly held the ax, and the dog stayed right at her side. "You will wait by the barn," she ordered.

He looked at her grimy hands. "Wash before you touch her."

She skirted around him and disappeared inside.

Steven stood outside and clenched his fists. He was a man who managed everything, but his world was spinning out of control. His heart and soul ached with an emptiness he'd never known. Just the memory of Jane stole the breath from his lungs. He was helpless—as helpless as his baby daughter. Their fate lay in the filthy hands of an ignorant, low-class farmer's wife.

◔♡◑

Lena lit the lamp and shut the door. She barred it and didn't care that she was wasting lamp oil when the sun still hung high in the sky. She didn't trust that man. How could he have humiliated her like that? She'd been working all day. Of course she was dirty. He'd asked an incredibly intimate favor, then had the unmitigated gall to insult her. If it weren't for the fact that his tiny daughter kept mewling so pitifully, she would have refused him.

Lena hastily stripped out of her clothes, used the water in the bucket by the stove, and washed up. She put on her clean dress, then went over to see the baby. The child was a newborn—barely a day or so, and born weeks before her time. Pitifully thin, she barely managed any sound at all. "Dear Jesus, help me to help her!"

Lena gently offered herself to the baby. She was so weak, it took patience, but soon she seemed to get the idea and did passably well at suckling. Lena burped her, then laid her in the cradle and picked up Johnny.

A fair bit of time passed—how much, she didn't know. Lena didn't own a timepiece. When both babies were fed and changed, she made sure all of her buttons were closed, then she ran a brush through her hair, plaited it into a thick rope, and left it to hang down her back. With a baby in each arm, she struggled to open the door.

The sunlight was bright after she'd become accustomed to the dim interior of the soddy. By the time she blinked and focused, the man had snatched his baby away. "Well? Did she eat?"

"Yes."

"Your boy is big, so he must have quite an appetite. Did you give her enough?"

Lena's arms curled around Johnny, and she stepped back. "Your baby is small, so she doesn't need much. Since she was very hungry, I fed her first."

"Good."

Good? Not, "thank you," but good? Lena barely held back a shocked retort. She stared at him, then said, "You still have a few hours of daylight. If you ride hard, town is south of here. You could get bottles from the general store and milk from the diner for her."

"She doesn't need that now that she has you."

"Mister, I think you'd better get on your horse and leave." She inched back from the doorway back into the shadowed interior of her home.

"I can't. Not yet. You managed to satisfy her and quiet her down." He pointed to two half-pint jars on the ground. "I found those in the barn. Doc said she has to eat every other hour. We'll stay 'til you feed her again. You can fill those up, and it'll get us through the night 'til I send someone over for more in the morning."

Lena gawked at him. "I am no milk cow!"

His face took on a thunderous look.

"I don't even know who you are, and you ask this of me?" Her voice cracked, "Do not come back here!" She hurriedly slammed the door shut and bolted it.

"Mrs. Swenson? Mrs. Swenson!" He pounded on her door.

She huddled on the bed. "I have a rifle!"

"You may as well load and use it on both of us. If you don't feed her, she's going to die. As for me—I've already lost my wife. If I lose my baby, I don't want to live, either."

Chapter 3

"Only for a week," she reminded herself as she stepped into Mr. Halpern's house. Lena looked around at the grand home and felt swamped by her inadequacies. She'd tried to wipe her feet, but her worn boots still left small clods and crumbles of dirt on the gleaming wooden floor. Johnny's clean gowns and diapers and her nightgown filled the burlap bag she clutched in a shaky hand. She didn't belong in such a fancy place.

"Mrs. Axelrod," Mr. Halpern ordered, "put Mrs. Swenson in the blue room. She'll stay with us for the next week. Move the cradle in there."

"Yes, sir." The portly woman studied Lena with undisguised curiosity. "Follow me."

Lena carefully balanced a baby in each arm as she went up a flight of stairs. She walked down a hallway, past several closed doors. Mrs. Axelrod opened a door and motioned her inside. "I'm sure you'll find this comfortable."

Lena tentatively shuffled in and looked all around. A blue satin counterpane covered a cherry wood sleigh bed. Wallpaper sprigged with blue columbines gave a dainty, fresh feel to the room. The washstand had a marble top, and the bureau boasted a snowy doily with a porcelain figurine on it. "I've never seen anyplace so beautiful."

The housekeeper nodded. "Mrs. Halpern was very particular. She loved making the house look perfect. You'll have to forgive the boss if he's grumpy these days. He loved her to distraction."

Lena crossed the floor and looked out the window. It was so nice to have real glass panes. She stared out in the direction of her farm and said very quietly, "I understand this kind of pain."

"Yes, I guess you do."

"I will do my best for his daughter. The farm—I cannot leave it even this long. He promised to have someone go tend it for me. After one week, I must go back to my home."

"We'll see."

Lena looked over her shoulder and said in a definitive tone, "One week. It is our agreement. I will not stay longer —I cannot."

Mrs. Axelrod opened the burlap bag and busied herself, putting Johnny's clothes in the second drawer of the bureau. She shook out the nightgown and laid it on the bed. "Did you bring anything else?"

Lena shivered. "My other dress is rolled up behind my saddle. Once the babies are asleep—"

"I'm sure Mr. Halpern will have it brought in."

"It is muddy. I need to wash it."

The woman cast a glance at her and said in a knowing tone, "No wonder, after last night's storm. I'll wash it."

"Oh, but—"

"You are here to see to the baby." The woman plumped

the pillow and flicked a nonexistent wrinkle from the bed. "Best you get that straight here and now. Bad enough Miss Jane didn't get through the birthing. Mr. Halpern's going to be a bulldog about the babe. You see to her; I'll see to the laundry."

Lena watched as the woman set her boar bristle brush on the washstand and the Bible on the bedside table. She'd been lucky to grab those last two things—Mr. Halpern had been in such a hurry, she'd barely been able to latch the soddy's door behind them.

The baby girl whimpered. Lena cast an apologetic look at the woman as she set both children on the mattress. It was a shame to mess up the perfectly smooth bed, but there was no chair in the room. Lena stooped, untied her boots, and took them off. She washed her hands and couldn't help noticing how the dainty columbines painted on the edge of the washbowl matched the wallpaper. The linen hand towel was such a fine weave, she felt guilty for using it. She went back to the bed, scooted so her spine rested against the headboard, and dragged a baby to either side.

The housekeeper stayed in the room. She'd gone over to the window, needlessly straightened pale yellow curtains, and then pulled on gold tassels to shut the heavy, blue brocade draperies. She turned back and granted Lena a tight smile. Lena held one hand over the buttons of her bodice and the other on the Halpern child. "I will take good care of her."

The housekeeper nodded. "I'll be back with the cradle."

In the middle of the night, Steven heard a baby. He worried about his daughter. The Swenson woman hadn't come down for supper. Mrs. Axelrod said she'd taken up a tray, and that ought to do. They'd need to feed the woman well so she'd be able to nurse both babies. In truth, she needed more to eat, just for her own sake. He'd lifted her into her saddle, and though she was tall and sturdy through the shoulders, the lean shape of her hips and waist made it clear food wasn't as plentiful on her table as it ought to be. When he sent her back home, he'd be sure to replenish her larder.

Her son was a solid tike—chubby and apple-cheeked. Whatever else she did wrong, one thing was clear—she did well by her child. Would she care for him first and neglect his daughter, though? Steven paced back and forth. A small wail hovered in the air, then died out. Should he go check?

Steven fought with himself. He had no business going into the widow's bedchamber; he had every right—his daughter was in there. After fifteen more minutes of grieving over his lost wife and agonizing about how best to see to his daughter's needs, he yielded to temptation. He lightly tapped on the door.

She gave no answer.

Quietly, he opened the door. No light shone inside, but she was probably like a mole or a cat—able to navigate in the dark, after living in that disgusting mud hovel. He set the lamp on the hallway floor and tiptoed in.

The top drawer on the dresser was open. The back of a chair sat beneath it for support. Why had she done such an odd thing? The cradle lay empty. His frown deepened and his nose wrinkled. Something stank. Diapers. A wad of them lay in a big bowl. The room was a mess. Jane wouldn't have ever dreamed of letting things get out of place like this.

He stepped closer to the bed. The scene stopped him in his tracks. Lena was asleep. Her hair billowed in a riotous mass all over the pillow. She lay on her back, her left arm bowed out a bit to hold her son close to her side. His hair was the same pale gold, so it was easy to spy above the dark-colored blankets. Steven's daughter lay nestled to Lena's breastbone. A pale flannel blanket covered her, and Lena's big, rough hand held her fast.

Pain laced through him. *Jane wanted this baby so badly. Jane should be holding her. Jane should be cherishing her soft skin and downy hair and fretting over each snuffle and squeak.*

Instead, a stranger, a woman who worked like a man and lived like an animal, held her. The baby made a soft sound. Even in her sleep, Lena tenderly patted his daughter. Obviously accustomed to dealing with the needs of an infant, she murmured soft hushes. A rough hand. An accent to the voice. It was wrong—all wrong.

Steven stumbled out of the room, through the house, into the yard. At his wife's graveside, he stared at the mound of freshly turned earth. Each breath tore at his throat. His chest burned. He leaned against the tree, let his head fall back, and groaned. There were no words for the grief and rage he felt.

༺♡༻

Lena woke early and fed her son, then settled him into the cradle. He could sit up, so she was afraid to use the drawer

199

as a baby bed for him. As she carefully tucked the Halpern girl into a fresh diaper, she whispered, "I don't know your name, Princess. I'll have to ask today."

Lena smiled softly as the wee one made a greedy little sound. It was her first, and it was a good sign. As tiny and tentative as she'd been, that reassurance was welcome.

After a while, Lena turned over and let her finish nursing from the other side. She whispered her morning prayers, then started to sleepily drift along. She'd missed out on a lot of sleep, nursing both babies during the night.

Mrs. Axelrod pushed open the door and bustled in with a tray. She took the baby and grinned. "No doubt it's my imagination, but I'd swear she weighs more today than yesterday."

Lena merely smiled and sat up.

Mrs. Axelrod burped the tiny girl and started to change her diaper. "I brought creamed oatmeal with your breakfast. Your son is old enough to be eating regular food."

Lena clutched the blanket to her chest and let out a small sound of distress. "I have enough milk. I am Johnny's mother—"

"Yes, you are. I just figured you'd been giving him rice or barley cereal because he's so stocky." They both glanced over at the cradle. "Your boy is going to grow into a sizable man. It's plain to see, he'll be able to do a man's work earlier than most." She looked down at the newborn. "On the other hand, this one is going to be a dainty little thing. Small as she is, she won't need much milk at all yet. I'm not worried about you having enough for both."

"No one has told me her name."

Mrs. Axelrod pursed her lips. "She doesn't have one yet. I suppose we'll have to ask the boss."

Lena reached over and tenderly caressed the baby's dark hair. "In the Bible there is a girl. Her name is not given. Talitha means 'little girl' and that is all we know her by. For now, I will call her this. When Mr. Halpern decides upon a name, please let me know."

"Talitha?"

"Yes. She was healed. It was a miracle."

"We surely could use a miracle or two around here," the housekeeper mumbled as she headed out the door.

Chapter 4

Originally, Lena agreed to only a week of caring for Talitha; but the baby thrived on breast milk, and she refused to suck from a bottle. Mrs. Axelrod truly tried, but it was to no avail. She lifted her hands in surrender. "I'm afraid you'll just have to keep feeding her. She's still so little."

Lena chewed on her lip and stared out the window. She needed to get back home today. There was so much work to do. . . .

Then, too, there was another problem. This home was like the Garden of Eden. Food was plentiful, and she had companionship. Something about Mrs. Axelrod's friendship after months of isolation drew her. Being able to lie down at night and not fear every strange sound counted for a lot, and she knew Mr. Halpern was more than capable of protecting them all. She felt strong temptation to try to fit in here, but it was wrong for her to relish the creature comforts of this place when she clearly did not belong. The wise thing to do was to leave before she yielded to temptation and tried to wangle her way into a permanent position in the household. Lena squared her shoulders. "I'll take her with me. There's no other way."

"Mr. Halpern won't cotton to that."

Lena carefully positioned her shawl and continued to suckle Johnny. The man who'd been sent to tend the crops couldn't be expected to do women's chores. If she didn't take care of her gardening and canning, she and her son would starve this winter. "Tell Mr. Halpern he has no choice. I am willing to take her for a time. When she grows bigger, he can have her back."

Mrs. Axelrod pursed her lips and left the room. Lena had barely finished buttoning up her bodice when the door flew open. Steven Halpern filled the doorframe. "You're not going anywhere! What kind of woman are you to abandon a motherless babe?"

She stood, popped Johnny into the cradle, and started to pack her belongings into a sack. "I am not forsaking Talitha. She still needs me, so I am willing to take her along."

In sheer desperation, Steven captured her shoulder. "No one is going anywhere!" He paused as his eyes narrowed. She'd gone perfectly still beneath his touch. The hectic color she'd sported just moments before drained clean out of her cheeks. Very lightly, he rubbed his thumb back and forth across her collarbone. She inhaled sharply and wrenched free. "Did that hurt? Mrs. Axelrod said the rifle bruised your shoulder when you tried to run those cows off your land—"

"It is not fitting to discuss my person, and I am quite well, thank you. Do not touch me again."

He scowled. "What kind of man do you think I am?

I loved my wife. I just buried her. You can bet I'm not looking for the likes of you to take her place!"

Lena stood even straighter. She looked at him with wounded dignity, then quietly said, "I know of the pain of losing a mate. I have tried to understand the hurt in your heart. When Lars died, my heart was empty. Each day, I wake and know the ache of loneliness. I am sorry for your loss. I did my best. I offered to still feed your daughter, but I must see to my farm, too." She turned and scooped up her son. "If Talitha needs me, you can have someone bring her to me."

☙♡❧

Steven gawked at her, then shot Mrs. Axelrod a horrified look. "Do something!"

The housekeeper watched as Lena walked off. She grimaced. "We can't make her stay. We'll come up with a schedule for taking Talitha to her."

"Talitha?"

"Mrs. Swenson said it's in the Bible. It means 'little girl.' "

"What business does she have, naming my daughter?"

"It's temporary—'til you decide on something. When she says it, it comes out sounding right pretty."

"Go make a bottle. I don't want that woman touching my daughter again."

☙♡❧

Lena was relieved to get home. True to his word, Mr. Halpern had a man there to do the chores. Lena thanked him and sent him on his way. Once he was gone, she took her horse into the barn and noted the cow still hadn't been milked. Her pitiful lowing let Lena know that had to be the first thing she did.

After milking the cow, Lena set the milk pail aside on her way to the house and ducked into the chicken coop. She found only two eggs—the man must have gathered the rest. From the looks of things, he'd done a fair job on the chores. Supposing the eggs were in the soddy, she lifted the pail and headed that direction. As soon as she entered the tiny room, she noticed a bowl full of fresh eggs on the table.

He'd slept in her bed and left it a rumpled mess. She shuddered and set Johnny into the cradle. In a rush of activity, she stripped the feather mattress and set the sheets and quilt to boil.

The ground was still damp, so he hadn't needed to water the crops. He'd visited her garden and staked up a few of the tomato plants. He'd carried the wood she'd chopped and stacked it by the side of the soddy.

She stirred the laundry, hung up the damp things on her line, then wrung out the bedding and hung it up, too. Boris trotted along with her and acted delighted to be in her company.

Lena collected Johnny and sat in the shade to nurse him. It was noon—time for her to make herself some dinner. She wasn't overly hungry, and it would be best for her to skip a meal whenever possible to conserve her supplies. *Jesus, help me not to feel bitter about Mr. Halpern's ingratitude. Please keep Your hand on Talitha and soften her father's heart.*

The ranch hand had left a mess on the table, so Lena scraped the dishes into a slop bucket for the pigs. With water scarce, she took the plates and skillet outside and used sand to scour them. While doing so, she tried to think of a way to make a box of some sort for Johnny. He'd soon be crawling, and she worried that he'd hurt himself while she was busy with chores. Lars would have built something special. He'd made the beautiful cradle. He was so good with his hands. Grief curled in her heart.

Distracted by her sad thoughts, Lena didn't hear the horse until Boris barked. Seconds later, she detected a high-pitched wail as she tucked the dishes into a basket, yet she didn't turn around. *Jesus, please help me act and speak with kindness.*

"What kind of woman are you, Lena Swenson, to leave a motherless baby to starve?" Steven's words stole her breath away. He sat in the saddle, glowering at her. He held his daughter as if she were a bale of barbed wire. His eyes were just as sharp.

Lena forced herself to stay silent. The dishes rattled as she put one last cup into the basket and got to her feet. Talitha's wails rose in urgency. Halpern dismounted and headed toward her. "Stop that infernal nonsense and do your duty!"

Lena turned to the side and plucked Johnny from his basket. Without a word, she headed for the soddy. Steven intercepted her. He stood between her and her home. "What," he demanded, "are you doing?"

Her chin jutted forward. "I am doing my duty. My son is wet and hungry."

"So is my daughter."

"Then change her."

"That's a woman's job."

Lena shifted Johnny's weight a bit and stared at her neighbor. "You may think I am cruel, but I will say this, for you must hear it and live by the truth. When your mate dies, there is no such luxury as having men's and women's jobs. Things must be done, and you are the only one who is there to accomplish them. For your daughter's sake, you must learn to care for her. You have no choice."

His face paled. The muscle in his cheek twitched. "Cruel doesn't even begin to cover what I think of you. If there were any other way for my daughter to eat, I'd gladly do it."

Lord, he's so bitter and harsh. Give me a soft word to turn away his wrath. "You brought her. I said if you brought her, I would feed her. Fetch a diaper from your saddlebag. Come inside, and I will teach you how to change her."

He stayed in her path and grimaced.

"Until you decide my home is good enough, I still must see to my own son. Excuse me." She slipped past him and went inside. Lena started to hum as she laid Johnny on the bare mattress and changed his diaper. A huge shadow suddenly blocked out the sunlight spilling from the doorway. She didn't look up. She kept humming a hymn under her breath.

"I didn't bring a diaper."

His confession triggered both pity and concern. How could he plan to keep his daughter when he was so inept? "Go get a diaper off of the clothesline."

He didn't say anything at all. He simply wheeled around and headed off toward the rope where her laundry snapped in the prairie wind. When he reappeared in the doorway, he balanced the laundry basket in one hand and the baby in the other.

"Bring her here." Lena dropped Johnny's wet diaper into a bucket and rinsed her hands in the washbowl. As she dried them, she said in a sad tone, "I am proud of my home. Lars built it for us, and we filled it with love. I know you are used to fancy things, but that is your life. Johnny and I are warm and happy here. If you wish me to help Talitha, you will have to accept me and my home."

"Listen, both of these kids are crying. Can't you feed them first and save your sermon for later?"

Lena stared at him in stunned silence. She went over, turned the rocking chair to face away from the door, and sat down. She pulled a shawl over her shoulder and self-consciously unbuttoned her bodice. A second later, Johnny stopped crying.

"Hey! I thought you said you'd feed my daughter first!"

"She needs to be in a dry diaper and gown."

"Don't tell me Johnny doesn't pee all over you."

"Sometimes he does."

"He'll eat everything. You won't have enough left."

"Small babes need very little. God will provide enough."

"Listen to her crying," he said in a nervous tone. "You can feed them both at the same time. Let her eat now, too."

Lena glanced down and readjusted the shawl. "Bring her to me as soon as you are done changing her diaper."

It wasn't long before she heard the ground crunch beneath his feet. He awkwardly changed Talitha, then shoved her into Lena's arms and hightailed out of the soddy. After she finished nursing the babes, she went back outside. He turned around, and his haggard look tore at her soul. "Mr. Halpern, I do not mind caring for your daughter, but I must still tend my land."

He nodded curtly. "Nights at my place, days here. She's mine. I want her under my roof and protection at night."

Chapter 5

Lena somberly stepped back into the columbine bedroom. Mrs. Axelrod stood in the doorway and pled, "Please don't be too hard on him. He's grieving for his wife."

Lena cranked her head to the side and swallowed a big lump in her throat. She'd been without Lars for eight months. She'd been terribly alone and afraid. Every day, she suffered the backbreaking farm labor and loneliness. Every night, she fixed supper for only herself. Her grief was still raw.

"I'm not trying to be mean, Lena. You don't understand—"

"I do not understand? I spent eight months in solitude and delivered my son on my own." Her voice broke.

Mrs. Axelrod sucked in a loud breath. "I'm sorry, Lena. Truly I am. You're so good with the babies and keep such a calm spirit, it's hard to remember you're freshly widowed."

"God gives me strength and comfort," Lena whispered.

"Poor Boss. He's shaking his fist at the Almighty for

taking his wife. I did the same for a good long while when my Sam passed on. It's a rare person who can endure grief like you have."

Lena settled into the room and confessed, "Each day, I have had to pray for help. It is like being forced to pull a heavy wagon alone when once there was another who shared the yoke. God only gives strength enough for each day, for each step."

Mrs. Axelrod shook her head and pulled Johnny away. "Speaking of strength, you look near worn to a frazzle. If I don't miss my guess, you did three days' work in one morning. You take a rest, and I'll change this one. He's wet as a leaky bucket."

❧♥❧

Steven couldn't sleep. He hadn't slept a night through since Jane died. He tossed, punched his pillow, and lay in the darkness. Unable to fill the aching void, he got up and paced out of his room.

Without thinking, he went to Lena's room. Once there, he glanced about and thought how impractical the furniture was. The washstand and sleigh bed were carved alike and useful, but everything else was far too ornate. He hadn't stepped foot in here since the day Jane finished decorating it, and now that he didn't have his wife beside him to distract him, he studied the room and found the whole affair far too fussy. Blue flowers, white lace, and blue ruffles made him want to bolt. Doodads rested on every available surface—little glass bottles, picture frames, porcelain statues.

The dresser top was different. It held only Lena's leather-bound Bible and a hairbrush. The stark simplicity of those two items jarred him. Sturdy. Practical. Like their owner. Ah—and there was a chair there—propping up the top drawer. Still. His scowl deepened as he realized his daughter occupied that makeshift bassinet. He'd get the boy's cradle over here today.

Steven peeked at both babies. They slept like angels. All he could see of Lena was her profile. She'd turned her face away. Her pale hair flowed over the pillows in an unrestrained mass. The sight was a beautiful one—but completely unexpected.

His wife had been proud of her hair. She made a show of taking it down each night, brushing it one hundred strokes, and plaiting it. There was something. . .wanton about a woman who went to bed with her hair unbound and wild. Jane had been far too mannerly and demure to do anything so impulsive. No matter what time of the day or night, she'd been a complete and total lady from the top of her perfectly coifed coronet to her narrow feet. This woman obviously hadn't ever been taught proper conduct. A wry grin twisted his lips. No husband in his right mind would point out that shortcoming and lose such a magnificent vision.

Traversing the room silently was no small feat. Afraid to make any noise or sudden moves, Steven navigated around a marble pedestal with a Grecian statue on it. He practically tripped over the tip of the cradle runner, then bumped into the bedside table. He fought the urge to start pitching all of the folderols and knickknacks on it straight out the window. Instead, he breathed a sigh of relief that Lena and both babies were still asleep. He lifted Talitha into his arms, tiptoed out, pulled the door almost shut, and headed for his bedchamber.

Feeling adrift, he paced over to the far side of the room and stared out the window. One work-rough hand cradled the babe to his chest, the other went up and tentatively touched the pane. He could see the tree from here. Jane was buried beneath it. In a grief-heavy whisper he said, "I'm doing the best I can for her, Jane. Her name's Talitha. It's a pretty name. Comes from the Bible." His voice broke. "Oh, Sweetheart, I miss you. We need you." He hung his head and finally let his silent tears flow.

A short while later, Steven took a deep breath and dashed away the proof of his raw grief. Sorrow weighted his steps as he went back to his bed. There, he curled next to his little blanket-wrapped daughter and finally slowly drifted off to sleep.

அ♡ஓ

Heart in her throat, Lena swept her shawl around her shoulders and ran out into the hallway. Talitha was missing! Lena looked about, unsure of where to go or what to do. She'd never explored the house, but she knew which chamber belonged to Mr. Halpern. Had he taken his daughter? She sped to his door and though he didn't respond to her knock, she heard Talitha's whimper. Relief flooded her. Lena let out a shaky breath and tapped on the door again.

Her heart nearly broke at the sight that met her when she hesitantly entered the room. Steven Halpern lay curled around a tiny bundle. His big hand cupped it and nestled it close to his heart. How many times had Lena done that with Johnny, herself? Snuggled her son to her breast and tried to mute the pain of losing her mate?

Talitha fussed a bit louder. Her father roused a bit and nuzzled her downy hair. Though Lena hated to part them, she tiptoed closer and whispered, "She's hungry."

He opened his eyes and canted up on one elbow. His other hand brushed the edge of the blanket from the baby's face, and he fingered her cheek. "Bring her back when she's done."

Lena did as he asked as soon as Talitha was full. She couldn't deny him that comfort. She slipped his daughter back into his arms. He said nothing, but the pain burning in his eyes and the almost desperate way he accepted his daughter spoke volumes.

A while later, Lena woke to find him standing over her. "I think she's hungry again. I changed her already."

She accepted the baby, but to her dismay, Johnny picked that moment to start fussing. "Stay put. I'll change him," Steven said. He lifted her son from the cradle, then changed him on the foot of Lena's bed. "He's a fine boy. Robust. Lars must have been proud."

Lena swallowed hard. "Lars never saw his son. You are the first and only man who has ever held Johnny."

"Other than Doc Willowby. . ." His eyes widened as she shook her head negatively. He pulled Johnny up into his strong arms and held him so gently, Lena's heart tripped over at the sight. "But, Lena—who? How. . .?"

She'd assumed Mrs. Axelrod had told him. Obviously, he didn't know. "Johnny was born the week before Christmas, during the blizzard. I was alone." Memories assailed her. Fear, pain, loneliness, joy. . . She gave him a sad smile.

"You did it all by yourself," he marveled under his

breath. He looked down at Johnny and thought aloud, "Being with child is hard enough on a woman. I can't fathom how you lived alone and managed your chores each day, let alone comprehend handling the birth all on your own. You are a remarkable woman, Lena Swenson. I don't know of another woman who could have done it."

"God gave me strength."

Pain replaced the admiration on his face. "Why," he rasped hoarsely as he put Johnny on the mattress close by her, "why didn't God give Jane strength?"

"I do not know. I am sorry. I do not know why He took Lars, either. Each day, I look at Johnny and try to be thankful for the time I had and the son that his love left me."

"That's not enough. It's not enough for me."

Lena didn't know what to say. He looked awful. His throat worked, and the muscles in his stubbled jaw twitched. The shadows beneath his eyes tattled on how hard grief rode him and robbed him of his rest. She reached out to touch his arm. Wordlessly, he jerked away, turned, and left.

Chapter 6

For the next three weeks, Lena rarely saw Steven Halpern other than at night when he snuck Talitha away. They'd come to a tenuous understanding. Lena slept beneath his roof but then took Talitha with her each day when she went home to work her farm. Because of the hours of work she lost by having to travel each day, Steven insisted on having one of his men stay in her barn and work as a hired hand.

From the pretty mahogany and porcelain mantle clock in her bedroom at the Halpern ranch, Lena had learned tiny little Talitha needed to nurse every hour and a half. Day and night, she had to halt whatever she was doing to take half an hour to feed the newborn. Each day, she looked about the farm and felt more discouraged. No matter how hard she tried, she couldn't keep up. Nursing another baby and traveling back and forth each day robbed her of too much time.

Even with the man helping her water and tend the crops, Lena had plenty to do. Storing and preserving food was a priority. She harvested truck from her garden, then canned. It was hot, time-consuming work to boil down the vegetables, sterilize, and seal the jars.

Each night, she left a bit later to go to the Halpern place. She'd wear Johnny on her back in a carrier she'd fashioned along the lines of the cradle boards Indians used, and she tucked Talitha in a sash of fabric she wore across her front. Steven insisted she ride his gentlest mare since her old plow horse was too slow to transport her satisfactorily. One night, Mrs. Axelrod met her on the kitchen porch and snatched Talitha from the sash as she hissed, "Mr. Halpern is in the study. He's fretting, you're so late!"

"I was busy," Lena said dully.

"He was ready to come after you."

"There was no need. I gave my word I would have her here each night, and I keep my promises. The tomatoes—"

"Tomatoes!" The housekeeper glared and warned, "Boss won't listen to flimsy excuses. His daughter always comes first."

Lena took the baby back and headed for the stairs. "Then you can let him know I've gone to my room to suckle her."

Since they were pressuring her to come home by sunset, Lena started rising even earlier. More than once, she dozed off in the saddle while the mare automatically carried her home.

On the rare occasions she saw Mr. Halpern, he was hollow-eyed with grief or occupied running his ranch. Lena prayed for him.

Mrs. Axelrod was far too busy, too. Cooking and cleaning was already a huge job—adding on laundry for another adult and two babies stretched her to the limit. Too tired to do much to help her, Lena tried to rinse and wash the children's clothes and diapers when she could. She insisted upon eating in the kitchen instead of having trays to make things easier on the housekeeper. At supper one night, Mrs. Axelrod asked, "How're things at the farm?"

"Dry. The drought, it is bad," Lena admitted. "That one rain we had, it was not enough."

"We need more," Steven agreed.

After blotting her mouth with a napkin Lena said, "When there is a need, God can use it as an opportunity to provide." Talitha started to cry, so Lena excused herself from the table.

Behind her, she heard Steven mutter, "God's taking His sweet time, and while we're waiting, her crops languish and my stock suffers." She didn't bother to turn and make a retort. She knew his pain and grief made him angry. With time and prayer, he'd come to understand the truth.

ℰ♡ℬ

A few days later, Lena got up and yawned as she changed the babies. Once fed, they both slipped back to sleep. She dressed and plaited her hair, then carefully wrapped Johnny into his cradle board and strapped it to her back. Talitha didn't stir at all as Lena lifted her into the sash so she could leave for the farm. Lena held a boot in each hand. Toeing open the door caused it to creak. Johnny let out a wail, and Lena winced.

Steven appeared in his doorway. His hair was rumpled, and his chin looked heavily stubbled. Bare feet stuck out beneath a thick robe. "Lena, what're you doing?"

"I need to go now. Soon the sun will be up."

He padded over, took her boots from her hands, and dropped them on the floor with a loud pair of thuds. In the next instant, he took Talitha from her. "She fussed most of the night. You have to be exhausted."

"I ate cabbage yesterday, and I do not think it agreed with her. I made the rest into sauerkraut, so you do not need to worry. I will not have it again as long as I feed her."

His brow furrowed. "Lena, I'll stock your place when you leave us. Stop preserving food and don't worry about firewood."

In an effort to pacify Johnny since he kept whimpering, she rocked side to side. "Already you have a man doing much good work with my crops. I cannot accept more!"

"Wait here." He walked away and returned a moment later without Talitha. With a few quick tugs, he untied the straps holding Johnny to her back. "He's winding up. Is he hungry?"

"He may be wet again." Steven carried the cradle board into her room and laid it on the bed. She plucked Johnny out and hummed a lullaby under her breath as she deftly changed him.

"You're always so patient with the babies, Lena."

She smiled at the compliment. "It is not easy some days, but they need to be loved, so I try."

When she moved to tuck Johnny back into the cradle board, Steven halted her. He swiped Johnny, slipped him back into his cradle, then turned to her. "I can't let you go back home today, Lena. You're plumb tuckered out. Go back to bed."

She cast a longing look at the bed, then decisively shook her head. "There is much that needs doing."

Strong, lean, tanned fingers captured her jaw. He turned her face ever so slightly toward the window so the first pink rays of dawn illuminated her features. "The dark circles under your eyes tattle, Lena. You're weary beyond imagining. This is ridiculous. If you fall sick, we'll have a real mess on our hands. The babies need you healthy."

"I am not sick."

"You're weaving on your feet!"

A gamine smile tilted her lips. "I am in the habit of rocking. It soothes the children."

"I'll pull a rocking chair in here for you."

"That would be most kind. Thank you."

"For now, you're going to bed." He swept her up and placed her in the center of the bed. Once he settled her there, he cupped her shoulders and gave her a stern look. "You desperately need sleep. Don't even think of getting up 'til noon."

"I am no slugabed!"

"No, Lena, no one could ever rightfully accuse you of sloth. Today, at least, you're going to rest up, though." He turned and paced from the room. Practical, ugly boots in the hallway stopped him. His heart twisted. She'd been tiptoeing out of here and putting on those ugly monstrosities downstairs to keep from awakening him or Mrs. Axelrod. She worked harder than any man he knew, yet she never complained. In fact, he now realized he'd leaned heavily on her, even though she'd suffered a recent loss, herself. From all accounts, she and Lars had a strong, happy marriage, yet she handled her grief with a dignity and serenity he could not begin to emulate. He envied her peace of heart.

He picked up the boots and took them back to her room. In the few moments he'd been gone, she'd turned onto her side, curled up, and already fallen fast asleep.

In the brief moment he'd lifted her, she'd seemed far too slight. Worried that she might be sickening, he summoned old Doc Willowby.

Doc sat in the parlor that noon. "Her son nurses about every four hours." He paused meaningfully and peered over his glasses. "Your daughter needs feeding every hour and a half."

Steven sucked in a noisy breath. "That was supposed to just be for the first few days."

Doc continued, "Your daughter came a full four weeks early, so she's a wee mite. Her stomach is small and can't hold much, but because she's premature, it takes her longer to suckle. She'll have to eat frequently for a good while yet. Don't get the wrong impression here—Lena didn't complain one bit, even though she's clearly reached the point of total exhaustion."

"Lena never complains." Steven said the words softly. Jane often pouted if she felt put upon, or she lamented little inconveniences. He'd needed to cajole her and placate her with tiny gifts and affection, but he'd figured it was a feminine trait. The realization that he'd made a comparison at all and his beloved wife hadn't been the victor sent pangs of guilt through him.

Doc adjusted his glasses. "You were smart to get Mrs. Swenson to stay in bed, and you are right to be concerned about how thin she's gotten. If she drops any more weight, she'll lose her milk. It's not that she's sick; it's like she's feeding twins, so she needs to eat like a field hand."

Steven groaned and thought of how Lena invariably ate every last morsel off of her plate. Jane always practiced perfect manners and left a few bites, so by comparison, he'd found Lena's manners wanting. Disgusted with himself, he realized aloud, "I've been starving her! Why didn't she say something?"

"I asked. The poor woman had to worry about having enough food on hand, so she never imagined anyone else had much more in the way of supplies. It didn't occur to her that you had more than what was put before her. Every single day has been a struggle for simple survival. On top of that, she's still suffering her own grief. The poor woman was already straining to keep her head above water. Taking on your daughter was the single most selfless act I've ever seen."

"We'll take care of her."

"She can still suckle the babies. In fact, if we take them away, she'll undoubtedly lose her milk in less than two days. Talitha still won't take a bottle, but she's thriving with Lena, so we need to safeguard them both. Food and rest—that's what she needs. Bible-reading time, too. Lena's one of those godly women who needs to nourish her soul to survive. It's undoubtedly what's gotten her through her trials."

"Whatever it takes, she'll have it. Thanks for coming by."

After Doc left, Steven trudged up the stairs. He'd considered Lena a sturdy farm girl until this morning. Wound up in his own sorrow, he'd failed to note how much of a strain he'd put on her. The doctor's words sobered him even more. He had to see her for himself. No noise came from the room, so he tapped lightly on the door.

Mrs. Axelrod opened it. She had Talitha over her shoulder and absently patted her to elicit a tiny burp. He glanced beyond them. Lena lay in bed, her braid once again unwoven so the tresses fanned out in a golden sunburst. Even in sleep, her expression was serene. Doc attributed that to her faith. Steven coveted the peace she had.

Steven stepped closer and intently studied the sleeping woman. Her hands were folded together under her chin as if she'd plummeted into sleep in the middle of a prayer. Deep crescents of fatigue shadowed her eyes. Her neck and hands were impossibly thin. The very thought of her toting buckets of water or chopping wood was completely ludicrous, yet he knew she had. The calluses on her hands were ample proof of that. For the first time, he was glad those were the hands that held and cared for his daughter.

Chapter 7

The morning sun cast a narrow strip of buttery light over the foot of the bed. Steven barely opened the door an inch and let out a sigh of relief. The room was quiet. Lena and the babes were sleeping. A plate had joined Lena's Bible and brush on the dresser. The crust of bread left there bore mute testimony to the fact that Lena had eaten the snack he'd ordered Mrs. Axelrod to take up each night. Steven gently fingered Talitha's blanket, then smoothed Johnny's cowlick down before he slipped away. He couldn't set out on a day's work unless he assured himself everyone was faring well.

He saw to a few matters around the ranch, then saddled up and headed for town. Folks murmured their condolences, and he accepted them grimly. Some of his old friends invited him to go into the Watering Hole and get rip-roaring drunk with them, but he exercised his self-control and refused. He had more pride and sense than that.

Watts' Mercantile sat between the bank and the diner. Hannah and Thaddeus Watts ran a fair place. They carried the necessities and offered them at a reasonable price.

Steven had always gotten his hardware, tools, and essentials here. The store smelled of pickle brine and lemon oil and brand-new leather goods. It always did, and the stability of that fact gave an odd comfort. Hannah stopped dusting off a shelf and gently rested her hand on his arm. "I'm sorry to hear of your loss. How are you and the baby doing?"

He cleared his throat and wished his eyes didn't feel like they had sand blown into them. "I—um, I have Mrs. Swenson there with the baby for the time being."

Hannah's face brightened. "There's a nice arrangement. With Mrs. Axelrod getting on a bit in her years and that great big old house to mind, she simply can't keep up with a baby. Waking up every couple of hours and having to warm bottles would wear her to a frazzle. Lena's young, strong, and has a real sweet way about her. You made a good choice."

Her words about Mrs. Axelrod flummoxed him. Steven had somehow assumed the housekeeper would take on the mothering responsibilities until Talitha reached her schooling years and needed a governess. Now that he pondered on it a moment, cooking, laundry, and cleaning kept Mrs. Axelrod busy morning 'til night. Chasing after a toddler would pose an undue burden on her. As soon as Lena weaned Talitha, he'd need to hire a nanny. Unthinkingly, he asked, "When do women wean their babes?"

Hannah blushed brightly. She dipped her head and murmured, "It's different with each baby."

He shared her embarrassment. Rattled, he blurted out, "I didn't know. Johnny is eight months, so I knew it was at least that long. Talitha is real tiny. She was too weak and small to take a bottle. She came early, you know, and I guess she might, um, need longer. . . ." His head dropped back, and he grimaced. Staring at the ceiling, he muttered, "Ma'am, could you do me the great kindness of forgetting this conversation?"

He could feel her lean closer. She whispered, "Mr. Halpern, am I to understand Lena Swenson isn't just minding your baby? That she's wet-nursing her?"

Steven straightened up and rubbed the back of his neck. He stared intently at the woman and wordlessly nodded. *I hope she doesn't gossip this all over the township!*

"Oh," she said in a tiny voice. "Women did that back in Bible times. Poor child! Is she improving at all?"

Paternal pride surged. "She's still a bitty thing, but she's not twig thin anymore. She's holding her head up, too."

Hannah beamed, "How wonderful!"

"Yes, ma'am, it is. I count it close to a miracle. She was so sickly at first, Doc wasn't sure she'd pull through. I owe it all to the very special care she's been given."

She winked. "It'll be our little secret."

He let out a relieved sigh. "Thank you. I appreciate it." Steven paused a moment, then lowered his voice even more. "Mrs. Watts, ma'am, truth is, I need to rely on your discretion on another issue, too."

"I assure you, I will hold your confidence." She hastily added, "Save for the fact that I do not keep anything from my husband."

Her addendum was so charmingly honest, it reassured him. Steven leaned a hip against the counter and silently handed her a slip of paper. It was too embarrassing to speak the need aloud, but Lena's clothes were ready for the ragbag, and she used a shawl because she had no robe. He hadn't noticed that last fact until Mrs. Axelrod said something right before he left this morning.

While he waited, Steven selected a few of the smallest baby gowns for Talitha and tossed a pair of the larger ones on the stack for Johnny. His mouth quirked upward. Johnny was an active little guy. A man would be pleased to have a strong son like that to leave his land to. As soon as the thought crossed his mind, he went somber. He'd secretly hoped for a son, and now he'd never have one. He couldn't imagine ever marrying another woman. He'd never be fair to her because he'd cherished Jane, and no other woman could possibly measure up.

"I think we're ready," Mrs. Watts called to him. The bell over the door jangled as she set a small stack of clothing on the counter. "Will there be anything else?"

Steven silently added the baby things and waited for her to wrap it all. He turned and saw two women gossiping furiously behind their hands. One pointed to the counter, and he realized they were gawking at the things he'd bought for Lena.

☙♡❧

Lena's cheeks scorched with color when Mrs. Axelrod dumped the contents of the package on the kitchen table. She gave Steven a horrified look. "Mr. Halpern, how could you do this? I cannot accept such fine things!"

"Those gowns cost only two dollars apiece! That's as common as can be." He scowled at the dress she was wearing. "Clearly, you need them."

She shook her head. "I am sorry, Mr. Halpern, that you are ashamed of me. I cannot change who I am or what I own. I do not have two dollars to buy a fine lady's church dress to wear so I can go home to clean the chicken coop and muck the stall."

He stared at her in utter silence. Finally he said, "Lena, I'm not ashamed of you."

"Yes, you are. You had a wife who had soft clothes and softer hands. I never met her, but I am sure you bought her many beautiful two-dollar gowns. I can see how much you cherished her and that you gave her many things. That was lovely, and she was blessed."

"But—"

"But I am a plain woman. My hands get dirty. Even when Lars was alive, we could not afford such luxuries. I did not pine for them. He chose the feed sacks with care because he loved to see me wear blue, and each time I wore my dress, he told with his eyes and words he was glad I was his wife." She gave Steven a bittersweet smile. "Fancy and expensive things do not suit me. Feed sacks are good enough. I do not need a two-dollar dress to be a happy woman."

He fixed his gaze on her and said slowly, "No, Lena, you don't. I can see you're a woman who finds contentment easily." He then turned to Mrs. Axelrod and silently pled for her to make the poor widow accept his paltry gift.

Mrs. Axelrod obliged. She held up the robe and declared briskly, "Now that we've established that you're not a gold digger, let's face reality. You certainly do need this."

Lena doggedly declared, "My shawl is enough."

Steven bristled. "Woman! Stubbornness better not be a trait passed on in milk, because if it is, Talitha is going to be a handful. Now stop acting so prideful and carry those things up to your chamber!"

Talitha started to cry. Lena lifted a shaking hand to her forehead as if she had a terrible headache. "Please take all of it back. I refuse to wear it and do not want to argue any longer. I need to change and feed the children." Steven realized he'd shouted his last words at her. Her muted response was far more civilized than he'd deserved.

He'd have never let anyone bellow at Jane like that. The woman was stubborn as an old mule and unreasoning as any member of her fair sex. Still, he needed to be careful not to upset her. "Sit down, Lena. Mrs. Axelrod, fix her some chow." He scooped up the clothes and headed for the stairs. "I'll take these things up for you. I'm sure you'll change your mind."

☙♡❧

Much later that evening Lena sought him out. "Could I please have a moment?"

"Sure."

She stared up at him, her eyes glistening. "Mr. Halpern, the sun has set."

Her comment seemed ludicrous. "Of course it has."

The corner of her mouth lifted into a wobbly, winsome smile. "The Bible says not to let the sun go down on your anger. I spoke angry words to you. They were honest ones, but I did not temper them as I should have. I know you are hurting in your heart these days, yet you tried to be generous. Please forgive me."

"You're making a barn out of a berry box, Lena.
Forget it. I raised my voice, and you got a bit huffy. It's
nothing. Just accept the clothes as an expression of my
thanks and go to bed."

᧖♡᧖

Steven knew he'd made a grave miscalculation early the
next morning. Lena's reaction should have warned him,
but he'd been too preoccupied to take the hint. The impact of his actions hit full force when Jane's parents arrived on his doorstep. Amabelle Maxwell swept past him
and looked about. "Why didn't your housekeeper answer
the door?"

Steven shut the door after Harold Maxwell entered.
He swept a hand toward the parlor. "Come on in. Our
neighbor's health took a bad turn yesterday, so Mrs. Axelrod went over to help."

The Maxwells didn't bother to go into the parlor.
They exchanged a wary look. Amabelle's tone went icy,
"Are you telling us you were here, alone, all night with
that woman?"

Harold Maxwell didn't even give Steven a chance
to answer. He raged, "Even with the gossip in town, we
thought to give you a chance. I can see now what they
were saying is true. Where there's smoke, there's fire." He
grabbed his wife's elbow and started tugging her out the
door. "Come, Amabelle."

Amabelle's eyes flooded with tears. "You lecher! Our
dear Jane, just buried, and you're already carrying on!"

"Now wait just a minute!" Steven gritted.

"We're not listening to any of your lies or excuses."

230

Mr. Maxwell pulled his wife outside and stormed, "You can bet we'll take legal measures to get custody of our granddaughter. We won't let you taint her with your wicked example!"

Chapter 8

L ena, we need to talk."

His heightened color and angry tone made her suck in a deep breath. Lena quietly took a seat and waited for him to speak. *What did I do wrong? Why is he so mad?*

"Jane's parents have petitioned to get Talitha." His eyes blazed as he bit out the words.

"No!"

"Oh, yes," he said bitterly. "Her daddy is a retired congressman, and he has some powerful connections. That wily old coot got the whole deal figured out. According to him, I'm an unfit father, so they should rear Talitha."

Lena shook her head. "That makes no sense. It is untrue. You are a good father."

"Oh, they're twisting things around. I'm afraid you're getting dragged into it, and it's dirty."

"Me? How can this be?"

His fist hammered a single, livid blow on the desktop. "The night Mrs. Axelrod went to help Mrs. Brown. They are casting aspersions about you and me being alone here."

Lena felt heat fill her cheeks. "This is silly. I will tell them I only feed Talitha. You and I—we never. . ."

"They won't listen to reason. They've publicly questioned our morals, and half the town is gossiping about how I bought you a robe. A stupid robe!"

"I am sorry. I do not want them to take Talitha from you." She stood. "I will pack and leave right away."

He wearily rubbed his hand down his face a single time. "Sit down, Lena." She complied, and he continued on in a haggard voice, "I don't have much choice. I went to town and talked to Judge Perkins. He said they have grounds for action, and I have call to be concerned. According to him, the only way to solve this is for us to marry." He looked at her and added somberly, "So I'm begging, Lena. Marry me."

His proposal stunned her. Lena couldn't form any coherent words. She silently shook her head.

He came around and towered over her. "I lost my wife. I can't bear to lose my daughter, too. I won't pretend, Lena. I don't love you. I never will. My heart is buried out there with Jane. I won't even lie when we have the judge hitch us. I'll vow to honor and protect and provide for you. You just tell me what you want." His hands fisted. "I'll do whatever you want, buy you anything your heart desires—but you have to marry me so I can keep my baby girl."

Lena's heart twisted. She wet her lips, but before she could utter a word, he blurted, "If you're worrying about your son, you have my word that I'll treat Johnny like my own. When he's a man, he'll get a full share of the ranch just like our other sons. I'll hire a sharecropper if you want to keep the farm going so he can have his father's legacy, too."

The distress on her features cut him to the core. Desperation made him push harder, "Lena, you've been good to Talitha. I know you love her. You do, don't you?" He already knew the answer, but she was honest enough to bob her head in confirmation. "This way, she'll be your daughter, too. You won't ever lose her, either. This way, we can both keep her."

The mantle clock struck the hour. Silence hovered heavily in the room. "I will have to pray about this."

"Pray? Woman, you won't ever be safe living alone. Men will think you're my cast-off mistress. For your sake, and your son's, you don't have any more choice than I do."

Lena slowly rose. Her knees shook so badly, they barely held her up. "I will pray and give you an answer later."

🖉♡🖉

She went to her bedchamber and prayed earnestly. As a clock struck eleven that night, she found Steven out on the verandah. Her voice was subdued as she quietly said, "I will marry you. Thank you for promising to be good to my son."

"You don't have any reason to thank me, Lena. I should have been on my knees, thanking you every day for saving my daughter's life and helping me keep her. Whatever I do for you, it'll never repay you for that. I'll send for Judge Perkins. We'll get married tomorrow." He turned away, went down the steps, and disappeared into the night.

Lena stood there and listened as the sound of his boots on the stairs grew quieter. Doing God's will had never been harder. Over the weeks, she hadn't just fallen in love with Talitha—she'd also come to care very deeply for

Steven. The terrible truth was, tomorrow she'd pledge her hand to a man who could never love her back.

ꗈ♡ꗇ

The next afternoon, Steven stood in the doorway and watched Lena stab one last pin into her freshly combed hair.

"That dress looks nice on you," he said in a gravelly voice.

She whirled around in surprise, then recovered. "A dress so beautiful would make a pig look like a princess."

He continued to stare at her. She wore one of the ordinary, two-buck dresses he'd bought that had gotten them into this fix. It was plain as could be, yet she acted as if a modiste in New York custom-made it for her. She looked like it, too. It wasn't the gown—it was the woman inside it. For the first time, instead of looking common, she looked elegant and refined. His wealth would provide every comfort for her—yet he knew full well she'd been content living in her soddy with Lars. *Because Lars loved her.* Steven knew then that she'd been much better off back then. This was different. Steven asked everything of her, and she'd consented. He did it for Talitha, but he wasn't proud of himself. Lena was a beautiful, warm-hearted woman. She deserved a husband who would love her. Still, she'd accepted his deal, and he was going to hurry her through the ceremony before she changed her mind. "If you're ready, let's go."

Instead of coming directly to him, Lena went to the cradle and lifted Johnny into her arms. "We're ready."

Pale and composed, she stood beside him in the parlor. Steven had summoned the judge to the house instead of

235

standing in the church before Preacher Durley. There were no friends or flowers. He wanted no reminders of what things had been like when he and Jane pledged their ever-lasting love. Instead of holding his hands for the ceremony, Lena held her son. It was just as well. Mrs. Axelrod stood off to the side and held Talitha. His daughter's nearness gave him strength to get through this sham.

When it came time, Lena took the traditional wifely vows to love and obey. Her voice shook, but she said them. He, on the other hand, had spoken with Judge Perkins and arranged for substitute words. Lena's arms tightened around Johnny's little body, and her gaze dropped as Steven vowed only to provide and protect. Once again, he knew he was cheating her, and he silently promised he'd provide her with all he could to make up for it. When she looked back up at him, her beautiful eyes swam with tears.

The judge sensed he'd best not push his luck and suggest a kiss to seal the deal. Instead, he cleared his throat. "Well, that's that. For what it's worth, I think what you did was right. Those youngsters need two parents. I'll stop off on the way home and make sure Jane's folks know Talitha isn't up for grabs anymore."

❧♥❧

Winter was mild. Steven spent most of his time outdoors. When he came in, he made every effort to be cordial to Lena. She saw to the children lovingly, and he found his only happiness in their presence. Johnny crawled about and began to walk by Christmas. Tucked in the corner of the sofa with the support of pillows or held in Lena's arms, Talitha cooed at Johnny's antics. When Steven shucked off his boots and Johnny tried to put them on, he laughed for the first time since Jane died.

Johnny weaned himself and took great glee in spilling his cup down the front of himself. Talitha still nursed, but she'd grown big enough to wake Lena only once or twice a night. Claiming she was well rested, Lena took over more of the household chores.

Out of deference for Lena's feelings, Steven took the tintype of his beloved Jane off the dresser in their bedchamber and put it on a shelf in his den. He couldn't bring himself to hide it away. He walked a tightrope between remembering the love he once had and trying to respect his new bride. Lena never spoke of his struggle, and she never mentioned Lars. It was as if they'd made a pact of silence.

He wordlessly unplaited her hair before they retired and temporarily lost his sadness in the tenderness she gave. In the dark of night, he still knew it was Lena, not Jane; but she was his wife now, and he let his barriers down in those private moments.

Once, she whispered her love in the aftermath of their intimacy. He pressed his fingers to her soft lips and shook his head. "No, Lena. Don't. We care about each other and for each other. That has to be enough. I have nothing else to give you." She'd compressed her lips, grazed his cheek with her fingertips, and turned away. In the light of day, they never acknowledged the fragile bond they shared. Even if he could not cherish her, he hoped she drew strength and comfort from him.

Lena knitted a woolen scarf for him for the winter, and each time he went out, she wrapped it about his neck. She got up early each morning to boil water just so he'd have warm water for shaving. She expertly mended his leather gloves and sewed clothes for the children. He knew she'd accepted her place—and that bothered him even more than if she'd railed against him for cornering her into a loveless marriage. Quietly, she cared not just for the children, but him, too. He didn't deserve it. . .but when he urged her to stay abed or sit and rest, she'd still carry on with the little things that she thought a wife should do. He saw emotions in her eyes that he wanted to ignore—the caring, the need for affection, the sadness; yet Steven also saw the hickory toughness in her, and he hoped time would allow her to adjust to their bargain.

One night, he watched Lena finish knotting off a length of thread. She'd kept her head bowed over whatever it was she'd been working on for the past several evenings. "What is that?"

Lena gave him a winsome smile. She held up a charmingly embroidered rag doll. "I thought Talitha needed one of these."

Steven thought of the dolls at the mercantile. They were fragile porcelain. When Talitha got much older, one of those dolls would be a cherished toy; but for a tiny girl who'd drag the doll about and abuse it, a soft, cuddly homemade cloth doll was far more practical. He smiled. "That's mighty kind of you, Lena. Little Talitha'll probably love the stuffing right out of it."

"I hope so." She set it aside and picked up a piece of muslin and started stitching it.

Her hands were never still unless they held her precious Bible. She read aloud to the babies every evening. It seemed silly at first, but soon, Steven made excuses to be present for those stories. Something about that Bible time eased a bit of the ache in his heart. One night, when he'd been out with an ailing cow, he came in and caught Lena's quiet voice. He stood in the hallway outside the parlor door. Something held him back from going into the room. He heard her close the Bible.

"So he loved Rachel with all his heart, yet he was married to Leah. Leah tried to be a good wife to him. The very best she could. She gave him many sons, too, but he never grew to love her."

It wasn't just the words. Lena's voice carried a distress he'd rarely heard. Steven quietly tiptoed away before she discovered he'd eavesdropped. Bad enough he'd trapped her into a loveless marriage and cheated her out of all a woman deserved. He could at least let her keep her dignity. He owed her that much.

For Christmas, he ordered new clothes and a beautiful brooch from a catalog for Lena. Lena thanked him sweetly and wore them with grace, but he realized she'd been just as queenly in her ragged feedsack calico.

She hadn't pitched her old gowns into the ragbag, either. One afternoon, he rode in after a few days out on the range to find Lena in her old gown, conscientiously walking one of his mares. "She got colicky. Mark was worried."

Steven took over. "Why didn't Mark walk her?"

Lena gave him a puzzled look. "I am able. Mark is needed for other things." She walked beside him for a while. He finally rested his hand on her shoulder and asked, "Lena, how can you be so calm and have a peaceful heart? You've kept on going in spite of everything."

He stiffened when she slid her arm about his waist,

but the horse still needed to stay in motion, so they paced along. Lena quietly said, "If I kept shaking my fist at God, how could I ask Him to hold my hand and lead me on?"

Her words stunned him. He said nothing, and she didn't seem to expect a reply. They continued walking in total silence, then she gave him a light squeeze. "I'll see you at supper."

"Fine."

"And Steven?" She let go and gave him a tender smile. "It is not easy, but you are not alone. God wants to comfort you and lead you on. Just as you want only good things for our children, God wants good things for you. Think on that."

Chapter 9

Spring passed, and summer scorched the land. Since winter had been mild, the water table was low. Heat shimmered on the land. Prairie grasses were dangerously dry. Steven worried over having sufficient water for the stock; Lena fretted over saving every last drop for her garden.

Johnny ran about and had taken to calling Steven "Daddy." Talitha now crawled and mouthed a few sounds. She had a specific one for Lena, "Mamama." They'd become a family, simply by virtue of the love they shared for the children. Though she hadn't given birth to Talitha, Lena knew the little girl was truly her own daughter. She also knew Steven thoroughly loved her son. Even if he didn't love her, she couldn't help loving him. He'd kept his vows and provided well. He'd given her the protection of his name. He didn't flaunt his wealth, but he was generous to a fault. His spiritual struggle hadn't grown any easier, so she faithfully placed him in God's keeping.

Late one morning, Lena glanced out the window and narrowed her eyes. The heat of the day was already brutal, and she'd started to pull the curtains to keep out the harsh sunlight, but an ugly gray-black on the horizon captured her attention. Mrs. Axelrod had gone to her sister's for a few days, so Lena was alone with the kids. Her mouth went dry. She had no help, and she knew what that darkness meant: *Fire.*

Both children were napping. She ran to the barn and hitched the wagon herself. Quickly, she drove it right to the verandah steps. With a glance over her shoulder, she checked the progress of the prairie fire. Lena knew she had precious little time. She pulled the drawer from Steven's desk that held all of his bookkeeping for the ranch. She put it in the wagon along with his moneybox, then ran upstairs. In a matter of moments, she dumped the children's clothing on quilts, tied the corners, and threw the bundles down the stairs. In her haste, she made one more bundle and included her Bible, then grabbed both children from their cribs and raced outside. Praying ardently, she put the children in the wagon, climbed in, and set the wagon careening for safety.

༄♡༄

"Fire!"

Steven squinted and caught his breath. Prairie fires moved lightning fast, and this one was no exception. He raced for his horse, vaulted into the saddle, and headed for home. Lena and the children were alone. *Dear God, keep them safe!* he prayed.

Every hoofbeat, every heartbeat drummed home his worry. Cattle stampeded and every beast of the prairie bolted in panic. Animals knew to run, but would Lena? Even if she realized the danger, she'd never be able to handle the children. Big as they'd grown, she couldn't carry them both. How could she possibly get away? The wind shifted and picked up. It swept embers and flames directly toward his home. Steven knew the creek lay in the path of the fire, but it wasn't wide enough to stop the flames. *God, please, please at least let it buy me a few more minutes to get to them!*

He coughed from the acrid smoke, leaned closer to his horse, and urged it on. His family needed him. Nothing else mattered—not the cattle, not the barn or house or machinery. Danger roared toward his wife and sweet babies. They must be so very afraid. . . .

Terror and relief mingled as he reached the edge of his yard. Steven rode straight up to the house and tied his antsy mount to the kitchen railing. "Lena! Lena!"

He burst through the kitchen and into the hallway. "Lena!"

No one answered. He hastily searched the house, yelling; but when he found the cribs rumpled and empty, he knew she'd taken the babies and fled. Steven ran back to his horse and spied the wagon tracks in the dirt out in front of the house. He followed them.

"Lena!" He called, but she didn't hear him. He watched as she veered off the road because the wind had shifted yet again. She'd exercised common sense and instinct to plot a course to safety. Steven closed the distance between them and jumped from his gelding onto the wagon seat, then took the reins from her. She let out a cry of gladness, then scrambled into the back to hold tightly to the children. He drove the wagon over the bridge and finally pulled it to a stop in a safe place on the other side of the river. Once he set the brake, he twisted around. "Are you all right?"

Lena gave him a quick nod. Both children clung to her. He didn't blame them in the least. He felt a mite shaky himself. He joined them in the wagon bed and pulled all three of them into his arms. "Jesus, thank You for keeping them safe!"

"He did keep us. I prayed, too," Lena whispered into his smoky shirt. "He took care of all of us."

For a while, no one moved. They all huddled together in a knot. When Talitha started to fuss, Steven scooted to the side a bit. Lena lifted her and crooned softly. Something stabbed Steven in the hip. "What is this?"

Lena wouldn't meet his eyes. "I didn't have much time. I couldn't save much. Clothes, guns, your books and moneybox."

Essentials. Lena had been so very practical. He could scarcely credit that she'd hitched the wagon and made an escape at all—but she'd even had the foresight to grab a few of the most basic things. His respect for her mushroomed. . .until he bumped a quilt and his desk drawer came into view. She'd not only brought his books—Lena had grabbed the tintype of Jane he treasured.

Steven stared at it and looked back at her. She turned away and busied herself by giving Talitha the rag dolly to gnaw on. "Lena, why? Of everything in the house, why did you save this?"

She shrugged, but from the tension singing through her body, he knew the gesture was not a casual one. "You love her. It was a little thing, but I knew you and Talitha would want it."

He cupped her chin and lifted her face. "Lena, I loved Jane. She was the wife of my youth." Pain streaked across her features. He hastened to add, "Young men grow up, Lena. Today I discovered I've been in love with you for a long while."

She pulled away and dumbly shook her head.

"No, Lena. Please hear me out. I don't need a decorative little woman. I need a wife. I need a helpmeet, a partner in life. You are that woman. Jane wouldn't have left the house. She'd have sat in the parlor and wrung her hands. She'd have collected her pretty clothes and treasures and waited there. You are wise and capable. You acted and saved the children and yourself. Things can be replaced; a family cannot. You'll never know the terror I endured trying to reach you."

He raked his hand through his hair and continued on. "Now I know the truth. God was never far from me. Even when He took Jane, He was good enough to provide you so we could carry on. In my ignorance, I raged at Him; but He never abandoned me, and He gave you and Johnny to me as a gift. In my times of sorrow and strife, God blessed me with a woman and two babies to love. He was never far away, Lena. He was faithful, and He was there."

"Yes, He was," she agreed.

The reserve in her voice tore at him. Steven knew why it was there. He got to his knees and settled his hands on her shoulders. Gently, he ran his thumbs up the beating pulse in her neck and lifted her chin. "I was a fool, Lena. I let you feel like Leah, an unwanted wife. Hear me now: You aren't Leah; you're like Ruth. She was a widow, too. God gave her to a man she barely knew, but they found grace and love. Let me be that kind of husband to you. Believe me, Sweetheart. I couldn't say it months ago because I refused to lie—now, I say it freely: I love you."

For weeks, he'd ignored the lovelight in her eyes, and she'd finally banked it. She went about, filling their home with her special warmth and tenderness; but he caught the quiet hurt in her eyes and carried terrible guilt in knowing he put it there. Even now, wariness painted her features.

"Lena, you once said every need gave God an opportunity to provide and bless us. You didn't tell me the other part."

"What other part?" The words barely whispered between her lips.

"With every sorrow, God takes the opportunity to comfort and draw us close to Him. He did that through you, Lena. God used you to console me and teach me to risk loving again. That lesson came hard. It cost you every bit as much as it cost me. Please, Sweetheart—let's both be whole again and of one accord as He wants us to be."

Tears sparkled in her eyes. "Is this what you truly want, Steven?"

"With all my heart."

He'd just finished kissing her soundly when Mark rode up. He was covered in soot. "Glad to see your family's fine, Boss, but the rest of the news ain't good." He grimaced. "Your place burned flat to the ground."

Steven cradled Lena close. "I have all I need, and God will provide."

Epilogue

From the ashes of their ranch house, Steven and Lena worked together to rebuild a home. During those months, their love blossomed and Steven found the serenity he'd been lacking. They filled the rooms of their new home with laughter and soon gave Johnny and Talitha a baby brother.

"He's a hefty little man," Steven said as he admired his newborn son. He tenderly tucked a damp curl behind Lena's ear. "I can only pray this one is half as smart and strong as our Johnny-boy."

"*Ja*, that would be a blessing." Lena gave him a weary smile.

Warmth filled his soul. Steven knew the Lord had blessed them with a deep and abiding love. God had been faithful.

Cathy Marie Hake

Cathy Marie is a Southern California native who loves her work as a nurse and Lamaze teacher. She and her husband have a daughter, a son, and a dog, so life is never dull or quiet. Cathy Marie considers herself a sentimental packrat, collecting antiques and Hummel figurines. She otherwise keeps busy with reading, writing, baking, and being a prayer warrior. "I am easily distracted during prayer, so I devote certain tasks and chores to specific requests or persons so I can keep faithful in my prayer life."

Cathy Marie's first book sale was published by **Heartsong Presents** in 2000.

Returning Amanda

by Kathleen Paul

Chapter 1

Sheriff Jake Moore carefully rolled the week-old St. Louis paper into a tight baton. He eased his shoulders away from the wooden slats of his office chair and swung his paper bat down against the heavy desk. Whack!

"Forty-three," he said, satisfied.

He flicked the fly carcass onto the floor, propped his boot heels back on the desktop, and unrolled the paper. Scanning the page, he found the article he'd been reading. Fool paper said those mechanical carriages would one day take over private transportation.

"Humph," grunted the sheriff. A scowl momentarily brought thick brown eyebrows down over his hazel eyes.

Jake picked up the bandana lying over his lap and made another swipe across his face, wiping sweat from his strong, squared jaw. A bristly stubble darkened his chin.

When had he shaved? About seven that morning. The four o'clock eastbound hadn't even blown its whistle at the crossing yet, and here his face already felt like sandpaper. Fortunately, the Wednesday night church social didn't require him to spruce up. If it were a town meeting, he'd make the effort, but not for the ladies of the church. It wasn't as if there was someone there that he wanted to impress. He'd go for the good eats, and maybe he'd corner Elder Kotchkis and get him going on predestination. Kotchkis was always open for a good debate.

Jake ran his hand over the stubble he did not intend to shave. It'd be better, he decided, if all those women thought the sheriff was too unkempt to take home for keeps. He was tired of being viewed as potential husband material for every single female in the county. How was it that this town had so many widows and unmarried gals anyway? He'd made it twenty-six years without a female's coddling, he could make it a few more.

A fly buzzed around his head, and Sheriff Moore watched it as he once again rolled the St. Louis paper into a weapon. His lean frame tensed as the fly landed on the Kansas map hanging on the wall behind him. It would be a stretch, but he had long arms to match his angular, tall body. Jake tipped his chair back another inch, pressed his lips together in concentration, and slowed his breathing. Waiting for just the right moment, he struck. *Whack!*

The chair slipped off the two back legs. Jake crashed to the floor.

"Ouch!"

He rolled out of his sturdy throne, feeling just exactly where the wooden arm had refused to flatten under the small of his back. He rubbed the spot with a strong hand. A small black speck lay a foot from his elbow.

"Forty-four," he muttered.

A soft knock sounded from the front door of the jailhouse.

Jake wrinkled his brow. Nobody knocked at his door—they just came tromping in with all sorts of complaints and problems. Twenty-eight dollars and fifty cents, plus room and board at Maggie's, paid Sheriff Jake Moore to worry about the citizens of Lawrence, Kansas, and their difficulties.

The knock sounded politely again.

Jake unwound himself, placed his hands on the edge of his desk, and raised up to see what matter of business had intruded on his formerly peaceful afternoon.

He looked out and saw no one, then his gaze drifted down from where he had expected to see a face. A small girl stood on the boardwalk porch just outside his door. Corn silk hair in tight curls billowed out of the bonnet topping the pudgy, frowning face. The bonnet matched the blue dress covered with tiny yellow flowers and petite green vines. She carried a doll under her arm and a small square basket by its handle.

"Are you the sheriff?" she asked. Her scowl lightened to a small smile as she took in the image of the man behind the desk.

"Yes, ma'am." Jake stood and righted his chair. He looked over the diminutive figure in his door. Her clothes looked expensive. Her speech was refined. Her face held an expression of intelligence. In a few years she'd be breaking hearts. Now, she looked hot and tired. Jake didn't recognize her as one of the town children.

He sighed, relieved that his visitor wasn't one of the older girls in town, one of the pesky females dogging his bachelor steps. Whoever this was, she most likely wouldn't carry the tale of his falling out of his office chair to wagging tongues.

"What can I do for you?" he asked the small stranger.

"I've come to report a robbery." Her hard black buttoned-up shoes tapped on the wooden floor as she stepped into the room and crossed to stand in front of his desk. Her smile wavered, and her forehead creased with worry. The proud little chin quivered slightly. She blinked deep chocolate eyes hard, pushing back tears.

Where did this filly come from? Jake took pity on the little mite. He pulled up the only other chair in the room and offered it to his guest.

"I don't believe I know you," said Jake.

She put down the basket to climb into the chair. With her knee in the oversized seat, she hoisted her chubby body up and twisted her backside into place. Plump legs encased in white stockings stuck straight out in front of her. She smoothed her skirts around them. She looked kind of cute in all her finery.

"I'm Sheriff Moore," Jake said. He winked at her, the way he did the small girls at church. He didn't mind flirting with the little ones. It was the bigger ones, the ones who dreamed about marriage. Them he avoided.

"I'm Amanda Greer of St. Louis, Missouri." She supplied the information with crisp, polite formality.

"And, you've had some property stolen?" Jake sat down in his chair, steepled his fingers, and leaned his elbows on the table. One tender elbow told him he must have slammed it on the way down. He leaned back.

The little face scrunched into a frown again.

"Not prop-er-ty," she said.

Jake suppressed a smile. With all her self-assurance, he found it humorous to see her puzzle over the unfamiliar word.

"Can you tell me what was stolen?"

Her lips snapped into an angry line, and she scowled at him.

Whoa, thought Jake, *she's got a temper.*

"Of course, I can," she answered smartly. But the flare of temper fizzled. The fierce pride on the chubby face melted. The little mouth softened, and the chin quivered. The dark eyes batted. Amanda Greer took a deep breath and let it out with the merest suggestion of a sob. She pursed her lips, breathed again, and spoke hurriedly, getting the two words out as quickly as possible.

"My sister."

Jake sat up and leaned forward.

"Where are your parents?" he asked.

"In New York City, New York." Her head bobbed as she said the words, and the profusion of golden curls bounced.

"Do you know who took your sister? Did you see it happen?"

She nodded, the curls again springing into action.

"Who?" he asked.

Tears pooled in the soulful eyes and spilled down her cheeks.

"The train." The words came out in a whimper, and Jake thought for a moment he must have misunderstood.

"The train?" Then it dawned on him—Amanda had been left behind when the train had pulled out of the station. She and her sister must've been traveling west together.

The curls bounced again. Amanda Greer pulled the doll into a tight embrace and buried her face in its cloth head. Jake froze, immobilized by the muffled wails punctuated with loud sniffs. The chubby little blond with an extra helping of dignity rocked back and forth with her dolly, her abject misery piercing the heart of one confirmed bachelor.

"Now, don't cry," Jake said, desperation shaking his usually solid baritone. "Your sister will realize that you've been left behind, and she'll probably get off at the next stop and come right back for you." He abruptly stood and paced to the door, away from the distressed child. He looked out at the dusty street, squinting into the glare.

Henry Bladcomb swept the stoop before his jewelry shop. Gladys Sence gabbed with Miriam Halley in front of the mercantile. The Jones kids laid ambush to the Whitcombs beside the livery. Was there any help for him among these fine citizens of Lawrence?

Jake looked on up the street to the station. A pile of luggage blocked his view of the telegraph office.

"Miss Amanda," said the sheriff, swiveling back to his weeping visitor, "we'll go right now to the telegraph office and send a telegram. That's what we'll do. That telegram will be waiting for your sister when they make the stop at Big Springs."

Jake jammed his hat on his head and grabbed the little girl's square basket.

"Come on, now," he urged. "Let's do something about this predicament. No use crying when we can do something."

Amanda bravely lifted her head, sniffing loudly. She delved into a side pocket of her dress and pulled out a white hankie edged in elegant green crochet. With a honk that certainly didn't fit her diminutive size, she blew her nose. Replacing the hankie, she gathered up her doll and hopped out of the chair.

"Sheriff?" she asked, tilting up her chin to look him in the eye. "I'm tired."

Jake didn't quite know how to talk to a yard-high person. He crouched down, almost sitting on his heels. The tears had left tracks on her cheeks. Her little shoulders sagged, and all the sparkle had washed out of her eyes.

"Let's go out to the pump and wash your face before we go," he suggested.

Amanda reached out a small hand and took his large callused one.

♋♡♌

How he came to be carrying the mite, he didn't know. But, there he was walking down Main Street with a chubby bundle of feminine sweetness. Not only did she ride in his arms, but she'd put her head down on his shoulder, and her soft breath tickled his neck.

Jake kept his eyes trained on his destination, giving only curt nods to those who tried to speak to him.

"Hello, Samuel," he said as soon as he reached the telegrapher's open window.

Samuel jumped. The balding man ruffled like a hen at the interruption. He scooted his small frame around on his wooden stool and lowered his glasses from where they rested over the top of his head to their proper position on his nose.

"Sheriff," he clucked, "you startled me. Need to send a telegram?"

"Yes, Samuel." Sheriff Moore nodded at the child

relaxed against his shoulder. "This is Amanda Greer. She was accidentally left when the westbound went through."

"Oh," said Samuel, alarmed. "I'll have to get the station master. Oh, he's not going to like this. Left, you say." Samuel tutted, starting up from his chair.

"Wait, Samuel," ordered Jake. "Before you go get Blake, send off the telegram. We may be able to catch the girl's sister at Big Springs."

Samuel plopped back down on his chair, shaking his head.

"Oh no, I don't think so," he muttered. "No, no, it's too late."

"Too late?" asked Jake. He tried to shift the dead weight in his arms and was rewarded with a delicate snore in his ear. He set the square basket on the wide sill that served as a counter and leaned against the frame with the shoulder that did not hold the sleeping beauty.

"Samuel, I need to find Miss Amanda's sister."

"Yes, yes, of course," agreed the telegrapher, pushing his glasses back up a fraction of an inch. "But, don't you see that the westbound went through around noon. That was almost four hours ago. The eastbound is due any minute. The westbound passed Big Springs, made Topeka, had a layover, and has left already for San Francisco."

"Samuel," Jake ground out the name, "wire Big Springs and see if a Miss Greer got off the train there and is taking the eastbound back."

"Yes, sir." Samuel turned back to his apparatus.

Just then the eastbound blew her whistle at the outskirts of town. Sheriff Moore abandoned Samuel and crossed the wooden platform. Maybe the telegram would be unnecessary. He peered anxiously down the tracks. A cloud of smoke puffed over the trees just before the four o'clock rounded the bend. It came huffing and hissing to a stop at the station.

A conductor jumped down and placed a step beside the metal stairs at the end of a passenger car. Jake held his breath. The conductor doffed his hat and offered a gloved hand to a matron as she negotiated the descent. A sprightly young lady with golden hair caught up under a wide-brimmed hat came next. Jake started forward, but a clean-shaven man hopped off behind her and, with a possessive air, tucked her hand in the crook of his arm, escorting her to claim their luggage.

Harold Smithridge got off. Jake hadn't known the banker was out of town. Two young men who Jake assumed were students at the University of Kansas hopped off and strutted toward town. Orville and Margaret Cullen got off, back from visiting their grandchildren. A man with all the earmarks of an elixir peddler got off, carrying a big black case. Jake hoped whatever he was selling wouldn't make people sick. The peddler was the last passenger off. Jake waited a moment, watching until he was satisfied Amanda Greer's sister was not on the train.

Discouraged and still carrying his increasingly heavy burden, Jake returned to Samuel's window.

"Oh my, oh my, broken foot," said Samuel, wagging his head from side to side.

Jake pinned him with an impatient look and waited for the man to clarify his statement.

"Miss Greer got off at Big Springs in a panic about her sister and broke her foot. Dear, dear, oh my! Doctor says she can't travel for a week. A week! Mr. Blake says to put the little girl on the westbound tomorrow, no charge. Can you imagine, no charge from Mr. Blake?"

"What am I supposed to do with her tonight?" asked Jake, more to himself than the distraught Samuel.

"Can't put her in jail, Sheriff." The man offered serious advice.

"I know that," snapped the sheriff.

"Better feed her and find some woman to take her in." Samuel nodded earnestly and his glasses slipped down on his nose.

Jake grinned, thinking of the church social and all those eager females.

"Thanks, Samuel," he said. "I'll do that."

Chapter 2

"A m I arrested?" Amanda's indignant question roused Jake from his paperwork. He studied the plump, disheveled figure sitting up on one of the padded cots in the first cell. The bonnet sat caddywumpus on her head. Maybe he should have taken it off of her when he laid her down.

"If you were arrested," Jake told her, "the door would be shut and locked."

"I'm hungry," she complained. She tugged at her bonnet, trying to straighten it.

"We're going to a church social tonight. There'll be lots of good food there."

"You said you'd get my sister back," she accused. Her hands left off fidgeting with the crooked bonnet and rested in her lap. She cast him a squinty-eyed glare with her lower lip stuck out to demonstrate her disapproval.

"She's waiting for you in Big Springs. You can get on the train tomorrow and join her."

"By myself?" she asked, obviously doubting him.

"The conductor will be sure you get there just fine."

She sat for a minute thinking this over. Jake watched

her anxiously. He didn't relish the idea of another bout of tears.

"All right," she said and kicked the towel off her legs. An hour and a half earlier, Jake had covered her with the only clean thing he could find. Amanda slid off the cot, gathered her doll and basket, and tapped across the floor in her ankle-high shoes. Maybe he should have taken those things off, too, when he laid her down. They looked mighty hot and uncomfortable.

The scorching summer afternoon had stilled into an oppressive swelter. Clouds gathered in the west. Rain would be welcome, as long as it came gently, good for the crops, not torrents to tear down the fields.

Amanda stood looking at him with solemn dark eyes.

"I have to go," she said.

"It's out back."

She stared at him.

"I'm not going with you," he said. "Go out that door." Jake pointed to the only door in sight. "Go around the building. You can't miss it." He looked back at the papers spread out on his desk, avoiding her eyes and hoping she'd go by herself. He heard the distinctive tapping of those awful shoes and breathed a sigh of relief.

ℭ♡ℬ

"Well, well," said Mel Kotchkis as he put down another stack of plates next to his daughter. She worked busily preparing the long table in the fellowship hall for the social. "Seems Sheriff Moore has finally come to a church social with a pretty gal on his arm."

Mel bit his mustached lip to keep from laughing as he watched his daughter, Pamela, react to his statement.

Her spine stiffened and her hands ceased the rapid arrangement of cutlery on the table. Slowly she reached for the stack of plates and moved them one inch farther from the edge of the table. Her capable long tapered fingers returned to fussing over the forks, precisely lining them up in a staggered formation.

Pamela sidled her trim figure down the table, carefully keeping her back to the commotion going on at the front door. Mel put his hand over his quivering lips and stroked his work-worn fingers through his full salt-and-pepper beard.

"She's darling," said Mrs. Sence, her chirping voice carried across the hall.

"Look at those precious curls," said Ruth Bladcomb in a stage whisper to her husband. The older couple stood at the far end of the table, mixing the punch in large glass pitchers. "I declare, did you ever see such fine clothes? She must be from the city. Where ever did Jake Moore come up with a little beauty like that?"

Pamela Kotchkis skittered back to the corner of the table, rounded it neatly, grabbed the box of knives, and shuffled them out onto the tablecloth. When the first row lay precisely as she wanted them, her blue eyes lifted, obviously drawn to the spectacle at the front door.

Mel watched his favorite daughter's stone face soften into a warm smile. That expression, so like his Maddie's, gladdened his old heart. What was it Maddie used to say when he was rocking one of their young'uns? Something about when a rough and tumble man cradled a wee child . . .that it could wrench the tender heart of any woman. The sight of rugged Jake Moore with the mysterious little girl in his arms had no doubt pierced the armor his headstrong Pamela kept around her heart. Mel sent up a fervent, though silent, *Praise the Lord!*

The old farmer watched his daughter lift a hand to the tawny curl dangling at her temple and tuck it back off her face behind her delicate ear. His Maddie had used the same nervous gesture. He loved this daughter and all the sweet recollections she brought to his mind, but it was time for her to make new connections. Pamela was twenty! She couldn't be Papa's girl for the rest of her life.

Maddie would be proud of this last gal. Of course, Mel was properly proud of all five. But the first four had married city men. His baby was the only one left on the farm. All grown up now and ready to find her husband.

Mel prayed that it would be a man willing to take over after him. His life's work had established Kotchkis Kansas Corn. Mel was proud of it. He wanted to know his grandchildren would grow up on the piece of land he and Maddie had claimed.

Just Pamela remained. Pamela, the last of Maddie's brood, Mel's last chance to bring a young man into the harness of a mighty fine farm. Pamela, stubborn and beautiful, prideful and charming, deeply fascinated by the handsome sheriff, and rigidly determined not to give in to her attraction.

Well, Lord, said Mel in a comfortable silent conversation with his God and Savior, *I've been praying for ten years. I watched each of our girls grow, fall like so many silly geese in love, and leave. Now, I'm satisfied with what You've done. You lead them well. I thank You. But, here's Pamela, denying she longs to take that young man's interest. To my way of thinking, Jake Moore is just the right suitor for our gal. He's a strong man, got a good handle on You being the God of the universe and all, understands Your Gospel, and is living under Your authority. I'd be mighty grateful if You'd give these young folks a nudge. In Your time, of course. But I reckon You know I'm getting a tad impatient. Amen.*

∂♡ß

With a concerted effort, Mel Kotchkis managed to snag the sheriff and get him and his pretty little charge seated at a table with himself and Pamela. It had been no easy task with those nosey, matchmaking women intent on cornering the poor bachelor. Sheriff Moore's face had flashed desperation as he'd been surrounded, and Mel thought of himself as the man's rescuer. Mel wished Maddie were still with him to enjoy life's little comedies. She'd been a woman who could laugh.

"Would you like butter on your roll?" Mel asked Jake's small companion.

"Yes, Mr. Kottis." Amanda nodded. "Thank you."

Mel grinned at her prim and proper mispronunciation of his name, took up her roll, split it, and spread the butter, replacing it on her plate.

Pamela turned to Sheriff Moore, her curiosity getting the better of her. She'd heard bits and pieces of the story from the other ladies as they worked together.

"How old is she?" she asked.

"Hmm?" Jake chewed on the large helping of beans he had just spooned into his mouth.

"Amanda," clarified Miss Kotchkis, "how old is she?"

Jake swallowed. "I don't know."

"You didn't ask her?"

"No."

"Oh."

Pamela pushed the peas around on her plate. She ate a couple of bites of the potato salad. Mrs. Sence had made it. She must get the receipt from Mrs. Sence.

"Why did she get off the train?" she asked.

Jake chewed and cast an anxious look at Kotchkis's daughter.

He swallowed, reached for his punch, and took a swig.

"She didn't say," he finally answered.

"You didn't ask?" A merry chortle escaped with her question.

Jake grinned. The deep dimples on either side of his mouth danced in his cheeks. "Guess I'm not much good at interrogating the young and innocent. Now if she'd been a mean hombre with a marked resemblance to one of the posters on my wall, I might have gotten more information out of her."

Their eyes caught, sharing the good humor of their conversation. Pamela watched the twinkle in his hazel eyes change subtly to a gleam of admiration. She noticed how the green irises held flecks of brown and a dark rim clarified the odd color. They were fine eyes, eyes she would enjoy looking into over the dinner table in the bright kitchen at home. . .

Suddenly, Pamela felt uncomfortable and pulled her attention away. She turned quickly and interrupted the conversation between her father and Amanda.

"Amanda," she said rather breathlessly, "Sheriff Moore doesn't know how old you are."

"I'm four, Miss Kottis." Amanda's cultured tones sounded so out of place coming from her round and adorable baby face that Pamela smiled.

"Does your mommy call you Mandy?" asked Pamela.

"No, that's not my proper name. Mother calls me by my proper name."

"Oh," said Pamela.

"What is your proper name, Miss Kottis?" Amanda asked earnestly.

"Pamela."

"That's very pretty."

"Thank you," said Pamela. Amanda Greer sounded like one of the old ladies around the quilting frame. This pert little girl had the same intonations of a dowager who had come into town visiting a relative. Pamela could just picture the little girl sitting with the matrons, replying to their inquiries with only the politest and tritest information.

"Is Pamela a family name?" asked Amanda.

"Well," said Pamela, "my parents wanted to name a son after my father. His name is Mel. My mother had all girls, and I was the last, so they named me Pamela because Mel is in the middle of it."

Amanda nodded politely. "My name is a family name. I have an older sister named Amelia and an Aunt Amelia. My oldest sister is Althea and my mother's name is Althea. My other sister is Augusta, which isn't a family name, but she was supposed to be born in August, and my father thought it fitting. Augusta came on the last day of July. Father said he wouldn't give in to her willfulness and named her Augusta anyway."

Pamela heard a snort that sounded suspiciously like a laugh cut short. It came from the sheriff, proving he had eavesdropped on their conversation. She chose to ignore him.

"And, do you have an Aunt Amanda?" asked Pamela.

Amanda nodded. "Deceased," she explained.

"Oh, I'm sorry."

Amanda nodded again and turned her attention back to the chicken on her plate.

"Remind me," said Jake in a low voice, "to bring you to the jail next time I've got an outlaw. You've pretty much got her family history."

"Hush," scolded Pamela and turned back to find Amanda scowling at her. The wrinkled brow and puckered lips looked adorable. Pamela fought the urge to scoop her up and give her a big hug to drive away that crosspatch glower.

Pamela carefully took a bite of peas instead. After a moment, Amanda politely asked for another helping of potato salad.

"This is quite good," she said. "I don't believe I've ever had potatoes fixed in this manner."

Pamela again felt like a little old lady occupied the seat next to her instead of a four-year-old—as if a very short adult dominated that pudgy body. Pamela wanted to talk to the child.

"I grew up with four sisters," said Pamela. "It's fun to have a house full of girls to play with." Pamela gave Amanda a friendly smile, hoping that the little girl would abandon her grown-up demeanor and chatter away like her nieces or the little girls she taught in Sunday school.

Amanda frowned again, thinking.

"My sisters do not play. They aren't girls," she explained after a moment of consideration. "They are grown-up women."

"Oh," said Pamela.

"I am a twilight child," Amanda explained further, and picked up the basket of rolls beside her plate. She took one and offered the basket to Pamela. Pamela took it in a daze and offered it to Jake Moore. Their eyes met again, and this time the look they shared held no humor. Pamela's eyes shone with sorrow as she imagined a little girl's life in a house full of adults who did not play.

♔♡♔

After the meal, the men moved back the tables and rearranged the chairs so everyone could enjoy the music for the evening. The ladies made short work of the cleaning up. Mel Kotchkis and Pamela sat in the seats to the side where they usually sat on social evenings like this. Several of the women Jake had ignored earlier noticed that Sheriff Moore and his little girl visitor had decided to sit with them.

"Who is going to take care of her tonight?" asked Pamela, referring to Amanda.

"I think I'll take her back to Maggie's with me," answered Jake. "Maggie will put her up." He'd changed his mind once he'd arrived and seen how the women carried on and fussed over the child. Amanda was much too sensitive a girl for such silliness. He would just keep her himself.

"I heard Mrs. Jones offer to take her," observed Pamela.

"Her kids are too rowdy. They'd scare Miss Amanda."

"And Mrs. Whitcomb?" said Pamela.

"Same thing," answered the sheriff without batting an eye.

"Surely, Mrs. Dobson and Mrs. Roper wouldn't scare her. The sisters are gentle and genteel."

"Too old," said Jake.

"Old?"

"What if something should happen? They're too old to take care of an emergency."

Pamela nodded her head at the sheriff, but one little dimple peeked out at the corner of her mouth. Jake watched that dimple quiver in and out of existence like a twinkling star—for some reason the sight of it reassured him. Pamela Kotchkis was a sensible woman, and she understood a child's needs.

She might laugh at him for being possessive with the little mite, but she understood. It didn't seem right to foist Amanda onto another family when she'd already been through so much today. Miss Amanda trusted him. He'd take care of her until tomorrow and put her on the train himself. Jake smiled back at Pamela Kotchkis, enjoying the laughter in her eyes and the gentle glow of happiness about her.

Beyond Pamela sat Amanda. Her eyes glowed as she listened to the spirituals and hymns. She'd crawled up into Mel's lap, or had he picked her up? They looked natural together. Mel had a lot of experience with girls, first his own and now his grandchildren. Jake admired him for the ease with which he held the little girl.

Jake turned his attention to the Burkett family. They'd gone to the front to sing a special together. The Burketts all looked alike with bushy blond hair and wide grins.

Jake noted the room full of families. That was the way it always was. He was the only single man in the bunch. There was nothing wrong with being single, he reminded himself. Being single had its advantages.

"Are you getting tired, Sweetie?" Pamela asked Amanda in a soft voice that warmed Jake's heart.

"No, Miss Kottis," Amanda replied. "I had a nap in the jail."

"You slept in the jail?" asked Pamela.

"Yes, ma'am. In Sheriff Moore's jail cell."

Pamela turned scandalized eyes to the handsome sheriff. He could see the gleam of mischief in her look.

"Sheriff, really!" she said, mocking horror, "that is not the proper place for a young lady to sleep."

"No, it isn't," he agreed. He feasted his eyes on her. Pamela Kotchkis would make a fine mother. She had a head full of tawny gold hair and blue eyes rimmed with dark lashes.

Would all her children look alike in the same way the Burketts resembled one another? Would they all look happy like Pamela did tonight? Or would they all be reserved, as she'd always been with him before this night?

The only thing he'd noticed about Pamela Kotchkis before was that she had good sense. The good sense not to bump into him "by accident." The good sense not to casually walk up and join in a conversation that had nothing to do with her. The good sense not to giggle and flirt.

Pamela Kotchkis turned and smiled at something her father said. *She's a pretty woman*, Jake thought, *a calm, serene, gracious woman. She's got dignity, but not too much. She has a pretty smile. And, that dimple. . .*

No doubt her children would play and laugh and know they were loved. Her husband would hurry home, assured that her warm sense of humor and gentle ways would welcome him. He looked at that tiny dimple that flashed so intriguingly at the corner of her mouth. Her lips were pink. They looked soft.

Jake heard the huge yawn and shifted his eyes reluctantly to the little girl who claimed she was not sleepy.

Amanda shook her head wearily. "That wasn't a proper place for me to sleep."

Jake had to think. What wasn't? Oh, the jail. His mind must have wandered.

Chapter 3

I need a nightgown," Amanda Greer announced stubbornly and not for the first time.

"Miss Amanda, I don't have a little nightgown," said Jake between clenched teeth. He bit back other more impatient words. "I don't have any nightgown, big or little. You are just going to have to sleep in your shift."

"It is not proper for a young lady to sleep in her shift. A young lady needs a nightgown." Amanda crossed her chubby arms across her chest, stuck out her lower lip, and frowned the fiercest frown she could summon.

Jake cast a look at Maggie. His eyes held equal measures of exasperation and desperation. Draped in her habitual black sagging gown, Maggie leaned squarely against her parlor door. She raised a scrawny shoulder in an expression of indifference.

Jake counted off with self-righteous indignation the number of times Miss Maggie Hardmore had made it clear she didn't appreciate his bringing the tired little girl to her boardinghouse. *There isn't an ounce of compassion in the woman's bony breast.* Obviously, he'd get no help from her quarter.

"I'll be right back," said Jake, and he bolted from the room, taking the narrow stairs two at a time. In a minute he thundered down the same stairs and burst back into the parlor. He held a creamy yellow shirt of soft material. He offered it to the midget minx who had remained like a stubborn statue anchored to the parlor room rug.

"This is my dancing shirt."

From her position by the door, Maggie rolled her eyes.

"Shirts do not dance," said Amanda.

"No!" barked Sheriff Moore. He took a cooling breath. "No," he repeated in a milder tone underscored by a heavy black line of forced patience. "It is the shirt I wear to dances." He knelt down and held the shirt out for the girl to feel. "It's soft. The ladies like it."

Maggie made a strangled chortle noise behind him. "Since when do you go out of your way to attract the ladies, Jake Moore?"

"Maggie, if you are not going to help, be quiet," said the sheriff.

Amanda touched the fabric with chubby fingers. Sighing in resignation, she took it.

"It's not a nightgown." She made one last protest.

"It's a nightshirt," conceded Jake.

The furrows deepened on Amanda's brow. "Father wears a nightshirt," she said. "I've seen it on the laundry line."

"Then you know," Jake spoke quickly before her mature little mind could reason out further objections, "he'd think it more proper for you to wear a nightshirt than a shift."

274

Amanda nodded.

"Fine," said Jake unfolding his body and stretching to his full height. He looked at Maggie, daring her to abandon him. He spoke to Amanda. "Go with Mrs. Hardmore and change for bed."

Maggie stretched out a hand hardened by years of housekeeping. Amanda crossed reluctantly, took it, and followed the old crow out of the room without looking back.

Jake took the stack of sheets and blankets, provided under protest by Maggie, from the chair in the corner and began making a bed for Amanda on the parlor sofa. Finished, he collapsed in the big overstuffed chair.

"Where am I going to sleep?" asked Amanda, standing at his elbow.

Realizing he must have dozed off, he looked her over with groggy eyes. She was dressed in the pale yellow shirt. The rolled-up sleeves came to her elbows. The hem dragged on the floor.

Maggie Hardmore had brushed the unruly curls and wrestled them into two short braids. Amanda held her doll tightly against her side with a grip around its neck that would have strangled any living creature. In the other hand she carried the square basket.

Jake leaned forward in the overstuffed chair. It had been a long day, and his own bed called to him. He rubbed a hand across his scratchy face and stretched.

"On the sofa," he answered.

"In the parlor?"

Jake didn't like the way Amanda had said the word "parlor." Somehow it sounded as though he was about to have trouble, and the trouble would be with a strong-minded little girl.

"It's a very nice sofa. Mrs. Hardmore is very proud of her company parlor and the furnishings therein. The sofa came from St. Louis."

Amanda took a couple of small steps across the dim room on silent bare feet. She stood next to the sofa and examined it thoroughly. Sad eyes traveled from one brocade-covered arm to the other. Her solemn face showed her disapproval.

Finally she shook her head. The short braids swung and thumped her on the cheeks.

"It's not proper for a young lady to sleep in the parlor," she said in a low, calm voice. "It's not proper for a young lady to sleep on a sofa. I want a bed. I want my room. I want Miss Kottis."

She turned mournful eyes brimmed with tears and faced down the sheriff.

"Miss Kottis?" Jake was surprised. "I mean, Kotchkis? Miss Pamela? She went home. She's miles away in a farmhouse outside of town."

"Miss Kottis knows what's proper for a young lady." Amanda hung her head and sniffed.

"This is just for one night, Miss Amanda," assured Jake. He pulled himself out of the chair and dropped to his knees. He put an arm around the stubborn, stiff shoulders of his little guest. "You must be a brave little girl and crawl into bed with your doll. At lunchtime tomorrow the train will come, and you can climb aboard and go to your sister in Big Springs."

Jake pulled the blanket back in an invitation to the

little girl to climb in. She looked at him with pity in her eyes and sighed. Shaking her head over his ignorance, she put her doll and the basket on the bed and knelt beside it. She seemed to be waiting for him, so Jake hobbled on his knees closer beside her.

"Heavenly Father," said Amanda with her eyes firmly shut and her hands clenched in prayer, "thank You for this lovely day. Please take care of Althea's broken foot. Please take care of Mother and Father as they travel to New York City, New York. Please take care of Amelia and her suitable husband, Mr. Beasley, and all the little beastly Beasleys. Please take care of Augusta and her ne'er-do-well husband, Mr. Jenkins, and my scoundrel cousins, James, John, Jordon, and Jacob. Thank You for the nice dinner and the sheriff and Miss Kottis. Keep me safe this night in this awful parlor and this awful sofa. Amen."

Amanda rose to her feet and took up the doll and basket once more. She stood in quiet misery, staring at the sofa while big tears coursed down her round cheeks.

"It's not that bad, Miss Amanda," whispered Jake, strangely moved by the silent tears.

"Do you have a bed?" she whispered in return.

"Yes, but I have slept on the ground outside on more than one occasion."

Amanda transferred the basket to the same hand that held the doll. She rested her free hand on the sheriff's shoulder and gave it a consoling pat. Clearly sleeping on the ground was worse than the awful sofa. Jake put his arm around the tiny figure, and she melted against his chest, burying her face against his shoulder.

"Please, Sheriff Moore," she sobbed, "find me a real bed, not in a parlor."

ᓀ♡ᓂ

Jake rode Dancer at a sedate pace through the muggy night air. Completely limp, the little figure sitting before him in his yellow dancing shirt sagged against him. He took the handle of the square basket from her fingers before she dropped it. They hadn't been a mile out of town before she relaxed, not two miles before her head lolled to one side and her mouth drooped with a whispered snore.

Now why, he wondered, was it not proper for a young lady to sleep in a parlor on a perfectly comfortable sofa, but it was perfectly proper to ride out of town in the middle of the night wearing his good shirt? Of course, he didn't point out the quirkiness of this reasoning to the mite sleeping before him.

Back in Maggie's parlor, overwhelmed by the child's tears, Jake had proposed taking her to Miss Kottis who knew what was "proper for a young lady." When Miss Amanda agreed, he scooped her up with the doll and basket, and made for the livery stable as fast as his long legs would carry him. She clung to him with those fat little arms, and he found himself holding her tighter as if to assure her that everything was going to be all right.

And everything was going to be all right. It wasn't really the middle of the night. The church social had ended around eight-thirty. He'd wasted a little under an hour trying to get Miss Amanda to bed at the boarding-house. It would be around ten o'clock when he reached the Kotchkis place. If he were coming calling, ten o'clock would be improper. But this wasn't a social call.

What did he care about what was proper and improper? He was just doing his duty, seeing that the little mite got a good night's sleep before her journey tomorrow. He'd sent a prayer up to God for an answer to his dilemma. Then he firmly put aside any thoughts about why the first face that came into his mind had a tempting dimple right at the corner of lips it would be improper to kiss.

When Sheriff Moore turned into the long drive between two rows of white oak, a few windows of the Kotchkis farmhouse still glowed with yellow lamplight. A couple of dogs barked a greeting. He reined in Dancer at the front porch. Carefully hoisting Miss Amanda up against his shoulder, he slid out of the saddle. He spoke softly to his horse as he looped the reins over the hitching post.

"This won't take but a minute, Dancer."

His boots clomped on the wooden steps, and the door opened before he had a chance to knock.

Mel Kotchkis walked out onto the porch, clapped Jake on the shoulder as if this were not only an expected visit but one with nothing unusual about it, not the hour of the night, nor the pudgy, miniature proper miss draped over the sheriff's shoulder.

"She wouldn't sleep at Maggie's," said Jake.

"Hmm? Gave you some trouble?" Kotchkis grinned amiably. "Little girls are like that. Pamela will know what to do."

Pamela, in a robe thrown over her nightgown, came rushing down the stairs.

She'd heard the exchange at the door.

"Carry her on up the stairs, Sheriff Moore," she spoke softly. "We'll try to put her down without waking her."

Jake followed, but Mel went to the kitchen table. His big Bible lay open to the book of Matthew, and he patted the pages as he sat down.

"Yes, Jesus," he breathed the words with a grateful sigh. "Just the right suitor for our gal."

❦♡❦

"In here, Sheriff." Pamela pushed the door wide open as she scurried into a room ahead of him. A lantern sat on a bedside table. A book lay open, face down beside it. The covers were turned back and pillows were stacked against the headboard.

Pamela grabbed the top pillow and pushed it to the other side of the double bed. She smoothed the sheet and pulled the covers back a bit more then stood aside for Sheriff Moore to gently put down his burden.

Amanda groaned, and he patted her back, speaking soothing words. When she settled, he stepped away. Pamela tucked the little girl in and turned down the lamp.

Pamela's tawny, light brown curls caught the glimmer of the soft light and surrounded her face like a halo. Jake smelled the clean fragrance of soap and rosewater on her skin. The soul-shaking thought that he was in Pamela's bedroom, next to the bed she must have hopped out of when she heard him at the door, enjoying the sight, the smell of her, and even relishing the sound of her breathing, nearly sent him racing from the house in panic.

He stopped in the hall, trying to think of a time when

his heart had last raced like that. When Tommy Blake holed up in the livery, and he had to talk the outlaw out so he could arrest him without bloodshed? No, this was different. This was a whole lot different.

"Sheriff Moore?" Pamela came out into the upstairs hallway and closed the door softly behind her. "Where are her clothes?"

"What?"

"Her clothes."

"Maggie has them." He turned to look at her—which was his first mistake. She was close and sweet and looking up at him with puzzlement in her eyes. The little furrow across her brow was just at the right height for him to kiss. If she tilted her chin just a mite, her lips. . . He couldn't kiss her! You don't kiss a woman in her nightgown and robe unless you're married to her. Where was Mel Kotchkis? His daughter was up here with a—a. . .

Jake stumbled on the first step but caught himself and hurried down the stairs. About halfway down he remembered he was supposed to be quiet or he'd wake Amanda. At the bottom, in the foyer's bright light, he felt like a fool for running from her. Pamela's slow and steady footsteps descended the stairs he'd just plummeted down.

"Thank you, Miss Pamela," he croaked. Jake cleared his throat and began again. "Thank you, Miss Pamela. Her train leaves at noon. If you don't mind, I'll come by at eleven to pick her up. I'll bring her clothes with me then."

"That will be fine, Sheriff."

"Evening." Staring at her radiance, he reached for the doorknob, missed, dragged his gaze away from that angel face surrounded by the halo of soft gold hair, and focused on the cold, round doorknob.

"Much obliged," he muttered.

Sheriff Jake Moore strode out the door, across the steps, and vaulted into the saddle. A kid's trick, but he wasn't trying to impress the woman. He was trying to escape.

Chapter 4

Nothing pressing came up to keep Sheriff Moore in town. He'd swept out his jail cells, strolled down Main Street, and checked with Widow Harper on whether Daniel Frigby had turned up to do the work the judge had sentenced him to do as punishment for public drunkenness. Going out to collect Miss Amanda happened to be next on his list of things to do. The clock said nine instead of eleven, but there was no reason to put off a chore just because the night before he'd thought he wouldn't get around to it until later in the morning.

Jake whistled "All Creatures of Our God and King," and when he got to the alleluias, he lifted his baritone voice to fill the gloomy, heavy morning air with his praise. As Jake turned his horse down the lane to the Kotchkis farm, he noted the sky's angry countenance. Black clouds churned overhead and fits of wind spurted across his path, swirling the dust across the road in hectic dust devils.

Jake looked over the vast field of corn. The crops needed rain. A gentle, all-day rain would do.

Miss Pamela sat on the front porch in a rocker, a

sewing basket beside her, and something pink in her hands. Miss Amanda scurried around the yard, dressed more like a young girl than the day before. She raised a hand to wave at him and went back to her present interest, chasing the chickens. She had a small bag Jake guessed was feed. Instead of standing still and throwing out the grain, the city girl cornered the hens and gave them their breakfast. From the saddle, Jake watched Amanda as she tried to force feed the hens. With a chuckle, Jake dismounted and looped his reins over the hitching rail. Digging in his saddlebag, he produced the tightly wadded bundle containing Amanda's dress, shift, stockings, shoes, and bonnet. He walked up the wooden porch steps and presented it to Miss Pamela.

She shook her head over the compressed and crumpled clothing. Glancing at Jake with laughter bubbling in her voice, she proclaimed, "She won't wear these clothes in this wrinkled condition, you know."

Jake plunked down in the opposite rocker and removed his hat. None of the previous night's awkwardness remained. He gazed over the white railing surrounding the porch, watching Amanda's fruitless endeavors to corner a hen.

"Where did she get those clothes?" he asked.

"We have an attic full of little girl clothes, Sheriff Moore," answered Pamela. "Remember I am one of five sisters."

Jake tossed her a charming smile with both dimples showing in his broad masculine cheeks.

"Miss Amanda," he called, stood up, and walked down the steps to his little friend. "You must entice the chicken to come to you." He stooped to talk to Amanda, putting his arm around the chubby shoulders covered with a plain brown smock dress. "Here, stand very still and sprinkle the grain over the ground around you. The hens have very small brains and will soon forget you've been trying to catch them. Look, see how they're eyeing your bag of grain? They'll come up and peck the feed right at your feet."

The fat hens soothed down their ruffled feathers and scuttled closer to the feed. Jake eased himself to a stand and backed off, returning to his seat beside Miss Pamela.

"You're not a town boy after all," she said.

Jake smiled easily at her, taking in the way little wisps of hair curled around her forehead with the moist heat of the day.

"No, I spent ten years on a farm in Indiana." He leaned back in the rocker and his eyes moved to admire the field of corn just beyond the barn. "It was my Uncle Will's place. I went to live there after my folks died. We raised corn but nothing as fine as this strain your father has developed."

"He'd like hearing that. He has a lot of pride in Kotchkis Kansas Corn."

"Rightly so," Jake said.

"So, you didn't like farming and looked for a town job?" Pamela asked.

"Not exactly," said Jake, rubbing his hand across his chin. "Uncle Will never made a secret of the fact the farm was for his boys. He has two, Bill and George. They had ten years on me and always carried fifty to a hundred pounds more muscle."

Pamela let the pink apron she was hemming rest in her lap. Jake's voice held a note of regret. She studied his profile while he peered out over her father's latest test field. The hybrid flourished with strong green stalks and heavy, full ears sporting golden tassels.

"So, you liked farming?" she prompted.

Sheriff Moore nodded. "Funny thing was that of the three of us, Bill, George, and skinny Jake, I was the one who took to the fields. I liked the smell of the dirt, the sight of the seedlings popping up in rows along a furrow."

"But you left the farm?"

"I left the farm." He nodded toward the field. "Your father and I talk about the corn. It brings up the old ache inside me. I get him talking about predestination so I don't have to think about it." Jake tossed the farmer's daughter a mischievous grin.

Pamela laughed and plied her needle once more. Jake watched her. It was a comforting sight, the pretty young woman doing something domestic, calmly rocking on the front porch. At Uncle Will's there had been no softening of a woman's touch since Uncle Will's wife had died some years earlier. A hired woman came in and did the laundry and some other chores twice a week.

In those bleak days, Jake had escaped to the fields to relish the beauty of tender shoots breaking through the dark soil and swaying in the gentle breeze. Out there he talked to God as his mother had done before her death. Out there he felt the presence of a loving Father who delighted in a young boy's company. In Jake's early childhood, his father had lifted him onto muscled shoulders and carried him down fully-grown rows of corn. Even on top of his pa's broad shoulders, only Jake's head peeked over the crop.

Living with Uncle Will had been a dry time. Young Jake Moore received his nourishment in the fields. There, memories of his past and the comfort of his Lord watered his thirsty soul.

A sudden gust of wind brought a spattering of mammoth plops of rain. Pamela jumped to her feet, throwing the apron into the empty rocker. Jake grabbed his hat as the wind shuffled it across the wooden porch. Pamela's skirts brushed past him as she hurried out into the yard. He looked up to see her gather Amanda into her arms. Amanda dug her fists into her eyes. Wind whipped dirt up into the air and it swirled against the little girl. She cried that it was stinging her skin and hurting her eyes. Pamela wrapped her body around the child, sheltering her from the bluster.

Jake took two steps down the wooden stairs and heard the distant roar of a train. For a split second he froze, knowing that no train ran close enough to the Kotchkis place to be heard. Then it dawned on him—a tornado.

Dancer reared, his high-pitched whinny shrieking with fear. Jake sprang into action, and with difficulty, he stripped away the saddle and dropped it to the ground. He worked against the nervous horse to remove the bridle and halter. Once free, Dancer rose up on his hind legs and beat the air with his hoofs. With one last roll of panicked eyes, he charged out of the yard down the lane, removing himself from danger. The wind had beaten Pamela and Amanda into a ball huddled against the ground. Jake fought against the brutal strength of the wind's onslaught and the flotsam flying with deadly velocity. Holding his arms up to block the debris, he managed to fall to his knees beside Pamela. He put strong arms around her, using his body to shield her, and pressed his face against her hair.

"Storm shelter?" he yelled.

She nodded and tried to rise. Jake scooped up Amanda, and she clung to him with her arms around his neck, her face buried in his chest and her legs wrapped around his waist. Pamela pressed against his other side. He had a strong arm around each female, but the force of the wind threatened to tear them from his grasp. A branch hurled across the yard and assaulted them. Jake and Pamela beat the whipping limbs off. The wind caught it and carried it away.

Stooped against the aggressive force, the three pushed around the side of the building where two slanted doors covered steps into the basement. Jake handed Amanda to Pamela and wrestled the door open. Turning back, he took hold of Pamela's arm to guide her down the stone steps. Just as he had the two far enough down to be out of the most severe gusts, a blast against the wooden door heaved it against Jake. He catapulted down the stairs. His head whacked a beam, and his unconscious body smashed against Amanda and Pamela, slamming them to the dirt floor of the cellar.

ᘓ♡ᘒ

The roar of the tornado above did not diminish in the

recesses of the cellar. Instead, the sound of the wooden structure swaying added to the horrible cacophony. Pamela covered her ears and prayed, "Lord, help us!"

She squirmed out from under the heavy sheriff and managed to roll him over onto his back. Amanda scrambled into Pamela's lap and threw her arms around her neck. Pamela could feel her shaking and knew the words of comfort she mumbled into her little ear could not be heard.

The impact of some flying object jarred the house. The wood above them squealed, straining.

The house is going to go, thought Pamela. *What should I do? Oh Lord, what should I do? Where is the safest place?*

Pamela searched the dark recesses of the cellar. *We've got to be against the wall,* she thought. *Which wall, Father?* she asked in prayer. The darkest corner where only a child's mattress stood against the wall beckoned her.

Pamela forced Amanda to let go of her. Then pushing her arms under Jake's shoulders and grabbing what she could of his shirt, Pamela began to drag Jake toward the corner of the cellar room.

Amanda took hold of Jake's belt and began to tug as well. Pamela realized with surprise the little girl was helping move the man to safety. With the winds howling, fear gave Pamela strength, and she soon dragged Jake across the dirt floor. She put Amanda right against the stone corner and then positioned her body in front of the child's. She pulled on Jake until she had his upper body in her lap, his head against her chest. Then, she prayed.

The crescendo of the storm pounded on their senses.

The house shuddered, the noise peaked. Amanda covered her ears and curled into a tighter ball. Pamela squeezed Jake in her arms and fought the terror by repeating a single sentence. *Lord, help!* She couldn't make her brain function any further to provide details. It seemed enough to just hold on to that lifeline to the heavenly Father.

The timbre of the roar changed. Pamela raised her head to listen. The clamor receded and the drone of torrential rain dominated. She turned slightly and gathered Amanda in her arms.

"We're safe," she said.

Amanda hugged her fiercely and whimpered softly against Pamela's side.

"It'll be all right now. Those kinds of storms only go in one direction. It won't turn around to batter us again. We're safe." Pamela kept up the flow of soothing words until the rain slackened. "We've got to see to the sheriff," Pamela told Amanda. She gently pushed the child away from her.

"Sheriff Jake." Pamela bent over the form still draped across her legs. She gently shook his shoulder. No response. She put her trembling hand behind his head and drew back when she touched something warm and sticky. "Oh, you're bleeding." She shifted him to one side trying to see.

"He's hurt bad," said Amanda in a small voice.

"Maybe not," said Pamela. "It's a head wound and cuts on the scalp bleed a lot, even when it isn't serious. I need to stop the bleeding."

"He needs a bandage?"

"Yes," said Pamela. "Here, Amanda, you hold his head in your lap, and I'll try to find something clean to press against the wound."

Pamela managed to shift Jake's heavy body, laying just his head in the little girl's lap. Then she crawled directly to a stack of trunks. Finding the one she wanted, she opened it and rummaged through the contents. She came back with an old tablecloth, tore a strip off using her teeth to get it started, then folded the strip into a pad. She pressed it against the sticky place on the back of Jake's head.

"Is it going to rain forever?" asked Amanda.

"No, honey," answered Pamela.

"Will someone come help us?"

For the first time Pamela thought of her father. He'd been out in the south field. Had he found shelter?

"Let's pray," said Pamela. "Let's pray for all the people who were out in that storm."

Amanda obediently folded her little hands, resting them on Jake's face. His head still lay in her lap.

"Dear Lord, that was a scary wind, and it's raining awful hard," Amanda said. "We thank You that we're safe and ask that You help Sheriff Moore wake up from sleeping because of his head wound and that his scalp will quit bleeding all over the place. And, for the chickens to be safe because they haven't finished eating their breakfast yet and for me and Miss Kottis to wait patiently while You do all the things You have to do to undo all the things that the scary wind did and please make it stop raining soon so we can get out of this dark place without getting all wet. Amen."

"Father in heaven," said Pamela, "thank You for keeping us safe, and I ask that You take care of my father and all the other people in the path of the tornado. Amen."

Slowly the sound of the heavy rain abated to a drizzle.

Jake groaned and lifted his head only to let it drop again. Amanda patted his face.

"You are going to be all right," she said. "We prayed."

Pamela changed the pad pressed against his bleeding scalp. His eyes flickered open.

"You hit your head when we fell into the cellar," she explained.

"Help me sit up," said Jake.

"Maybe you should just lie still for a while," suggested Pamela.

"No, there are people out there who need help. My head's hard. I can make it."

Both Pamela and Amanda helped the sheriff sit. Once up, he had to rest against Pamela as the room swayed and darkness threatened to engulf him once more.

As soon as his head quit swimming, he tried to stand.

"Wait," said Pamela. "Move over closer to the steps where it's lighter. I'll bind a bandage to that thick skull, and then you can try to get up."

Jake obediently crawled across the dirt floor of the cellar and collapsed against the wooden boxes next to the steps. A fine mist from the still falling rain blew in. Everything was wet and debris covered the steps.

While Pamela fixed a fresh pad to the oozing wound

and wrapped a narrow strip of the tablecloth around Jake's head to tie it on, Amanda began pulling bits and pieces of wood, tree limbs, hay, and shredded plants off the lowest steps.

Just as Pamela tied off the ends of the cloth, Amanda stopped and dug around in the clutter.

"Look," she said, holding up her find, "a china teacup."

Amanda held it out to Pamela. She sat back on her heels and took it carefully in her hands. Pamela examined the blue forget-me-nots decorating one side and the fluted handle with a thin line of blue accenting the curve. The small bone china cup had not a nick or crack.

"Gladys Sence," she said, "this belongs to Gladys Sence."

The picture of Gladys Sence proudly pouring out tea from the matching teapot sprang into Pamela's mind. The Sunday school teachers met once a month in Gladys's homey little kitchen. The cup in Pamela's hand proved with a certainty that the Sence home had been shattered by the tornado.

She put the cup on a wooden crate so her shaking hands wouldn't drop it. Then she stared at the unharmed cup and imagined the wind ripping through her friend's home and carrying it here. She shuddered, wrapping her arms around her waist and bending forward to ward off the horror. She began to sob.

Jake's strong arms gathered her up. He rocked her and spoke words of comfort just as she had rocked and soothed Amanda almost an hour before.

Amanda put down the limb she used as a little broom

to knock things off the step. She settled down beside the two adults and leaned against them. With one chubby, grubby hand she stroked Pamela's arm.

"We should pray again," Amanda said, looking up at Jake's pale face.

He nodded and his soothing baritone filled the dim and dank cellar with hope.

Chapter 5

"Pamela! Pamela!" Mel Kotchkis's voice boomed across the empty farmyard.

Pamela jerked out of Jake's arms and scrambled to the steps. She peered up at the opening, disregarding the light rain misting over her upturned face.

"Here, Pa," she called. "We're in here."

Mel appeared at the top, his scratched and dirty face beaming relief with a wide grin.

"Jake is hurt," she called.

Mel's smile disappeared, and he plunged down the steps, pushing branches and debris out of his way.

The older man knelt beside the sheriff.

"It's nothing but a knock on the head, Mel," reassured Jake. "How is it out there?"

Mel leaned back and inspected the sheriff with a knowing eye. Satisfied that the young man didn't seem to be seriously hurt, he turned his mind to what he'd seen, and his huge work-hardened hand went up to his forehead. He made a swipe downward across his face as if to wipe the memory away.

"It's bad," he said. "Let's get you up into the house." He

reached to support Jake as he stood. "Our house has some broken windows, and there's a huge sycamore standing upside down, leaning against the back. But the roof is still on, and even the porch doesn't look like it's suffered much. I want to get over to the barn and see to the animals now that I know my Pamela and our little guest are all right."

They struggled up the steps.

"Do you know which way it went?" asked Jake.

"I don't think it hit town, but I'd say the railroad track is gone."

"Why is that?"

"My south field is riveted with railroad ties stuck in the ground like so many toothpicks. When I crawled out of the ditch and saw those heavy ties poked in the ground, some buried two or three feet by the force the tornado hurled them at the ground. . ." Mel paused and shook his head, still in a daze by the power in that awful wind. He shook his head again and cleared his throat. "Well, I praised God for protection and then hightailed it back to the house. I had to see if Pamela was all right." He laid a hand on Amanda's curly-topped head. "And, our Miss Amanda."

She beamed at him with the smile of a little girl who'd fallen in love with a grandpa. She took his hand, and they went around the house to the front porch. One rocker out of the three still stood. The flowerpots filled with marigolds were gone. A bedraggled set of long johns dangled from the eaves.

Mel chortled as they passed the red underwear. "I sure hope those were hanging on somebody's clothesline this morning and not on one of my neighbors' skinny hides."

Inside the house they found water standing on the floor

where rain had blown in through the broken windows.

Amanda let go of Pamela's hand and raced upstairs. A moment later she came down carrying her doll and the square basket.

"I won't go to Big Springs today, will I?" She cast a worried glance at Sheriff Moore.

Jake squatted to put a hand on her shoulder and look her directly in the eyes.

"I'm sorry, Amanda," he said. "I can't return you to your family today. I can't put you on the train as we planned, and I can't take you myself. I need to go help some people."

She patted his arm. "That's all right. I need to help Miss Kottis clean up this mess."

Impulsively, Jake gathered the dirty little mite into his arms and gave her a big hug. Amanda returned the hug full force.

"I was scared," she whispered in his ear.

"I was, too," he admitted. He leaned back from their embrace and looked into the solemn little face. "Right now, Mr. Kotchkis and I have to go see if there are some other scared people who need our help."

She gave him a serious nod and released him. Jake stood up and looked at Pamela. He stood transfixed by the beauty of her eyes. What was it the Bible said? In Genesis, wasn't it? "And the Lord God said, It is not good that the man should be alone; I will make him an help meet for him." Never before had Jake felt those words were for him. Now as he looked into the clear blue gaze of Pamela Kotchkis, he felt the terrible aloneness God never meant for His children to endure. He suppressed the urge to take her in his arms with the same ease he had gathered up the little girl. He knew that to give and receive comfort from Mel Kotchkis's daughter was not his privilege. He'd held her in the cellar, and it had felt right. Now he had to turn away and get busy with the things God had set before him to do this day. Mel cleared his throat. "Before we go out," he said, "let's take a minute to pray."

꒰♡꒱

Amanda and Pamela spent the next hour cleaning. That included bathing and changing clothes. They sat down to dinner alone, but before they'd finished, homeless neighbors began to arrive. Her pa and the sheriff were directing people to their door. By supper, the Kotchkis farmhouse sheltered women and children from three houses torn apart by the tornado.

Amanda bustled about the house as a born hostess, making sure the visitors had drink and food and a comfortable place to rest. Never shy, she addressed adults and children alike and carried messages to Pamela who worked in the kitchen.

"We're going to have a dance," Amanda announced as she brought in an empty plate from the parlor.

"A dance?" Pamela put the hot pan of muffins down on the kitchen table. "When?"

"Saturday night," said Amanda, crawling up into the chair beside the table and watching as Pamela carefully plucked out the fresh muffins.

Pamela sunk into the chair beside her and leaned on her elbows.

"I can't imagine why people are talking of a dance," Pamela said. She poured a glass of milk for herself and a smaller one for Amanda and put a muffin before the child.

"It seems a mighty poor time for frivolity."

"People are going to bring things for the people who lost everything. The dance will be a place to collect and dis—distri. . ."

"Distribute?" Pamela supplied a word.

Amanda nodded, her blond curls bouncing.

"I suppose that's a good idea." Pamela took her glass of milk and went to the window over the sink. She looked out toward the road. Another family limped toward the house. It was Gladys Sence and her children.

"Why are you smiling?" asked Amanda.

"I see the lady who owns the teacup coming down the lane," answered Pamela.

"I thought you saw Sheriff Moore coming."

Pamela turned to look at Amanda with a puzzled frown wrinkling her brow. "Why would you think that?"

"My sister Augusta smiles when she sees her husband, Mr. Jenkins, coming. Mr. Jenkins is a ne'er-do-well," said Amanda before taking a bigger-than-polite bite of muffin. Pamela grinned. Amanda's city manners were dropping away. Perhaps the softer, more comfortable clothes allowed the little girl to be less stiff. Perhaps just being surrounded by more casual adults made the difference.

"Do you like Mr. Jenkins?" asked Pamela.

Amanda's head jerked up, and she studied Pamela's friendly face. After a moment she nodded cautiously, still examining Pamela's expression. The little girl chewed slowly and swallowed before making any comment.

"Mr. Jenkins tells stories," she said, the tone of her voice condemning such a practice.

Again Pamela felt her face wrinkle as she tried to

decipher the statement. "He tells lies?" she asked.

Amanda vigorously shook her head, sending the curls wildly dancing. "No, real stories," she explained. "About fairies."

"Where do the Jenkins' live, Amanda?"

"In St. Louis, Kansas," answered Amanda. "They don't live on the right side of the river."

"The Missouri side is the right side?" Pamela raised her eyebrows at this petty prejudice.

Amanda nodded. "We live on the Missouri side."

"Of course," observed Pamela, trying to remember that Amanda was merely repeating what she'd been told.

Gladys Sence bustled into the room, coming directly over to Pamela and giving her a hearty hug. She then sank into a table chair and removed her bonnet.

"Such a day!" she exclaimed. "Such a day! What wonders I have seen. Pamela, three of your silly-looking Banty chickens are sitting at the very top of the post oak tree down by the river. Probably scared to death, never been up so high in their lives. Certainly didn't fly up there."

"Oh dear, my Banties," moaned Pamela.

"Well, don't carry on," admonished Gladys, her usual smile brightening her face. "That father of yours and the sheriff are trying to get them down. All the work that needs to be done and they're taking time out to fool with some plaything chickens."

Pamela laughed at Gladys's good-natured fussing. No one in all of Lawrence had a bigger heart than Gladys. Her face sobered as she remembered the teacup.

"Gladys, was your house hit?" she asked.

Gladys nodded her head in amazement. "That twister

aimed for my house, and that's God's own truth. But, God did like He did to Job, and said, 'Go ahead and take those boards, every pillar and post, but you can't have my servant Gladys Sence!'" Gladys clapped her hands together. "Fred hadn't even gone out to the fields yet 'cause he was working on the old plow harness that needed repairing. He came charging in the house, gathered us all up, and rushed us out to the banks of the river. I wanted to go down into the cellar and he said, 'No!' And, he can't tell me why he knew to go to the river instead of down in the cellar, but it's a good thing. What pieces of our house that didn't scatter all over the fields fell into the cellar."

"Oh, Gladys, praise God," Pamela whispered, and her hand moved to her throat as she realized what a close call it had been for her neighbors.

"You're right about that, Pamela," answered the older woman. "And, I'm thanking Him that Fred is such a put-it-off-till-tomorrow man."

Pamela nodded and then giggled at the look of pure mischief in Gladys's eye.

"If he had built that extra bedroom like I've been after him to do for two years, I would have been vexed to see it blown up like that." She shrugged. "Now he'll be building a whole house, and it can't be too much trouble to put in another bedroom for my girls."

They laughed together. Gladys jumped to her feet.

"Well, Pamela, tell me what you want me to do." She gestured toward the other room where people gathered to talk. "You'll be feeding that whole crew tonight, and probably tomorrow. Do you want me to mix up some biscuits?"

While the women worked together, Gladys told all the bits of news she had gathered, whose farms had been hit and what people had been injured. She talked of who was out helping people and where the injured had been taken.

᭡♡᭡

Pamela vacillated between the blue dress that brought out the blue in her eyes and her favorite yellow dress. When she tried the yellow dress on for Amanda and did a twirl in her bedroom, Amanda clapped her hands with enthusiasm over the way the skirt swung out.

"That one's the prettiest," she said, "and it matches Sheriff Moore's dancing shirt."

The two young ladies dug around in the attic trunks and found another party dress for Amanda to wear.

᭡♡᭡

Mel escorted them to the dance on Saturday night, and then left them to their own devices as he took up his fiddle and helped provide the music.

Pamela politely asked Amanda for the first dance, remembering when her older sisters would partner her at the community dances. Pamela guided her little friend over to the square where adults and children laughed together. Amanda curtsied with skill, but then just stood there as if she knew none of the steps. Everyone in the square took pleasure in helping her through the formations. Three dances passed before Pamela insisted they go get some punch.

The refreshment table sat under a huge sweet gum tree. Amanda drank her punch quickly, leaving a red mustache across her upper lip. Pamela laughed as she watched the little girl scurry off to join some other children playing nearby.

Pamela took her cup of punch and sat on one of the wooden benches along the outside wall of the town meeting hall, away from the small crowd around the refreshment table. She picked up one of the large star-shaped leaves of the sweet gum tree and gently crushed it between her fingers. It released the pleasant fragrance that gave it the sweet part of its name. Pamela inhaled deeply, enjoying the essence of the beautiful night.

A breeze riffled the leaves above her, and she saw stars peeking through the branches of the tree. A three-quarter moon gave some silvery light, adding to the golden glow shining from the windows of the well-lit hall. The magical night hummed with the life of people coming together to help one another. Pamela thanked God for the farmers and townspeople willing to give of themselves in a time of need. The tornado had reminded her how generous her neighbors could be.

Pamela leaned back against the building, her head resting against the boards, but her foot tapping on the dirt. She could feel the wood vibrate with the strong beat of the hoedown and the rhythmic movement of the dancers within. She imagined the building itself would like to join the dancing, just as her feet couldn't seem to keep still.

Amanda skipped back to her side and proudly displayed a ribbon one of the older girls had fastened in her hair.

"Do you like it, Miss Kottis?" she asked breathlessly.

"Yes, it's very pretty."

"I got it from my friends." Amanda's eyes glowed with excitement, and she rushed back to join the square they were forming to dance under the trees.

"What are you doing out here?" asked a familiar low voice from the shadows.

Jake's voice made her heart leap, and she felt her face flood with an expectant blush. She'd always been so careful to keep from falling under the sheriff's spell. She'd kept her distance and thereby kept her dignity. She'd always felt contempt for those girls in town who blatantly flirted around Jake Moore. Now, she hoped she could at least behave with some decorum, because her heart wanted to betray how she felt.

Smiling cautiously, Pamela turned to greet the sheriff as he sat on the bench beside her.

"We were hot so we came outside." Pamela nodded toward Amanda who had joined hands with the other children and moved as the circle rotated with the music. "Amanda is playing. I didn't want to leave her out here alone."

"She's not quite the stuffy little city miss she was four days ago." Pamela studied him as he watched the children. The girls in town made a point of being available as he finished each dance. She couldn't blame them. He seemed to find pleasure when he danced with the homely, awkward gals as well as with the pretty ones. And he danced as easily as he walked. The joy and fun he expressed as he whirled one partner after another around the hardwood floor caused many a girl to swoon over him.

She'd noted that where he carefully avoided the women when at church, he had no problem dancing with every female in sight at the community dances. He'd even taken the preacher's wife to the floor and danced with the elderly sisters Mrs. Dobson and Mrs. Roper, both widows in their sixties.

Pamela had never been his partner. Her careful adherence to the code of dignity had cost her that privilege. Pamela sighed, and the mournful sound on the night air caught his attention.

Jake turned to see the soft light of the moon bathing her gentle face. She smiled at him, and he spotted the dimple that had on occasion bewitched him. The dance inside had ended, and the violin played the first notes of the next, more sedate tune.

"Miss Pamela," said Sheriff Moore, "may I have this dance?"

Pamela nodded, and he took her hand. They stood and faced each other in the golden light spilling out of the open window. She put her hand on his shoulder. He put his on her waist, and they waltzed under the trees. Neither noticed the children pairing off to do an ungainly imitation of the dance. Pamela only knew she danced with the most wonderful man she'd ever met. Jake felt his heart surrender.

Chapter 6

The railroad crews settled into work, but a train wouldn't run for at least a week. The telegraph lines still lay on the ground, but riders carried messages to the neighboring towns. Most folks had started their repairs or the clearing away of the debris for their new houses. Monday morning had brought enough regularity to the community that Jake felt he could now leave to return Miss Amanda to her sister in Big Springs.

As he'd talked over his plans with Mel Kotchkis after church the day before, the farmer had offered his surrey for the trip.

"It's a fine rig," he explained. "Got it for the girls when there were so many of them at home, always getting rigged up and prettified for the church socials and community shindigs. It has genuine leather seats, silly little fringe dangling off the roof, and yeller wheels. Miss Amanda will feel right comfortable in that fancy wagon." Mel grinned at the mention of it. "And if you wouldn't be opposed to it, my daughter Grace lives in Big Springs; you could take Pamela along to help you with Miss Amanda and it'd give Pamela a chance to visit her big sister."

Jake, who at first had thought the surrey sounded like more trouble than putting Amanda across the front of his saddle on Dancer, suddenly took a hankering to driving the fancy rig and two charming ladies to Big Springs.

෧♡ව

Jake rode past the Kotchkis cornfields headed once more for the farmhouse. This morning the sun kissed the corn, urging the battered plants to stand straight. The blue of the sky sparkled its hue over the meadow to one side of the road. Milking cows lumbered without hurry over the lush green grass. A warm, light breeze ruffled the hair on Jake's neck and he pulled his new hat firmly down to keep it from blowing off.

Jake lifted his hearty baritone voice, singing "Sunshine in My Soul." With each verse his voice grew stronger, and when he reined Dancer to a halt before the Kotchkis hitching post, he heard Mel's tenor and Pamela's soprano join him in the chorus.

Amanda danced out onto the porch, laughing at the grown-ups' happy song.

When they ended on a ringing chord, Mel standing in the door of the barn, Pamela on the porch, and Jake still sitting on his horse, the little girl doubled over with mirth.

"I want to sing the words," she chirped as soon as the laughter left her throat. "Teach me!"

"We will," said Jake, "on the way to Big Springs."

"We have a picnic basket," Amanda squealed. "With tarts! I helped make them. Miss Kottis says we have to watch you because the knave of hearts steals the tarts!" She jumped up and down in her excitement.

Jake leveled his gaze at his accuser. "So, I am the knave of hearts."

"Yes, yes." Amanda clapped her hands. "But Miss Kottis is not the queen."

"She's not?"

"No, 'cause she doesn't want to be married to the king who beat the knave full sore."

"Ahh!" said Jake as he swung down from Dancer's back. "She's too softhearted."

"Yes," answered Amanda. "Do you want to know what kind of tarts they are?"

Jake came up the porch steps and he swept Miss Amanda up in his arms for a big hug.

"What kind?" he asked.

"I won't tell," said Amanda. "You have to wait for our picnic."

"You're a tease, Miss Amanda," Jake protested, laughing.

She giggled and squeezed his neck in a tight hug. "Let's go. We're ready. Miss Kottis and I packed two bags, one for her and one for me, and a big picnic basket."

"Whoa," said Jake. "We're going to have so much to tote, we won't have room for one little girl, and if we don't take the little girl, we don't need to go."

Amanda laughed and squirmed to get down. She raced past Pamela and into the house.

"Are you ready to go, too?" Jake asked Pamela, his hat in his hand, his eyes taking in the fresh beauty of her as she stood on the porch.

She nodded, smiling with only a hint of her joy getting past the shyness that suddenly enveloped her.

"I'll get our things," she said. "Pa's coming with the surrey."

In a manner of minutes, Jake had turned Dancer out into the near pasture and had swung his saddlebags into the back of the surrey, putting them on the floor in front of the second seat. Two bay horses were harnessed to the rig and they stamped their feet, seemingly as anxious to get started as Amanda. Amanda had set the bag of clothing Pamela had given her and her little square basket on the floor beside the saddlebags. She clutched her doll, waiting for the adults to finish with their good-byes. In the end, she gave Mr. Kochkis one more big hug as he lifted her into the front seat.

"You write me a letter," he admonished her. "And when your sister's foot gets better, you talk her into coming to visit us."

Amanda waved until they turned the corner, out of the farm lane and onto the main road heading west.

"How long before we get there?" was her first question.

Pamela laughed. "We just started. We won't get there until late afternoon."

"Does Althea know I'm coming?"

"She knows you're coming this week," said Jake. "I sent a letter with a fellow who was riding that way. But I sent it Saturday, before I knew just which day I'd be able to get away. She'll be surprised to see you so soon."

Amanda chattered for a while and then remembered the hymn Jake had been singing when he arrived at the farmhouse. They spent an hour going over the words, and toward the end Pamela and Jake harmonized, making Amanda clap her hands with enthusiasm.

When they took their first break to let the horses rest, Pamela took Amanda behind some bushes and introduced her to the reality of life without a privy. Amanda stamped back into the clearing, scowling as she marched up to where Jake sat on a log. She stood before him with her hands on her hips.

"What's the matter, little mite?" asked Jake.

"I like traveling on a train better than this," she said.

Jake raised an eyebrow at her. "You do?"

She nodded vigorously. "Except I do like the horses."

"Uh-huh," agreed Jake.

"And the surrey is pretty," she added.

"Uh-huh," agreed Jake again. He caught the glimmer in Pamela's eye and had to look away to keep from laughing.

"And I like it better being with you, Sheriff Moore, and with Miss Kottis," she smiled at her friends. "And, of course, I like the picnic."

Jake nodded with a solemn air.

"And the surrey bumps and rocks you and I like that 'cause the train jiggles and jostles and jambers your nerves."

"Jambers?" asked Jake.

Amanda nodded hard twice, making her curls bounce.

Pamela came from behind her and sat on the log with Jake.

"Why did you get off the train, Amanda?" Pamela asked.

Amanda's face went red. She looked over at the bushes and then back at her friends. Her face reflected a war between telling and not. Finally, she giggled and climbed into Pamela's lap.

"I was looking for a fresh privy," she said. "The one on the train smelled."

Pamela admirably did not show any amusement at this confession. Jake took sudden interest in a hawk flying over the field.

"Where was your sister?" asked Pamela.

"Sleeping."

"And did you find a privy?" asked Pamela.

Amanda nodded. "There was one at the station, but it wasn't much better, and when I came out, the train was going away with my sister on it."

"And, so began," said Jake in a deep dramatic voice, "the Adventures of Miss Amanda Greer of St. Louis, Missouri."

Amanda laughed and wiggled out of Pamela's lap and into his. As the child passed from one set of arms to the other, the looped crocheted edging on Pamela's cuff snagged on the sheriff's gun belt.

"I'm stuck," said Pamela.

"Hop down, Miss Amanda," said Jake.

Amanda looked on as Jake carefully disengaged the delicate threads from the belt at his waist. She didn't notice how quiet her two friends became. She didn't see the flush spread to Pamela's face. She certainly didn't understand why the sheriff held Miss Kottis's hand carefully in his after he succeeded in freeing her sleeve.

જ♡ஐ

As they went farther down the road, Jake told stories about going to school in Indiana with his cousins, Bill and

George. His cousins had been larger than he was and twice as ornery. Jake had had to use his wits to survive. Amanda listened attentively and laughed when Jake got the better of his cousins in their childhood pranks.

"Sheriff Moore," she asked, "didn't you go to a country school?"

"Yes," he answered. "Remember I said there were four grades in one room and four grades in the other. I never could get away from those rapscallion cousins."

"Rap-skal-yun" echoed Amanda, letting the unfamiliar word roll over her tongue.

"Mischief makers," explained Jake.

Amanda nodded. "Father is going to send me to a first-class private school for girls of refined civility in St. Louis." Amanda looked puzzled. "Father says that you can't learn to talk right, or act right, in the common schools."

Jake and Pamela exchanged a look over the head of their passenger.

"You talk proper," said Amanda to Jake with a sigh.

"Actually," said Pamela, "I've noticed that, too. You do speak with more precision than most farmers."

"Well," said Jake, "I always knew that I wouldn't be on the farm when I grew up. So I took pains in my studies at school and visited with the two schoolmasters, Mr. Ted Bishop and Mr. Edward Bishop, after school and sometimes on Sunday afternoon for extra tutoring. They were brothers and had more books than a library. They gave me odd jobs to do around their place. I cut their wood and such—neither one of the brothers were very strong. And, I ended up with good grades and came to Lawrence to go to the University."

"You didn't?" exclaimed Pamela.

He looked sharply at her. "You don't believe I'm smart enough?"

"No, that's—that's not it," Pamela stuttered in confusion. "I just—I didn't think. . . ." She broke off and looked at him. "Did you finish?"

"No, I took a job as a deputy because I was studying law," he explained. "Then I discovered I liked arresting the criminals better than defending them."

"Jake Moore, I'm impressed," said Pamela.

"Because I went to the University?"

"Well, that," she admitted, "but more because you did what you wanted to do. You went to school when you wanted to, and I'm sure you had to work to make the grades and work to make the money. Then you had the gumption to take another course when the first one didn't turn out to be what you expected. Some people just decide to do things and even when they know it's not what they wanted, they just plow ahead."

Jake grinned at her. "Well, I'm glad I told you. Next time I get to thinking I'm not as good as I should be 'cause I dropped out of college, I'll remember that you think I made the right choice."

"Well, I do!" she exclaimed. "God wants us to enjoy this life He's given us and that means doing a life work that gives us pleasure. He's just as delighted with a shoemaker who makes a good boot and enjoys his trade as He is with the President of the United States."

Jake laughed out loud. "Sometimes I'm sure He's more delighted with a shoemaker, especially if the lowly man is walking in the Light."

"Walking in the Light?" asked Amanda, her face turned to Jake's and a furrow on her brow.

"It means following Jesus," he explained.

Amanda shook her head. "You can't follow Jesus. He doesn't go anywhere."

Jake grinned at her. "Following Jesus means finding out what He wants from reading your Bible and praying. His Holy Spirit helps us to understand what we read, and guides us in our decisions."

"I have a Bible," said Amanda.

"You do?" said Pamela.

The little girl nodded her head, causing her silvery blond curls to bounce. "In my basket," she explained. "Pastor Jarmin talked about journeys the Sunday before Althea and I left on our trip. He said God would protect our steps so we wouldn't get lost. I packed my Bible and carried it with me so Althea and I wouldn't have troubles." She sighed. "It didn't work. I got lost from Althea, Althea got hurt, and the tornado nearly swooped me away."

" 'Order my steps in thy word: and let not any iniquity have dominion over me,' " quoted Pamela. "Psalm 119:133."

Jake looked at Pamela and shrugged. He didn't have any inspiration, so he willingly let her handle it.

"Amanda," said Pamela. "That text and many like it tell us to choose to do things that God has told us are good. The Bible tells us how God thinks about things, which things are good and which are bad. When a person chooses to do bad, then the bad things get control of him, and he can be very unhappy. This is important. God says it often in the Bible, so He must think it is very important.

You must follow the paths that He has labeled to be good. If you do that then you will be a happy person, and you will know God is helping you."

"But I still have troubles," lamented Amanda.

"Yes, but you have God watching over you. Carrying the Bible doesn't make Him closer to you," Pamela explained. "You have to carry Him in your heart. You have to love Him. Being a Christian isn't something you can pack in your basket. It's your attitude toward your heavenly Father."

"You started out on a journey," said Jake, "thinking the Bible in your basket was going to keep you safe. If you had left that Bible on the train, God still would have led you to my office. He still would have given you shelter during the tornado. He still would have put people in Big Springs to take care of your sister. The things that happen aren't dependent upon your having the Bible; they're dependent on God. You can't put God in a basket, or leave Him behind on a train."

"Yes," said Pamela, "and that is so much better, because no matter what happens, you know He is there with you."

"So my journey can have bad things happen, but I still have God," said Amanda.

"Right," said Jake. "And the Bible also tells us that all things work together for good for those who love Jesus. I know that's true because even though getting left by the train was a bad thing, look how much good came from it."

"I have new friends," said Amanda.

"Yes," agreed Pamela.

"And I get to ride in a surrey," she continued.

"Yes," said both adults.

"And you and you get to go on a trip with me." Amanda clapped her hands together.

Jake turned a smile filled with admiration and charm to his female companions. His eyes rested on Pamela, and she blushed under the warmth of it.

They stopped for lunch under willow trees by a stream. Amanda proudly displayed her peach tarts, and Jake ate his dessert first which made both of his women companions laugh.

"I won't eat my tart first," said Amanda in her old stuffy voice. "It isn't proper."

"Being proper isn't necessary on a picnic," said Pamela, as she took a huge bite of tart to prove it.

Amanda gasped and then giggled. She ate her tart first as well.

After cold, fried chicken and baked potatoes filled with cheese, Pamela and Jake rested, leaning against the trunk of the tree. Amanda played for a while with her doll.

"I need to go freshen up," she announced to Pamela.

Pamela started to get up.

"I can go by myself," said Amanda. "I'll go wash my hands in the stream, and then go over there for the other." She pointed to some bushes not ten feet away.

Pamela looked at the gentle brook, debating whether it was safe to let the girl go alone. It was deep enough to be dangerous.

Jake took hold of Pamela's arm so she couldn't rise.

"All right, Amanda," he spoke to the child while tenderly keeping Pamela by his side. "Miss Kotchkis will sit with me, and you can call if you need anything."

Amanda thrust her doll into Pamela's arms and skipped

off to the water's edge.

"Don't worry," said Jake. "We can see her from here if she falls in, and nothing is going to happen to her in the bushes."

They fell into conversation again. Pamela kept an eye on the little girl as she dawdled by the water, more playing than washing.

By the time Amanda skipped over to the bushes, Pamela had relaxed again against the tree trunk, listening to Jake tell of one of his classes at the University.

"What did she say?" asked Pamela abruptly.

"She's talking to herself," answered Jake. "If she was in trouble, she'd yell."

"She's talking to someone," insisted Pamela.

"An imaginary friend," said Jake, but he cocked his ear toward the bushes.

"Here, kitty, kitty," he heard Amanda call. He started to rise.

Pamela had heard her, too.

"Don't touch a stray kitten, Amanda," she called. "It may not be friendly."

"Come see him, Miss Kottis. He's pretty," said Amanda. "He's all fluffy and very little. I think he's lost. Here, kitty, kitty."

Jake put out a hand to help Amanda stand. They started toward the bushes.

"Oh! Nasty kitty!" cried Amanda.

Jake and Pamela quickened their steps, but they knew before they rounded the bushes what kind of cat Amanda had found. Amanda held tight to the small black-and-white critter even as the air took on a most horrendous odor.

"Put the baby down and let him go back to his mother," said Jake.

Amanda bent and released the "kitty" as she was told, but tears filled her eyes. The skunk scurried into the underbrush and disappeared.

Chapter 7

W e can't return her to her sister like this." Pamela crossed the little clearing to stand next to poor Amanda, but she couldn't bring herself to embrace the sniffling child.

"You've got a suitcase," said Jake. "Doesn't she have something else to wear?"

"That's not going to solve the problem," snapped Pamela. "She'll still stink."

Amanda gave up trying to be brave and started crying.

"Oh, dear," said Pamela, and crouched down beside her. "I'm sorry, Amanda. I'm not mad at you. I know you're miserable, and Sheriff Moore and I will think of something."

"We can rinse her off in the creek," suggested Jake.

"Yes, that will help some," agreed Pamela. "Don't cry so, Amanda. We'll take off this dress, and Jake can bury it."

She started untying the pinafore and glanced up at Jake who seemed to have frozen on the spot.

"Sheriff, do you have any soap in your saddlebags?" Pamela asked.

"I have a cake of shaving soap."

"That will have to do," said Pamela.

Amanda took a couple of big sniffs. "I have pretty soap," she said.

"You do?" asked Pamela.

Amanda nodded. "In my basket. A lady takes her own soap so she doesn't have to use the soap in the common washroom."

"Well, then," said Pamela, "we'll use Sheriff Moore's soap first, because it is probably stronger, and then we'll use your pretty soap because it probably smells nicer."

Amanda sniffed and nodded again. Jake went off to find the soaps and the clothes.

Pamela removed her own shoes, socks, and skirt. That left her clothed decently enough, she decided, with her shirtwaist, shift, and bloomers. She coaxed Amanda into the stream.

The water was warm from the hot summer days. Pamela held both of Amanda's hands as they waded deeper into the gently flowing water. Once it was up to the little girl's waist, Amanda began to treat her stream bath as an adventure. She let go of Pamela's hands.

"Look, I can dog paddle," Amanda demonstrated her splashy technique.

"Very good," said Pamela. "But let's take off that smelly shift."

"All right." Amanda put her feet back down on the sandy bottom and tugged at the wet shift, trying to get it over her head.

"Let me help," offered Pamela. She took a step forward and at that moment the shift slid over Amanda's head and slapped Pamela in the face. Pamela sputtered and fell. She landed on the bottom of the streambed, sitting with her head and shoulders above the water. Amanda grinned and slapped the water to splash her friend.

"Amanda, stop it," said Pamela, grabbing Amanda playfully. "We've got to get that smell off of you."

"I've got the soap." Jake's voice startled Pamela. He stood, looking tall and handsome, at the edge of the stream with the two suitcases at his feet. Pamela looked down to make sure the murky water covered her.

"I can't come get it," she answered.

"I'll toss it to you," said Jake and swung his arm back to pitch the first cake of soap.

"No," she squealed. "I'll drop it in the stream."

"Then I'll just have to bring it to you." Jake sat down and began pulling off his boots.

"Sheriff Moore," protested Pamela, "this isn't proper."

Amanda bubbled over with giggles. "Sheriff Moore doesn't know what's proper, Miss Kottis." She hopped up and down in the water. "He can't take a bath with us, but he can come swimming. I've gone swimming with my cousins, James, John, Jordon, and Jacob, and even their father, Mr. Jenkins, and my sister, Augusta."

Jake threw down his last sock and stood up.

"Here I come," he warned.

"Splash him! Splash him!" squealed Amanda, and she did her best to scoop up the water and send it flying across to the advancing sheriff. Her efforts weren't very threatening until Pamela joined the onslaught.

Jake laughed and plunged on. He put the cakes of soap in his shirt pockets. Then, with his hands free, he shoveled water fast and efficiently, sending it showering over

Pamela and Amanda.

The ladies shrieked and splashed all the harder as he came near. The fun continued even after Jake brought out the soap. Amanda wiggled as the two adults soaped her from head to toe, twice with Jake's shaving soap, and twice with her perfumed soap from the finest mercantile in St. Louis.

"Now, you must go up to the horses," said Pamela.

Jake laughed at her with a roguish twinkle in his eye and the two dimples deeply set in his smiling face.

"Why?" he asked.

"Because," Pamela said, her own face beaming with the joy of his teasing, "Miss Amanda and I want to get out of the stream and into some dry clothes."

"You have to go, Sheriff Moore," insisted Amanda. "Miss Kottis and I are proper ladies."

Jake leaned back in the shallow water and let his body float. "I'm not finished with my swim," he said.

With one swift movement, Pamela reached over and dunked the sheriff's head under the water. While he sputtered, she grabbed Amanda and plodded through the shallow water and up the bank. She put Amanda down and snatched the suitcases, hustling her little charge into the bushes.

Jake trudged to the bank and came out dripping. He grabbed up his boots and socks, but he couldn't resist rattling the bushes as he went by.

The girls squealed and he chortled. Without stopping, he made his way back to their picnic sight.

"You're no gentleman, Jake Moore," Pamela called after him.

Jake turned on his heel and walked backward a few steps as he answered, "Never said I was, ma'am."

He stretched out on the blanket in the sun, hoping to dry some while he waited. He closed his eyes and felt the warmth of the sun on his face. He couldn't imagine a more perfect afternoon, smelly skunk and all. *Dear Jesus, You have awakened a desire in my heart this past week. I find myself thinking, dreaming of this woman. I watch her every move, knowing I'm letting myself get drawn in closer and closer to that sacred state of matrimony. I don't want to hurt her or do anything that will shame You. I'm expecting You to give me a peace about this decision. I don't want to be guilty of taking this holy covenant of marriage lightly. Guide me. When I listen to her speak, may I hear words of encouragement from You. Amen.*

Jake wrinkled his nose as Amanda approached.

"Sit here in the sun next to the sheriff, and I'll comb out your hair," said Pamela.

Amanda plopped down on the blanket. Pamela sat behind her and started gently working the brush through the wet tangled locks.

"Where's my own clothes?" asked Amanda with a pout.

"Remember? They blew away with the tornado," answered Jake. "They might have flown right back to St. Louis, Missouri. They might have landed right in your very own backyard and hung themselves up on that laundry line you spoke of, right next to your father's nightshirt."

"I don't think so." Amanda squirmed under Pamela's brushing and yawned. "Althea isn't going to like this dress. Althea has good taste. She's very par-tic-u-lar about her attire."

"I think," said Pamela, "Althea is going to be so glad to see you're safe that she won't fuss about what you are wearing."

Amanda leaned sideways against Pamela's lap, and her head sank down on her folded arms.

"Augusta says Althea can fuss better than a flock of hens. She says Althea has taken fussing seriously as if it were an art form."

"And what does Althea say about that?" asked Jake.

Amanda yawned again. "Althea says, 'What can you expect from a woman who lets her husband call her Gussie?'"

♥

Finally, the tangles were out, but Pamela continued to stroke the brush through Amanda's curls.

"She's asleep," whispered Jake.

"It's been a long day for her, and she usually takes a nap," answered Pamela. She put down the brush and smoothed the curls back from the sleeping child's face. "Isn't she adorable? She bounces back and forth from acting like a little old lady to the little girl she is. I would love to keep her and give her the chance to get dirty more often."

"As long as it's dirty and not smelly," said Jake.

Pamela giggled. "She does have rather an air about her still."

"Should we load up the sleeping beauty and get back on the road?" asked Jake.

"Oh no," said Pamela, looking off toward the stream. "I've spread our wet things on the bushes to dry, and you could use some time to dry as well."

"We're going to be late getting into Big Springs."

"Does it matter?" asked Pamela. "Amanda's sister isn't expecting us today, so she won't be worried. My sister isn't expecting us, either. I'd rather stay here." She didn't say that she wanted the day together to last as long as possible, but she looked back at Jake stretched out on the blanket, and her eyes took on the softness of thorough contentment.

Jake gazed at her for a minute and then shook himself as if trying to awaken from a dream.

"We better move her out of the sun, then, or she'll get a burn." He quickly rose, and with Pamela clutching the blanket on one side and he the other, they moved it under the shade of the willow again. Settling down on either side of the sleeping child, they spoke quietly.

"All of your sisters have moved to cities, haven't they?" asked Jake.

Pamela nodded. She leaned back on the blanket and studied the trailing limbs of the willow that nearly surrounded them as a leafy bower.

"Do you want to leave the farm, too?" asked Jake.

Pamela's head jerked around to look at him. "No, not at all. I'm the youngest, and I think I missed the worst hardships during the early years when Pa was building up the farm. I've heard the stories about how grueling it was, and my older sisters relish the comparative ease of living in town. But, by the time I was old enough to take note of things, Pa's farm was well established. It's still a hardworking life, but not nearly what it once was. Now he's doing well enough to have hired help.

"I love the farm. I love gardening and my chickens and the excitement of harvest time. I want to stay."

Jake nodded. "It is hard work, but it's good work. It would be my first choice." He shrugged and gave her a wistful smile. "Maybe someday I'll figure out just exactly what it is God wants me to do with my life. At first I thought it was farming because I took to it so natural. Then when Uncle Will's constant reminders that the farm was going to his boys finally sunk in, I thought it was being a lawyer. I thought maybe I'd be a lawyer for the Grange Movement, or the Farmer's Alliance, but God didn't seem to be directing me that way either. I'm twenty-six years old, Pamela, and still living day by day with no vision of what the Lord wants me to do with my life."

"Patience, waiting, longsuffering," said Pamela. "I think that's the hardest thing God asks us to do."

Jake nodded.

"But it'll come, Jake." She smiled at him. "I know you've been faithful with the small things, living the day to day life of a Christian without any fanfare. Someday, God will lay a purpose on your heart, and you'll be ready."

Jake could only nod in her direction. He didn't have all the words he wanted to say to tell her how grateful he was that she understood. He didn't think he could explain how, through her words, she had just answered a prayer.

He leaned back and folded his arms behind his neck, looking up into the branches of the tree. He spotted a squirrel jerking its bushy tail and eyeing them. He pointed the saucy animal out to Pamela.

During the comfortable quiet that followed, Jake turned over the conversation in his mind. Pamela Kotchkis understood his frustration and didn't condemn him for having no goal in life. She was right that he had to wait on

God's leading instead of forging ahead on his own. God had made him the sheriff, and he would be a good sheriff until another door opened up.

Jake rolled on his side to speak to her, but saw she was asleep. She had turned on her side, facing Amanda. The breeze lifted the small curls on Pamela's forehead. The cinnamon-brown lashes of her eyes lay in a fringed semi-circle across each cheek.

"Pamela," Jake whispered. She didn't stir. "Pamela," he whispered again, just because he liked the sound of it. She'd called him Jake instead of sheriff, and he'd forgotten the formality of Miss Kotchkis, or even Miss Pamela. He felt comfortable with Miss Pamela Kotchkis, and as soon as they returned Amanda to her family, he intended to court the lady in a proper fashion.

A smile hovered on Pamela's lips as if she dreamed of something pleasant. The dimple flashed. Jake moved to his knees and leaned carefully over Amanda so as not to disturb her sleep. With great care, he stretched an arm over to prop himself. Slowly, not wanting to disturb either sleeper, he moved in and laid a gentle kiss on Pamela's lips. She responded slightly to the kiss, and Jake jerked back. He searched her face, thinking he must have awakened her. She didn't move. He sighed and leaned back on his heels. A small giggle caught him off guard, and he looked down into Amanda's laughing eyes.

"Shh!" He put a finger to his lips.

"You kissed Miss Kottis," whispered Amanda.

"Her name is Miss Kotchkis," said Jake.

"Kost-sis," repeated Amanda.

"No," said Jake patiently, "Kotch-kis."

"Kot-kis,"

"No, Amanda. Think about playing a game of tag. If I was it and I chased you and caught you, I would say, 'Caught cha.' Can you say caught cha?"

Amanda nodded. "Caught cha."

"That's good. Now, say caught cha real fast and leave off the uh at the end. Like this, caughtch."

"Caughtch," she repeated perfectly.

Jake grinned. "Now, just add kiss. Caughtch-kiss"

"Caughtch-kiss," said Amanda and clapped her hands, delighted with her success.

"It sounds like you two are having a sneezing fit," said Pamela as she sat up.

"Miss Kotchkis! Miss Kotchkis!" Amanda turned and threw her arms around her friend. "I learned to say your name. Sheriff Moore taught me 'cause I caught him kissing you. Kotchkis, Kotchkis, I caught cha kissing Miss Kotchkis."

She bounced out of Pamela's lap and tackled Jake, knocking him over so they rolled on the ground. He tickled her, telling her not to tell secrets. Pamela crossed her arms over her chest and watched them. When they settled down a bit, she addressed the child.

"Amanda, would you please go see if our clothes are dry and pack them in the luggage? I need to talk to Sheriff Moore."

Amanda scrambled to her feet and started for the bushes.

Jake sat up and reached for his hat. He concentrated on putting it on, smoothing his hair, setting it in place, taking it off, and replacing it a tad farther back on his head.

He finally looked at Pamela.

"Well?" she asked with an eyebrow raised.

He blushed and started to rise. "Perhaps I'd better help Miss Amanda. We don't want her picking up any more country kitties."

Pamela put a hand on his arm and stopped him.

"Why did you kiss me?" she asked quietly.

Her voice had a bubble of enjoyment in it, and Jake looked directly into her eyes, trying to decipher its meaning. The irrepressible dimple hovered at the corner of her lips, and her eyes twinkled with amusement over his discomfort.

"It was your fault," he said.

"Mine!"

"You've got this dimple that invites me to kiss you," said Jake with a certain amount of phony priggishness. "I've done my best to resist temptation, but when you start winking that dimple at me even when you're asleep. . . what's a man suppose to do?"

Pamela's mouth dropped open in outrage, and she snatched his new hat right off his head. With mock anger, she bludgeoned him with it. He raised his arms to ward off the attack, and when he saw an opening, he reached past the flailing hat and grabbed her around the waist. With a twist, he had her pinned to the blanket. She laughed so hard he had no trouble reclaiming his hat. With one hand, he jammed it on top of her head, still keeping her arms captured.

"You have no right to be battering an officer of the law that way, Miss Kotchkis."

"It was you who trespassed against me while sleeping,"

Pamela laughed and continued, "I have a confession to make, Sheriff."

"Yes?"

"I wasn't asleep."

She laughed again at the expression on his face.

"Miss Kotchkis, I fear you must be punished by the law for your trickery."

"Oh, dear," she sighed. "What is my punishment?"

He didn't answer but lowered his head to touch his lips again to hers. The tender kiss led to another. That one led to one less tender and more urgent. Somehow her arms escaped, and she wrapped them around his shoulders. He leaned back and gazed into the dreamy expression in her eyes. He shifted his weight to free her and pulled on her arms so that she sat beside him.

Just then Amanda came struggling through the bushes, dragging a suitcase. She stopped and looked at the happy couple.

"I caught cha kissing again, didn't I, Miss Kotchkis?"

Jake stood in one swift movement and easily lifted Pamela to stand beside him. He wrapped an arm around her waist and addressed Amanda.

"I've decided I must change her name, Miss Amanda."

Pamela looked up at him with suspicion in her eye.

"If she'll have me, I'm going to marry her so her name will be Moore, and not Kotchkis anymore. I'd hate to think she was going around all over Kansas being caught kissing." He turned to look again at the smiling face he adored. He cleared his throat. "Unless it was me she was kissing."

Pamela shook her head slightly. "That may cause us

more problems, Sheriff," she said.

He frowned.

"I might become demanding," she explained. She stretched up on tiptoe and kissed him quickly on the lips. "I might start demanding Moore, Moore, Moore." She punctuated each pronunciation of his name with a kiss.

"Are you going to marry the sheriff?" asked Amanda.

"Oh yes, most definitely," answered Pamela.

"Can we go to Big Springs first? I want to tell Althea about the tornado and the china cup and feeding the Banty hens and dancing and the skunk. She'll never believe it all."

"I think she'll believe the skunk, Miss Amanda," said Jake as he bent to pick up the blanket and fold it.

Amanda pouted.

"Never mind him, Amanda," said Pamela. "Right now he's pretty full of himself. Let's gather up the rest of our things and pack up the surrey. We still have a fine bit of traveling to do to get to Big Springs tonight."

Amanda nodded. The curls were dry and bounced a happy rhythm around her face.

"Yes," she said. "We can't forget to do our duty just because we're having a grand time."

Jake looked at her, puzzled. "I guess I've been having too grand a time, Miss Amanda. Just what is our duty today?"

Amanda placed her hands on her hips and announced loud and clear:

"Returning Amanda!"

Kathleen Paul

Kate lives in Colorado Springs—"You can see Pikes Peak no matter where you are in the city"—with her eighty-four-year-old mom. "I was a single mom for thirteen years and Mom helped me balance my life. What a blessing to have her support as I raised my children." She has a college-aged son and a recently married daughter. Then there are the two dogs—Gus and Gertie, one big, one small, both full of mischief.

Kate dabbles in oral storytelling. She's used these skills in teaching elementary school, Sunday school, and AWANA and anywhere she found herself surrounded by children.

"I read the accomplishments of my colleagues in the Christian writing field and I am humbled. I am a very ordinary person. But I count myself extraordinary in that God loves me and has given me a ministry."

Kate's first novel was *Escape*, which was released by **Heartsong Presents** in 1999.

A Letter to Our Readers

Dear Readers:

In order that we might better contribute to your reading enjoyment, we would appreciate you taking a few minutes to respond to the following questions. When completed, please return to the following: Fiction Editor, Barbour Publishing, Inc., P.O. Box 719, Uhrichsville, OH 44683.

1. Did you enjoy reading *A Mother's Heart?*
   - ❑ Very much. I would like to see more books like this.
   - ❑ Moderately—I would have enjoyed it more if _____
   _____
   _____

2. What influenced your decision to purchase this book?
   (Check those that apply.)
   - ❑ Cover   ❑ Back cover copy   ❑ Title   ❑ Price
   - ❑ Friends   ❑ Publicity   ❑ Other

3. Which story was your favorite?
   - ❑ *One Little Prayer*   ❑ *The Tie That Binds*
   - ❑ *The Provider*   ❑ *Returning Amanda*

4. Please check your age range:
   - ❑ Under 18   ❑ 18–24   ❑ 25–34
   - ❑ 35–45   ❑ 46–55   ❑ Over 55

5. How many hours per week do you read? _____

Name _____

Occupation _____

Address _____

City _____ State _____ Zip _____

If you enjoyed

A Mother's Heart

then read:

♋♡♋

mother's wedding dress

*Four Romantic Novellas
Linked by Family and Love*

Button String Bride by Cathy Marie Hake

Wedding Quilt Bride by Colleen Coble

Bayside Bride by Kristin Billerbeck

The Persistent Bride by Gina Fields